**Kimball Library**
**5 Academy Ave**
**Atkinson, NH 03811**

W9-CCN-464

*Stay*

## Also by Deb Caletti

# Stay

by DEB CALETTI

Simon Pulse
NEW YORK  LONDON  TORONTO  SYDNEY

*To Jen Klonsky—*
*For all that you do to bring our books into the world, and for doing it*
*with such respect, care, and sisterly good fun . . .*
*my thanks. This one's for you, Pal.*

This book is a work of fiction. Any references to historical events, real people,
or real locales are used fictitiously. Other names, characters, places, and incidents are
the product of the author's imagination, and any resemblance to actual events

or locales or persons, living or dead, is entirely coincidental.

SIMON PULSE

An imprint of Simon & Schuster Children's Publishing Division

1230 Avenue of the Americas, New York, NY 10020

First Simon Pulse hardcover edition April 2011

Copyright © 2011 by Deb Caletti

All rights reserved, including the right of reproduction in whole or in part in any form.

SIMON PULSE and colophon are registered trademarks of Simon & Schuster, Inc.

For information about special discounts for bulk purchases, please contact

Simon & Schuster Special Sales at 1-866-506-1949 or business@simonandschuster.com.

The Simon & Schuster Speakers Bureau can bring authors to your live event.

For more information or to book an event contact the Simon & Schuster Speakers Bureau

at 1-866-248-3049 or visit our website at www.simonspeakers.com.

Designed by Mike Rosamilia

The text of this book was set in Scala.

Manufactured in the United States of America

2  4  6  8  10  9  7  5  3

Library of Congress Cataloging-in-Publication Data

Caletti, Deb.

Stay / by Deb Caletti.—1st Simon Pulse hardcover ed.

p. cm.

Summary: In a remote corner of Washington State where she and her father have gone to
escape her obsessive boyfriend, Clara meets two brothers who captain a sailboat, a lighthouse
keeper with a secret, and an old friend of her father who knows his secrets.

ISBN 978-1-4424-0373-4 (hardcover)

[1. Fathers and daughters—Fiction. 2. Secrets—Fiction. 3. Islands—Fiction. 4. Dating (Social
customs)—Fiction. 5. Stalking—Fiction. 6. Washington (State)—Fiction.] I. Title.

PZ7.C127437St 2011

[Fic]—dc20    2010021804

ISBN 978-1-4424-0375-8 (eBook)

## Acknowledgments

Deepest gratitude, as ever, to Ben Camardi. My thanks, too, to my book family at S&S, and to the terrific people at Brilliance Audio—to each and every one of you who handle my work, you are so appreciated.

Always love and thanks to my family—Evie Caletti, Paul Caletti, Jan Caletti, Sue Rath and gang, and our far-flung clan. What would I do without you? We have a great family. Sam and Nick—you give me reason every single day to count my blessings. Oh, you are treasured. And gratitude, gratitude, gratitude to my husband, John Yurich, and to the fates that brought us together. I am now a believer in true love.

# Chapter 1

First off, I've never told this story to anyone. Not the entire thing anyway, and not entirely truthfully. I'm only telling it now for one reason, and that's because an untold story has a weight that can submerge you, sure as a sunken ship at the bottom of the ocean. I learned that. This kind of story, those kind of things kept secret—they have the power to keep you hidden forever, and most of all from yourself. The ghosts from that drowned ship, they keep haunting.

So here is the story. Sit back and make yourself comfortable and all that.

I met him at a basketball game.

Wait. You should also know that another friend of mine, Annie Willows, had asked me to go with her and her friends to El Corazon that night to hear some band and that I didn't go. If I had gone, all this might never have happened. The way two people can end up in the same place, find each other in a crowd, and change their lives and the lives of the people around them forever . . . It makes you believe in fate. And fate gives love some extra authority. Like it's been stamped with approval from above, if you believe in above. A godly green light. Some destined *significance*.

Anyway.

My school was playing his, and I was there with my friend Shakti, who was watching her boyfriend Luke, number sixteen, who was at that moment sitting on the bench and drumming his fingers on his knee like he did when he was nervous. Inside the gym there was that fast, high energy crackle of competition and screaming fans and the squeak of tennis shoes stopping and starting on shiny floors.

He was with another girl; that was one thing. I was aware of her only vaguely as she moved away from him. She maneuvered sideways through the crowd, purse over her shoulder, heading to the bathroom, maybe. His eyes followed her and then landed on me, and by the time she came back, it was over for her, though she didn't know it. That sounds terrible, and I still feel bad about it. But something had already been set in motion, and I wonder and wonder how things would have been if I'd have just let that moment pass, the one where our eyes met. If I had just taken Shakti's arm and moved off, letting the electrical jolt that passed between us fade off, letting the girl return to his side, letting fate head off in another direction entirely, where he would have kept his eyes fixed on the girl with the purse or on another girl entirely.

My father, Bobby Oates*, said that love at first sight should send you running, if you know what's good for you. It's your dark pieces having instant recognition with their dark pieces, he says. You're an idiot if you think it means you've met your soul mate. So I was an idiot. He looked so *nice*. He *was* nice. After Dylan Ricks, I was looking for nice. Dylan Ricks once held my arm behind my back and then twisted so hard that I heard something pop.

"Thirsty!" I yelled to Shakti, and she nodded. I moved away from her, followed the line of his eyes until I was standing next to him. I wish you knew me, because you'd appreciate what this meant. I would never just go walking up to some guy. I would never ignore the fact that his girlfriend was right then in the bathroom putting on new lip gloss. Never. I was nice and my friends were nice, which meant we lacked the selfish, sadistic overconfidence of popularity. But I didn't care about that girl right then. It's awful, and I'm sorry, but it was true. I kind of even hated me for it, but it was like I *had* to do what I was going to do. I can't explain it. I wish I could. He was very tall and broad shouldered, white-blond hair swooped over his forehead, good-looking, oh, yeah, with those impossible, perfectly designed Scandinavian features. Still, it wasn't just his looks. It was some *pull*. The ball hit hard against the backboard, which shuddered and clattered. The ref's whistle shrieked and the crowd yelled its cheers and protests.

I held my hands up near my ears. "Loud," I said to him.

He leaned in close. His voice surprised me. He had this

...................

* It sounds familiar because you *have* heard of him. Crime writer, or, as the critics say, "contemporary noir." *Her Emerald Eyes*, among others. Yeah, you saw the movie, too.

accent. It was lush and curled, with the kind of lilt and rich-
ness that made you instantly think of distant cities and faraway
lands—the kind of city you'd see in a foreign film, with a snow-
banked river winding through its center, stone bridges crossing
to an ornate church. Ice castles and a royal family and coats
lined with fur. The other guys in that gym—they watched ESPN
and slunked in suburban living rooms and slammed the doors
of their mothers' minivans. See—I had already made him into
someone he would never be, and I didn't know it then, but he was
already doing the same with me, too.

"I don't even know what I'm doing here," he said. "I actually
hate sports."

I laughed. "How many people here are secretly wishing they
were somewhere else?"

He looked around. Shook his head. "Just us."

I was wishing that, all right. I was wishing we were *both*
somewhere else. A somewhere together. A warm heat was starting at my knees, working its way up. "I've got to . . ." I gestured
toward Shakti.

"Right," he said.

I made my way back to Shakti, who was standing on her toes
at the sidelines, trying to see Luke, who had been called in to the
game and who was now dribbling the ball down the court in his
shiny gold shorts. "He's in," she said. "Oh, please, God, let him
not do what he did last time."

But I was too distracted to actually watch and see if Luke
would accidentally pass the ball to an opposing teammate as
he had during the last game. My focus had shifted, my whole

focus—one moment he wasn't there and then he was, and my mind and body were buzzing with awareness and hope and uncertainty. You have ordinary moments and ordinary moments and more ordinary moments, and then, suddenly, there is something monumental right there. You have past and future colliding in the present, your own personal Big Bang, and nothing will ever be the same.

That was the point, there, then, when I should have shaken it off and gone on. I see it like an actual road in my mind, forking off. I should have kept my eyes on Luke with his sky-length legs and skinny chest; I should have cheered when he passed that ball just as he should have, to number twenty-four, who shot a clean basket. I should have stayed in that moment and moved on from *that* moment, when Shakti grabbed my arm and squeezed. Instead, I watched him as he headed through the crowd, and he looked back at me and our eyes met again before he disappeared.

It was already too late. Basically, two springs and two summers and the sea and the haunting had all already happened.

# Chapter 2

That was before.

But after, as that second summer approached, my father decided we needed to leave. It felt too dangerous there. We rented our house to a researcher doing work at the university. Something scientific. It was hard to imagine a science guy in our house, which overflowed with my father's books and papers and his collection of ship lanterns and paperweights. My father would be leaving behind his cherished and tangled grapevines, which grew over a large arbor in the yard and which he tended to lovingly with clippers and a careful eye. We'd be back in time for their ripening, in time for him to make his home brew wine. I thought my dad drank too much, for one thing.

I stood in the open doorway of his office, the large old

French doors swung wide. His reading glasses were on a chain and hung down on his chest.

"It all seems too big," I said.

We were trying to hurry, but I couldn't seem to get going. My father was shoving things into a box. "Don't get stuck, Clara Pea. Get a move on."

"How do you pack for three months?" I asked him. I'd never been gone from home that long. Everything about the trip seemed hard to grasp. My mind felt lately like a building destroyed by a natural disaster, where all I could do was walk around the rubble and wonder what I could possibly do next.

"Just bring the things you love most. You've got to have good things around you now, right, Pea? Your favorite shoes, your favorite sweater. Shirts, T-shirts. You need anything else, God forbid, we can go shopping." Dad hated shopping. Malls, cell phones, and reality television—don't even get him started.

"You bringing that?" I asked. He was wrapping one of his paperweights, one of the largest, shaped like an old typewriter and just as heavy.

"I'll keep it under the bed since I don't have a baseball bat."

My stomach dropped. His eyes were bright and he was grinning, but I thought he might be serious, too. He felt that same shadow looming that I did. One time I actually drove too fast and turned down some crazy street because I thought I was being followed. Looking at Dad then, I felt guilty suddenly, or rather, *again*, for this leaving. He had a book due by the end of the summer. He had every reason to stay here where he was.

"Pea, you know I can write anywhere," Dad said, reading my mind. He was good at that. He was someone you couldn't hide from. "I could write in the back of a pickup truck driving across the country. Who could have complaints about the beach, Pea? I just might want to stay."

"God, Dad." I rubbed my forehead. "This is all so strange."

"It's good for both of us," he said, even though there was nothing good about what was happening. He finished wrapping the paperweight in newspaper and set it in a wide leather bag. I could see the fat pages of a manuscript there, too, and a stack of index cards wrapped in a rubber band. "You need a place you can breathe for a while. *I* need a place you can breathe for a while." My father knew about recovering yourself after you were sure you were lost. He had taken a trip like this once. Different, though. It was more about grief than guilt, and it only lasted the two weeks he thought he could be away from me, since I was young and needed him. I had stayed with JoJo Dean, a friend of my father's, as my father mourned my mother in private.*

"You went away to a beach before," I reminded him.

"A different beach. Not one I want to go back to." He closed the zipper of the bag. "Haul ass, kid," he said.

And so I did.

......................

* Yes, this story has a dead mother. Mine. She had a sudden aneurysm when I was barely four. Died before she could even get to a hospital. Dead mothers have become a story cliché thanks to Disney movies and novel writers. All the dead mothers in books, you'd think it was a common occurrence. Even Dad's books have them. But mine was real. She was no cliché and neither am I.

* * *

We left the city behind us and drove north, until the land flattened into farms and pastures and tulip fields. And then east, down two-lane roads forested on each side, full of tall evergreens and dark, mossy places that made the air feel suddenly cool. Little towns appeared at stoplights, three or four buildings at most, a church, a café, sparse I-wonder-who-lives-here-and-why streets. And then forest again.

"Do you remember the bridge?" my father asked. The car smelled like french fries, and the backseat held the crumpled-up bags from our lunch stop.

I looked around. "Bridge?"

"Not yet. This is one you wouldn't miss. It's the bridge over Deception Pass. We came here a long time ago. I carried you in a pack down to the beach. After we hiked up to the car again, we realized you'd lost your sandal. Your mom ran all the way back down the trail to get it. I said, Leave it, we'll buy her new ones, but she ran the two, three miles down there anyway. Came back with that shoe." He smiled. "A triumph."

I smiled, too. The windows were rolled down. He was shouting a little. He didn't like air-conditioning when you could get the smells and feel of the real outside right there in your face.

"Okay, be ready."

He was right. Deception Pass—you couldn't have missed that bridge spanning those waters. It was almost shocking the way nature can be so suddenly before you in all its enormity and beauty. Out of the forest, and then—wow. Just, wow—this deep,

Deb Caletti

steep down-ness, this drop to the sparkling waters of Deception Pass, a thin bridge spanning the impossible distance.

"Let's pull over. This is a bridge you have to walk across."

"Got it. A metaphor, right?" Dad was a writer down to his cells, and he loved metaphors. Everything was a metaphor. Your dirty laundry could be one. Unexpected encounters with dog shit, definitely.

"Ha, I didn't even think of it," he said. He'd already unbuckled his seat belt and had flung his door open in the small crescent of gravel that was the lookout point. "Deception Pass. How does one make *that* crossing, at least permanently?"

"You're asking *me*?" I said. We wouldn't be standing there right then if I understood how to manage deception and my own self-lies. I stepped outside. I breathed in—the air felt huge. The blue-gray-green waters that stretched out before us sparkled in the sun. It smelled great out there. "I keep feeling like we have to *go*. Like we have to *hurry*."

"We can relax now," he said. He took a big dramatic breath. "Ah! This is magnificent, eh? Christ, I should set a book out here."

He was right. The rock wall that dropped to the water was sheer and craggy, and as we stepped out onto the narrow footpath of the bridge itself, my stomach seemed to tumble and fall the million miles down to the jagged waves below. The landscape was moody and dangerous. "I can't look," I said. It was too far down. We were safe; our feet were on the solid ground of the bridge and I gripped the iron rail, but my heart still felt the long, long drop.

"Look right at it. Know you can," Dad said. "Look right at that fear. Fear is the biggest bullshitter."

*Stay*

This was not just some motivational rah-rah to get me through what was happening right then. This was how my father talked a good lot of the time. His words had layers—they went two or three directions when other people's words went one. He was curious and playful and hungry for meaning, and his speech reflected that. My friends said he sounded like a writer. I didn't know what this meant until I stayed over at Annie's or Emma's or Shakti's houses, where dads either asked you about school or didn't say much at all.

You had to walk single file on that bridge, and so I followed him across, the cars whipping past us on one side, the sheer drop below us on the other. We made it to the far end, where a matching set of warning signs were posted along the cliffs, as if anyone would be stupid enough to climb there. I felt a little sick and a little proud. It had a sort of significance, though I didn't know what kind. It had to—you didn't cross the perilous distance over Deception without it meaning something.

We got back in the car and wound our way down the island. You could practically follow the wet and salty air and that tangled underwater smell right down to the sea. The house was small and gray and shingled and sat at the tip of the peninsula. In spite of everything I felt excited, like I wanted to run out and explore the place, like you do when you're a kid on vacation. My father had found the house in the back of *Seattle* magazine, where the travel ads are. Some guy was renting it out while he was working in California. We left the car packed and my father unlocked the front door, and I checked it all out—the small kitchen and the closets and the little white bedroom with white curtains that would be mine and the bigger paneled bedroom that would be my father's. The man who owned the house had good taste—his shirts were expensive and the cupboard had flavored vinegars and fancy olives and a bottle of Scotch.

"Something to do with the film industry," my father guessed. "California, right? It makes sense." He was standing by the bookshelf, the first place he always went to find out about a person.

I looked, too. "*The Elements of Screenwriting. Elia Kazan: A Life*; *The Making of Citizen Kane*. But wait. Zig Ziglar's *See You at the Top*? *The Art of Closing Any Deal*? Some sort of businessman? What do you know about the guy?"

"Not a thing," my father said, pleased. This was a game that could last us the three months, easy.

"We could just look him up on the Internet," I said.

"Cheating!" he said. "Don't you dare. I'm going to get the bags. Feel free to gather more clues about our host."

Instead of gathering more clues, though, I sat down on the bed in my crisp, clean room. The bed had the kind of sheets and down comforter you could sleep years in. I wished I could sleep years, that's how tired I was. A million years tired. The sheets smelled good, like spring. I looked out my large window, trimmed in blue paint. I could see the coastline from my bed, the blue-gray sea, though that night after dinner, it would become unbelievably dark out there. The dark of the ocean was an endless dark.

It started to sink in: no one knew who I was here, and no one back home knew *where* I was. It was a fantastically freeing feeling. I could be anyone at all. I could be someone with an entirely different past, and a wide open future.

You'd imagine with a feeling like that, a person could sleep easy. I guess I was thinking, though, that if someone were walking around outside, even right outside my window, you wouldn't hear those footsteps in the soft sand.

# Chapter 3

Of course I went to the next basketball game our
school played against his. The minute I got home that first night,
I'd looked up the game schedule to see when we'd be playing his
team again. I thought about him every day until then. I started
having those conversations with him in my head that you have
when you first meet someone you sense is going to be important in your life. I told him things about me I thought he should
know. That I was a mostly shy person concealing that fact; too
straight, probably. Never tried pot and never wanted to but had
several times been to parties and pretended to drink something
I wasn't really drinking. I read too much. I was scared of spiders
but once was stung by a hundred bees and didn't cry. I told him
I loved the butter lake you could make in mashed potatoes with
the back of your spoon, and the way lumberyards smelled, and

goofy dogs, but that I didn't know what I wanted to do when I "grew up." Something with words like my father, I said to him in my head, because words were hills and valleys you traveled, so lovely sometimes that they hurt your eyes. I told him I felt sure there was a true and right place for me I hadn't found yet.

I imagined him telling me other things. His first memory. Who had hurt him and who had loved him best. His dreams. It was stupid, and I'm not that kind of person, but I even imagined us living somewhere together. I imagined us traveling to the place he had come from. We would visit museums with paintings in heavy gold frames or watch the northern lights with wool mittens on our hands.

I had decided what to wear three days before*, but once I had on those jeans and that shirt I decided it looked like I was trying too hard because I *was* trying too hard, and that ignited one of those clothes crises that can get a person seriously panicked, where you feel the slick, precarious slope between having it all together and being completely out of control. Clothes piled up and I knew I was going to be late, and finally I put on something I wore all the time—my old jeans and a soft green shirt, my hair taken from its barrette and worn straight. Right away I felt better—feeling confident at a time like that was hard enough without having to get to know some new outfit, too.

I borrowed Dad's car, listened to my favorite girl power CD for a little musical rejection-proofing. I checked my reflection in

..........................

* Okay, I had actually bought something new.

the rearview mirror at the stoplights. My stomach felt giddy and tumbling. All this, and he probably wouldn't even be there.

The parking lot was packed. I think we were in some sort of basketball playoffs—I could never quite follow all of the specifics when Shakti told me. It was dark already and there was that parking lot excitement of a big event, headlights and shouts and loud laughter, people crossing into the paths of idling cars and running to the curb. Shakti met me out front by the bike rack, our usual place. Her eyes were bright in the streetlights.

"This is it," she said, and gave a little squeal. Shakti wasn't the squealing type, and neither was I. She was smart and thoughtful and dinners at her house were careful and quiet, though the huge plates of food served by her mother were steaming and delicious and somehow passionate. Shakti had dreams of medical school and would no doubt get there, unlike Luke's friend, Sean Pollard, who talked about going to Harvard Law School, but who thought a tort was one of those fancy desserts.

"Is Luke nervous?" I asked.

"Oh, God, Clara, he looked ready to puke. There's a million people in there."

"Poor guy," I said. But I didn't *feel* "poor guy." What I felt was my own disappointment. A million people. The chances of me seeing him again in a crowd like that were next to zero.

We squeezed our way through the mob. Our band was playing a pounding, rousing something, and your ears just thrummed with *noise*. The blare of contemporary tribal warfare. Shakti had her place she liked to stand, right near the team benches, where she could keep an eye on Luke and on the assistant coach, our old history teacher, Mr. Dutton. Mr. Dutton's face showed every emotion, and Shakti was sure she could read his game plan for Luke in his expressions. This was fine by me. We'd made an agreement in my head, the boy-from-somewhere- else and me—we'd meet again in the same spot. It was the only likely way we'd run in to each other again. I'd walk over to him, just as I had last time. I had it all planned out for us.

The whistle screeched; the game began. There was the rumble of running and the slams of the ball being dribbled down the court. Everyone was shouting. But I was in that strange place of heightened awareness that makes you feel both more a part of your surroundings and completely lifted out from them. The scoreboard was flashing and Shakti shouted things my way and one of our good friends, Nick Jakes, came over to stand with us, but I felt only that single presence in the room somewhere, his eyes on me, that sense of being watched that makes your every move feel acted out with a charged self-consciousness. He was in the room, I was in the room, and we both knew it.

I kept scanning the crowd, looking toward the place he'd stood with the girl last time. He wasn't there. He wasn't anywhere. The first quarter was over. We moved toward the end of the second. I was starting to lose my energy for this game, the one I alone was playing. Disappointment and the ways I'd been foolish were starting to sneak in around the edges of all that hope and buildup. I was beginning to rewrite the whole deal. So, we'd said a few things to each other, so what. So, it meant more to me, obviously, than it did to him. That happens, right? No big loss. I was glad I hadn't worn that other outfit. That outfit would have felt humiliating as I walked back to the car.

Nick bought Shakti and me a Coke, two sloshy drinks in paper cups. His fingers passed mine as he handed it to me. I hadn't realized it before, but I think Nick liked me. We thanked him. We stood and yelled stupid jokes about the other team's mascot, who wore a costume that looked like a gopher on steroids. I said something that made Nick laugh, and he put his thumbs through my belt loops and gave my waist a shake. The clock kept ticking. I was reluctantly letting go of the stupid fantasy I'd had.

And then I felt a tap on my shoulder, two light hits with a rolled-up program. I turned my head.

"Still wish you were somewhere else?" he shouted.

My heart, which had slunk off somewhere safe, now had some catching up to do. It zoomed to its rightful place and started beating madly. Some people can be disappointing when you see them again after spending time with them in your imagination. They can look younger and act it too, or have some strange mole or weird teeth you wish you were generous enough not to care about. But he was not disappointing. Not at all. That silky, white-blond hair, those blue eyes. And he smelled good. Good enough that the warm buzz began again; it started at my knees, worked its way up.

"Hi," I said.

"Hi."

We just looked at each other and grinned as if we'd just pulled off something great, some great heist or magic trick. Then he gestured his head toward the door. "Let's."

*Stay*

"I'll be right back," I shouted to Shakti and Nick. I still held that Coke Nick had bought for me. It was now a cup of mixed emotions with crushed ice. Shakti looked at this stranger and raised her eyebrows—curious, but also disapproving. We didn't know this guy. This wasn't the kind of thing either of us would do. Then again, we *had* known Dylan Ricks and look what had happened there.

I admired him from the back—those broad shoulders, snug T-shirt, a butt you didn't mind one bit walking behind. It was the kind you'd want to put your hands on, let's just say that. The gym doors were propped open for air, and outside there was the sudden freedom of the cold night mingled with the smell of someone smoking far off. A car engine revved, and a girl shouted something. Someone laid on their horn, yelled *Fuckers!* and laughed loud.

As we walked toward the track, the pulsing energy and sounds of the gym fell back. I wasn't sure who was leading, but it must have been me. It *was* me. I was leading the whole time, see? That's what I'm trying to say. The track bleachers were a good place to talk. I led him through the dark ticket gate, and we sat down on a cold metal bleacher seat a few climbs up. He was there right next to me, after being in my head for weeks. It was hard to believe. The air smelled like fall—orange leaves piled upon orange leaves making their own scent that rose up in the October night. It felt surprising and unreal, one of those times you feel like you're in someone else's body. It wasn't how I imagined it going, but it would do just fine. Better.

"You smell really good," he said. Ah, that voice.

"I was thinking the same thing about *you*," I said. "Clara. We don't even know each others' names. Clara Oates."

He didn't ask about my father, as some people did when I told them who I was. You could tell he hadn't been here very long. "Christian Nilsson. Do we shake now?" he teased. I saw his eyes laughing. I held out my hand to shake, to tease back, and he took it. Ran a finger down my palm before letting it drop.

It made me shiver. Christian. The name felt surprising. There was his actual *name*, who he was, a piece of information that meant there were a thousand other pieces of information about him I didn't know yet. It felt like a door to another land. "That's a beautiful name," I said. My words sounded stupid to me suddenly, and I felt myself blush. It *was* a beautiful name, it sounded like a designer scarf, and I was just me, and I hadn't come from anywhere special.

"Who was that guy you were with?" he said.

"Nick? Just a friend."

"Ah," he said, as if there were likely more to that story, which there wasn't. He looked out over the empty track. Dylan Ricks had been on the lacrosse team. I had sat in that same spot to watch him play before. "I was hoping you'd be here tonight. I don't give a shit about that game."

He made the word *shit* sound luxuriant and striking, something you wanted more of, please. If nothing else, you could love him for that voice.

"I was hoping to see you too," I said. I was bold. The moon was big and white. I could hardly believe what was happening.

Dylan Ricks had been my only boyfriend before this. I'd gone to the movies with Terrence Hilligan, out for coffee, that kind of thing, but I hadn't wanted to kiss him. Harrison Daily for homecoming. I'd once gone to a movie with Dean Yamaguchi to be nice. It felt like my life was changing.

"I don't normally go hunting down girls like this, just so you know."

He looked at me expectantly. I knew what I was supposed to say—that I didn't do that kind of thing, either. It was the truth, so it was easy. But I could feel his need to hear it, his need for my reassurance, and that need made me feel . . . large, maybe. In a way I hadn't before. But he didn't know that. For all he knew, I was always that large. It felt good. Fun. Unexpectedly large is sudden, magic levitation—you're high, an impervious Balloon of Joy. So instead, I teased. "Well, I don't go hunting down *girls*, either. But guys . . ."

"Oh, I see," he said. "You're that kind." He looked at me with those blue, blue eyes. I kept watching his mouth. You'd want to bite that bottom lip. I wanted to right then. This was the way I had never felt about Terrence Hilligan. I don't think I'd ever felt that way about Dylan, either.

"Okay, obvious question," I said. "Where are you from?"

"Texas," he said. He grinned at me, and I laughed. "No, Copenhagen. My mother married an American. She was a journalist. They met here, in California. We moved to the states three years ago, but my mother hated Los Angeles."

"Wow," I said. "I can't even imagine Copenhagen. But my father is a writer, too. Novelist. Mysteries, crime . . ."

"We don't read many paperbacks," he said.

I felt my father's reputation unfairly plummet, from bestselling author with countless fans* to some writer of supermarket books with gold foil covers, sold used at flea markets for a quarter. My own defensiveness prickled, and I was about to blow it all by counting off various honors my father had earned when Christian took my hand. I could see he didn't mean anything by his comment. He held my hand in both of his. This wasn't something boys here would do either. He held it like something precious.

"I'm just glad your mother didn't like L.A.," I said.

He looked into my eyes, way down in, and I was sure he could see all of the important things there. He looked and he understood and maybe even had the ability to know me like no one else had before. I didn't feel like a seventeen-year-old girl, the sometimes brave but mostly searching girl that I was. I felt fully formed in ways that someone, a man, could respect and desire. I felt all that right there on the cold bleacher seat. I was much more than I normally was, that was for sure.

And his eyes, blue—if mine were all at once known, his were all things unknown. The wide unknown, long plane rides, a country of Vikings and midsummer, of beautiful blond people

..........................

* Including, you probably remember, the crazy one who tried to replicate in real life the plot of *Fine Young Woman*, but who thankfully was caught before anyone was hurt. If you saw my father trying to cook and talk on the phone at the same time, you'd be shocked at the power he holds over people. He'll go around with his T-shirt inside out too, and not even notice, the little flap of a tag getting a thrilling new view of the world it didn't ordinarily get.

and old royal castles and the white, icy shadow of Greenland. Busy streets winding irrationally, brimming with people and the smells of promising new foods. Our own streets were dull and quiet except for the beep of the crosswalk sign that thoughtfully let blind people know they could go ahead. We were vanilla here, and the rest of the world had all the other flavors.

Those things—they sat there like an invitation. To a party you never thought in a million years you'd be going to but suddenly felt ready for.

He leaned forward and I could feel his warm breath. He was going to kiss me, I thought. He waited, and so I leaned forward, too. I wanted that kiss. He moved toward me and our mouths met and our tongues entwined and it got hot right away. Jesus. I stopped.

"I've got to get back," I said. My mouth tasted different.

"Let's walk, then."

I felt awkward being so suddenly set free. My legs were wobbling walking down the bleachers. The night had seemed almost graceful and fluid, which did not match with the clumping of my shoes on the metal seats as I made my way to the field. Before we got to the gym doors, he stopped.

"I told myself not to be an idiot and forget your phone number this time."

"You're right. What if we forgot?" It was so new and fragile it could easily disappear like melting snow, like spoken words, like a dream upon waking. You needed ways to pin it to the ground, ways like phone numbers and addresses and plans to see each other again. I looked around in my bag for paper, but no luck. I found the business card of the guy who had just fixed my dad's transmission, *Jake Ritchee, Smith and Gray Auto*, where I'd dropped the car off as a favor to my dad. I drew a line across the front, wrote my name and number and e-mail address on the back.

Christian took my pen, then turned my palm upright and wrote his number there. "It's on you forever now," he joked.

"Okay," I said. It was that awkward good-bye place. A kiss or hug would have been too intentional then.

"All right," he said as if we'd decided something important. He grinned, but his self-confidence had shifted slightly. He looked stunned, dazed. I had affected him. Knowing it felt vast and shimmery. He thought for a moment. "You let me kiss you."

"And I'd let you again," I said.

He turned and headed back to his car. He *hadn't* cared about that game—he didn't even return to it. But I did return, with his number on my palm, black ink that looked as permanent as a tattoo. I had forgotten my Coke cup back there on the bleacher seat, I realized.

I found Shakti where I'd left her. She stood there now with Akello, a friend of ours from Uganda. Nick had moved on.

"So who was *that*?" Shakti asked.

"Christian. He's from Denmark."

"Hmm. Watch out," Akello said. "Lots of consonants shoved together, those people. And Abba."

"Weren't they Swedish?" Shakti said.

"'Dancing Queen, long and mean, give it the Dancing Queen,'"Akello sang. His made his voice really high. He shimmied around a little, with his arms up.

"Abba Greatest Hits Gold," Shakti said, in an announcer voice.

I rolled my eyes at them. Shakti gave me a look that said we weren't through talking. But I didn't want to share everything yet with anyone, even her. I needed that time alone with it first, that delicious time where you replay every moment, where you make what has happened more real and also less—it becomes fact the more you repeat it, but it becomes story, too, with all the characters and plot and fictional truths.

I didn't even know what the score of that game was. I drove home. I lay in bed in the darkness, bringing the night from start to end in my mind again and again—*You let me kiss you. And I'd let you again.* My words had felt daring and right (and lucky, too, given how the right words usually came to me only when it was too late), and his had seemed grateful and a little awestruck. It was powerful to make someone feel awestruck. It was new, and I liked it. I was sure that feeling of power could make me bold again and *more* bold, too. I was not somehow smaller than him, or less interesting. He wasn't so large to be beyond me—he didn't see me that way, not at all. This was what confidence felt like. It was swirling upward inside of me, and that was the irony. The biggest feeling I had that night was of my own power.

Maybe he felt that, too. Maybe that was the seed. My power, his sudden powerlessness. This, too, is the ugly little heart of my guilt. I was the one who led, I was the one who stepped into that power and owned it and liked it. But then again, I was maybe only drunk from that kiss; my dark places were meeting his dark places, and I could only see his words as *awestruck.* I didn't see the accusation there. It was already right there, wasn't it, from the very beginning? Did that mean it would have been there no matter what I had done or said or felt? Could it be that there was never actually an *escalation* that I had caused, but instead only the ways he increasingly revealed himself?

I wouldn't see the accusation in those words until I had played that scene so many times in my mind. And many more times still, the way you do when you are trying and trying to understand the senseless logic of tragic things.

# Chapter 4

When I woke, my new bedroom in the rented house was white with hazy morning sun still hid by clouds. I had left the window open, and the breeze coming through smelled damp and salty. I put on my robe, looked out to the long stretch of sand, twice as deep as the night before now that the tide was out. My heart did a little leap, that heart swoop that meant there were still things to look forward to. We were right to come here, if only because the ocean reminded you that impossible things were possible. Miles and miles of the deepest waters that moved like clockwork were possible. Creatures like jellyfish and sea urchins were, too. Millions and jillions of the tiniest grains of sand to form one long, soft beach—yep, even that was possible.

Or maybe it was just the smell of bacon cooking that made me feel so good. Dad had the radio on, too—NPR, by the sound of it. At home, he drove me crazy with the sound of that NPR, but I liked it right then. It was familiar but new in this new place. Pans were clattering, which meant French toast, too, and I could hear him whistling. I hurried, and for the first time in a while I was hurrying because of something good in front of me instead of something bad behind me.

"The great day waits, Sweet Pea," my father said happily. He was wearing drawstring striped pajama bottoms and a white undershirt and was wielding a spatula. He had his scuffers on, which is what he called those old slippers of his with the open backs. His black-gray hair was longer than usual, though his beard and mustache were kept trim, and he had on the rectangular black glasses he wore in the mornings or when his contacts were bothering him. His nose was big, and he looked a bit rough, but women thought he was Italian because of his olive skin. They *liked* his edge, and he often got letters from them based only on that black-and-white jacket cover photo.*

"That looks so good," I said. "I'm starving."

"I'm glad. You're looking too thin. It makes me think of your mother."

My mother. Rachel Fournier Oates. It was true, she had been thin, I could see that in the pictures. I resembled her, not Dad, with her light brown hair, angled face, and serious eyes.

........................

* Which, by the way, I took in our backyard. If you look closely at the photo credit, you'll see that it reads *Photo by S. P. Clara*, which is the name we gave me. The "S. P." stands for Sweet Pea. Pretty good photo, right? My mother was a photographer, and Dad says I have her eye.

She wore her hair long and straight, though, or in a ponytail down her back, whereas mine stops right at my shoulders.

"They're all thin on that side of the family," I said.

"Nerves," he said. He didn't elaborate, and I didn't want him to. My mother's family hated him, and it seemed like the feeling was mutual. Still, they were our relatives, hers and mine.

I snitched a piece of bacon right off the plate. "Bacon makes you believe in God."

"A pig would disagree. See if he's got any hot sauce around here," Dad said, which meant he would be making eggs, too. "You'll never believe what I found on the shelf above my dresser." He gestured toward the table, where a thin leather photo album sat at what I guessed was now my place.

"Jackpot," I said. "We know what he looks like now."

"Not so fast," Dad said. "Hey, take a look at these knives. The guy likes only the best."

I grinned at Dad brandishing the silver knife with the black handle, looked down at the album. I opened the cover, expecting to see our mystery host in full color, but instead there were only dim, square photos from the 1970s—blond boys with shaggy, feathered hair, flannel shirts tucked in to flared jeans with wide belts. I turned the page. The same blond boys with groovy, 1970s parents in front of a Christmas tree flocked white. Some family trip to some unidentified state capital. "All we know is that he's blond," I said.

"And a little younger than me. You think?" Dad said. "He's probably in high school there?"

My father was loving this. Maybe he liked not knowing, or

maybe he liked finding out. We once followed a searchlight for miles until we ended up at a Fred Meyer opening in Lynnwood. Dad wasn't even disappointed. "I guess. Ooh. Looking hot here." I held up the album so he could see a teenage couple in front of a purple backdrop with a gold moon. School dance. "Three-piece suit in high school? He's wearing a *vest*."

"He's not *hot*. He's a *stud*. And she's a *fox*. They're about to leave that idiotic dance to get it on in a Chevy van. Have you noticed that no one gets it on anymore? No one is funky? No one gets down?" My father was on a roll. He cracked eggs into a pan, and they started to sizzle in the melted butter. He picked a bit of shell out with the edge of his finger. "We could feed the fire department."

"No one boogies . . ." I added. I remembered my friend Danisha's mother, listening to the oldies station every morning when we carpooled to middle school.

"No pretty mamas no more," Dad said. You could tell he liked how the words sounded. I did too.

We ate that enormous breakfast. Dad slapped more French toast on my plate because we needed to *eat up* for a *big day*. I groaned when Dad said this. It was the kind of heavy meal that makes you feel in need of a nap. Food coma. I didn't see how truck drivers did it. I'd pictured lying around on my white bed in the white room, reading books off of the mystery man's shelf. "Don't you need to work today?" I asked.

"Explore the town," he said through a mouthful of eggs. "Find the library. Bank. Grocery store. A job for you."

I pushed my plate away. "God, no. Dad—"

"If you think you're going to laze around pondering the

miserable state of your life all summer, it's not going to happen. Job, and maybe those waylaid college applications, right? It's for your own good. Note that this is often what parents say when it is also for *our* own good. I can't work with a human weather system in the next room."

"There's miles of beach," I tried.

"Forget it."

"Did you see how big that town was? What are the chances of even finding a job?"

"Zero, if we don't look. You're not the depressed type, C. P. When have you ever been the depressed type? We Oateses are sturdy folks. There is an *after* you have to plan for, here. Bus is leaving, ten minutes." He shoved his chair back and stood. For a minute I thought he might pound his chest like an alpha male gorilla. It was puffed out like that, anyway. "God, the ocean is energizing," he said.

The library was the first stop, as it always was when my father was in a new place. He visited libraries like other people did museums or historic churches. The Bishop Rock Library was so tiny, it could have fit into the children's room of the Seattle branch. He bullshitted with the librarian who followed him out with her eyes, I noticed. I told you, women looked at him like that. He checked out a large, hefty book on the history of revolvers (that thing weighed fifteen pounds, I swear) as well as several novels, and I did the same.

"She said to check the taffy shop for jobs," my father said when we emerged and found ourselves back on the main street. "Did you know Bishop Rock taffy is world renowned?" He smirked with a bit of superiority, but I could tell he liked this small town. We walked down the sidewalk, past a tiny grocery and a store selling souvenir T-shirts, and finally arrived at the candy shop, which had a yellow striped awning and a sweet, buttery smell oozing like sugar lava from the doorway. Dad stopped, but only for a second. "Come on," he said, and we walked past that place. It was one of the good things about him—my father understood the fine shadings of feeling, the sense you had in your gut but didn't have words for. The yellow awning and the bins of sunny pastels and the matching yellow aprons and the optimism of taffy were impossibly surreal and strange against the backdrop of what had happened—think pop music in a funeral home, or a brand new baby dressed all in black. I could never work there, not then. Cheer and despair don't like to sit that close together.

Across the street there was a small marina, a dock of parked fishing boats, and a small, dilapidated tug. There was a second dock filled with sailboats and cruisers and motorboats. A huge sailboat was moored at the very end, with a mast straight to the sky, and you could see a guy on the deck, shading his eyes to look at another guy, who was hanging way up in a harness on that mast.

"Look," my father said.

"Beautiful," I said.

"Let's go see it."

"Dad . . ." I hated when he did this. He wasn't just going to go see it—he would talk to those guys. He *had* to talk to people. All people, anywhere, people in movie lines and airports, chefs and taxi drivers. He learned things, great, but it always felt a bit embarrassing. Did they even *want* to tell him their life stories, or how a propeller worked, or how many miles they guessed they'd driven that taxi over the years? "I've got to find a job, remember?" I said. But he had already tossed our bag of books in the car and was crossing the street, heading toward the marina and that gorgeous sailboat.

I followed him. I could feel the dock moving under my feet. The water sloshed below, and you could smell its salty green depths and the deadness of seaweed washed ashore. There was a small hut at the end of the dock, a ticket booth. The boat was a tour boat. A majestic blue hull, with the name in script on the side. *Obsession*.

"*Obsession*, eh?" my father shouted to the guy on deck.

The guy turned. I was surprised to see he was not much older than me. Eighteen, nineteen. He had cargo shorts on, no shirt. Tousled black hair, the scruffy start of a beard, the kind of eyes you'd call sweet. "It was named before the perfume," he said. "You folks want a ride?"

"I won't step one foot on a boat," my father said. He didn't mind looking at the water, he just wouldn't get in it or on it. No way in hell. I had no idea why. Childhood trauma, general fear, who knew.

"We'd make sure you didn't fall in more than once," the other guy said from above, his legs dangling down. They had to be brothers. They looked just alike, with that same dark hair and scruff, though the one above us was older, leaner. Longer hair. Sunglasses that hung from a leather lanyard around his neck, a pair of keys on it, too.

"She's beautiful," my father said. "Is she *your* obsession?"

"I guess you could say that," the guy on deck said. "Tours are an hour, hour and a half if we like you." He looked at me when he said that. My stomach did a little flip, and I cursed it. So what if he looked like that. "We go out past Possession Point. Got good wind."

"Possession Point?" I said.

"Out there. That bit of beach that juts out?"

I nodded. Sure we knew it. It's right where our house was.

"How fast does she go?" My father was still stuck on that boat.

"Oh, she's gone twenty-five knots downwind with the spinnaker up. Ten to twelve on a usual day."

"Fast for a boat that big."

"We race her in the off-season. Crew of eight, ten guys."

Dad shook his head. "How big? What, maybe fifty feet?"

"Seventy."

Dad whistled. He was loving this, the short clip of guy talk. He could edge right in and make it work. You'd never guess he was the same person who could speak in loops and swirls that were basically poetic. "The mast?"

"Ninety."

Dad shook his head with appropriate appreciation. I did the same, though numbers were as hazy and hard to grasp for me as ideas were for other people. Ninety, okay. It was tall. Really tall. And that guy was hanging up there like it was nothing.

"If you change your mind . . ." the guy above shouted. He took out his wallet from his back pocket as he dangled there. A business card fluttered down and landed in the water. A seagull paddled over to see if it was something he could eat.

"Moron," the guy on the deck shouted up. He took out his own wallet, handed my father a card, and then another to me. *Finn Bishop*, it said. *Sailor*.

*Stay*

"Bishop?" my father said.

"The old dead captain was some sort of relation, though my mother always gets the story screwed up."

"Pleasure meeting you guys," Dad said.

"You too." He paused for a second. Grinned. "Hope you'll come for a sail sometime," he said to me.

My stomach flipped again, making its point. I looked down, smiled in spite of myself, and then we waved and crossed back over the dock. I was blushing, but I hoped Dad didn't see. Oh, Jesus. I didn't need to worry about Dad, though—he was in his own world, as usual. He turned back around and shouted. "You guys know where someone could get work?" He crooked his thumb my way.

"Dad, for God's sake," I hissed. Shit, he could be so embarrassing. I know parental embarrassment usually stops somewhere at fifteen, but he just kept on giving me good reason. I tugged at his arm, waved my hand at the guy to indicate he should just ignore him. Too late; the guy was already shouting back.

"Try the lighthouse. Sylvie Genovese. She's always firing someone."

"Thanks." Dad waved his arm again.

We had a humiliating and lengthy wait at a DONT WALK sign, with not a car in sight for miles. Dad was a priss about jaywalking.* Finally, we were back on the other side of the street, and

..................

* Or maybe he just liked to stare down what he'd testily call the "grammatical error sanctioned by the state." There is, of course, no apostrophe in the DONT WALK sign.

then at our car. "Great. Always firing someone. Makes the taffy place sound like a haven," I said.

"Come on, you could charm the skin off a snake," he said.

We got back into Dad's Saab. I may have slammed my door. My good mood was shriveling right up. Some combination of shame and humiliation in front of really cute guys mixed with the oddness of where we were and why and the caffeine from the morning's coffee wearing off.

But maybe it was something else. "Possession Point, Dad? Jesus."

"I didn't know," he said. "How was I supposed to know?"

"Obsession? Possession? Deception Point? You're telling me it's all an *accident*? How many places could we have gone?"

"Swear to God, Pea," he held up his hand. "I'd have to be a sick bastard to knowingly put us in a house on Possession Point." He started up the car. I couldn't believe it; he started to laugh.

"Dad!"

"You gotta admit, it's kind of funny." His shoulders were moving up and down. Having himself a good old moment of hilarity.

"It's not funny at all."

Which of course made him laugh harder.

I was mad. I tried not to smile. "Okay, it's a little funny," I said.

"Holy Christ, fate's got a fucking sick sense of humor," he chuckled.

We headed out to the lighthouse, a drive that took us across a windswept road out to a high, rocky cliff that dropped down to the beach. The lighthouse was pure white, and the way its column stood against the sky made it seem proud and lonely and important. The keeper's house was white, too—two stories with red trim and a steep sloping red roof and narrow rectangular windows. A big old sip-lemonade porch sprawled a welcome in front. There was a small garden around its perimeter, with bright green grass and flower baskets. I had gotten twisted around as to where we were after that winding drive, but when we stepped out of the car, I realized we weren't that far from our house—I could see the jut of land that was Possession Point not far from the cliff where we stood. From that height, I could see that we weren't entirely alone out there either, at that lighthouse. A few gray shingled houses dotted the beach, as did a small single shack that looked like it could be done in by a strong wind.

"Clara!" Dad called from where he stood in front of a large white sign. "Clara Bell, come and see this."

I jogged over, because it was a place that made you feel like running. It was like one of those adventure places—an old military fort or a red barn in a pasture, where you felt eight years old again. You wanted to climb and make discoveries and play pirates of the Caribbean.

He was grinning wide. He pointed at the sign. "Another meaningful word! Honey!"

"Don't even joke," I said. I looked. PIGEON HEAD POINT LIGHTHOUSE. "Very funny," I said.

"Very sca-ry . . ." He was so pleased with himself. "Pi-geons! Oooh-eee!"

I ignored him. "They've sure got a lot of 'Points' here," I said.

He started to read aloud. "'Pigeon Head Point is an elevated area on the western edge of Bishop Rock, with eighty-foot bluffs that drop into the inlet. The first Pigeon Point Head Lighthouse (also known as the Red Bluff Lighthouse), was built in 1860, and . . .'"

I walked to the keeper's house. Dad was the kind of person who read every word on every plaque in every museum, zoo, or historical site. He couldn't be like us regular people, who only read the first line or two. This meant that going with him to those places was a lengthy and painful process. In fact, he was still reading aloud right then for my benefit, but I pretended I couldn't hear.

There was a sign on the door of the keeper's house. VISITOR HOURS. The place should have been open, but it didn't look like anyone was there. And another sign in the widow, handwritten: PIGEON HEAD POINT LIGHTHOUSE AND GIFT SHOP NOW ACCEPTING EMPLOYMENT APPLICATIONS. INQUIRE WITHIN. The sign looked yellowed, as if "now accepting" was a permanent condition. I cupped my hands against the glass and tried to look inside.

"No one home?" Dad said.

"Doesn't look like it."

"Let's go around the back."

We made our way around to the rear yard. There was a white arbor along the length of the house and a fenced garden back there. A door on the second story that led to a deck was propped open.

"Hello?" my father called.

No answer.

"That's okay, we'll come back," I said.

"Grapes," he pointed. "How the hell do you grow grapes here?"

"Vegetables, too." I pointed.

"That's some kind of green thumb. Let's wait a few minutes."

My good mood was returning, and there was no reason why we shouldn't wait. There was nothing we had to do here anyway. There was no school or work or room to clean. No friends to call and meet for coffee, no concerts to go to, no movies to pick up at Total Vid. No future to plan just yet. We'd agreed that I would tell my friends we were traveling in Europe for Dad's book research, so no phoning or texting. No e-mail. We couldn't chance letting anyone know where we were. I didn't even tell Shakti the truth. My friends were on one planet, going out and taking last trips together and packing for college, and I had dropped onto another planet, where it was just us knocking around in this empty in-between, this temporary new life. It was lonely and strange and liberating.

We walked over to the edge of the bluff. The ocean was wide, wide around us; the white waves curved in a majestic arc around the bay, and the sky tried to compete, showing off with bold stripes of white clouds. The ocean roared and you heard a couple of seagulls calling as they looped in circles above. Inside the house, a dog barked.

My father was quiet, for once. Suddenly quiet. His arms were folded across his chest. His thoughts were a million miles out to sea.

"Why don't you like the water?" I asked.

He thought. He did an evasive word-dance. "I love the water. You can't not love the water. Seventy percent of our planet is water. Seventy percent of our own *bodies* are water. It's what we *are*."

"We can dislike what we are."

He ignored this.

"You won't go on boats . . ." I tried again.

"I've made peace with the water. I figured out how to love certain parts while I hate other parts."

"That doesn't sound very peaceful."

It was obviously something he didn't want to talk about. He probably didn't know how to swim and was too embarrassed to say. He looked at his watch. "If your new boss isn't back here in fifteen seconds, we're heading out. I'm starved."

"I can't believe you're hungry after this morning."

He watched the second hand of his watch without speaking for fifteen seconds exactly. "Sea air is famishing," he said.

We headed to the grocery store to stock up on food, and then we stopped at a shack near the beach that sold fresh fish. We bought crab wrapped in newspapers, and later that evening we unwrapped it and laid it right out on the table, cracking the legs and dipping the sweet white meat into melted butter. The clouds came in—we watched them approach from far off. After dinner, Dad went for a walk, his pants rolled up to his shins, his shirttail out. I went to my room and lay on my bed and started one of the new books I'd gotten from the library.

I heard Dad's heavy steps on the deck when he returned, then the bottoms of his sandals being clapped together to free the sand. The door slid open and shut, and then a moment later, open again. A deck chair scraped against the wood. He was just sitting out there, watching the sea. I set my book open at the edge of my bed and got up.

"What's he going to think when his good scotch is all gone?"

I said. Dad's feet were on the railing, knees up. He swirled a bit of brown liquid and ice in his glass.

"I'll buy him a new one," he said. Defensive.

"Fine. Whatever."

"If you've come to interrupt my peace with your parental attitude, I do hope you'll cease. In case you haven't noticed lately, I'm the father here."

I sat down. "The new book's not great," I said. "Kind of shallow."

"Mmm," he said, and shook his head. "Too bad." His regret was sincere.

"I'm going to give it more of a chance."

"There are so many that are *yours* just *waiting* . . ."

We always argued about this. I tended to give a book a chance and another chance and another, sometimes seeing it all the way to the end, still hoping for it to turn out different. Maybe I was confused about what you owed a book. What you owed people, for that matter, real or fictional.

He tinked those ice cubes in that glass. It was the second time in one day I'd seen that look on his face.

"Are you okay?" I asked.

"Yep." He took a swallow. I once tasted that stuff, just to see what it was like. It burns your throat like a lit match. He moved his free hand in and then out, like the tide. "The ocean . . . It gives, and then it takes. Gives. Takes."

It made me uneasy. Maybe he was drunk. I never really saw him drunk, even though I saw him drink often, often enough that it seemed bad for his health. Health, you might guess, was pretty important to me. I had no wish to be an orphan. But if I were being honest, I knew it wasn't the alcohol that was bothering me right then. It was something in his face, and the time before, too, at the lighthouse. Something closed off and weighty. It was a shut door, and shut doors meant things kept to yourself. There were reasons you kept things to yourself, and they usually weren't good, happy, open-air sort of reasons. Still, I didn't want to see behind that door. You think you want to know everything there is to know about everything there is to know. But you don't. Not really. I had pried the lid off of the dark places of another person before, I had seen inside. Down deep. You don't want to look at what's rotting there.

I left him to brood and went back to my room. My book had fallen to the floor. It said something about where my mind was right then that my first thought was that it had been moved. I even looked around, just in case. I feel ashamed to admit it, but I checked the closet, which only held boxes belonging to our mystery host, labeled WINTER CLOTHES. It's what I used to do when I was a kid, check the closet before I went to sleep. Making sure there were no robbers there. I wasn't a kid who believed in some kind of monster.

I got into my p.j. shirt, brushed my teeth. I was suddenly exhausted. I came back to my room and sat at the edge of the bed, took that business card from my book, where I'd used it as a bookmark. *Finn Bishop. Sailor.* I tried to make the simple typed words tell me more that they did, but they just sat there without giving. I couldn't imagine his life or who he was beyond the kind eyes and the strong hands.

And then the business card reminded me of another business card. *Jake Ritchee, Smith and Gray Auto,* because that's how it works after something terrible has happened. You know this is true if something terrible has ever happened to you. A thousand objects take on new meaning. Everything is a reminder of something else. A business card will never be just a business card. A handful of change will not. A rope will not.

# Chapter 5

Christian called me the next morning after that basketball game, like I knew he would. I was sure of it. Every moment
from the time he kissed me, from the time he drove away in
his car after that basketball game—it felt like waiting. I think
even in sleep I was waiting, and he must have felt the same. My
phone rang at two minutes after nine, which probably meant he
had told himself not to call until then.

"It's crazy, but I already miss you," he said.

"I know. Me too. I could hardly sleep."

"Your voice. Morning voice. Husky."

"I haven't talked to anyone yet," I said. I was still in bed. I was
lying down, tucked into the covers.

"It's sexy."

I felt that way, talking there in bed. I felt like warm liquid, languid.* He was somewhere, who knew, but I was lying in bed, and it felt intimate. "Where are you?"

"I'm at . . ." He paused. I imagined him looking up at the street sign. "Ravenna and Fifteenth. Several blocks from Mr. Hooper's house."

"Mr. Hooper—wasn't he on Sesame Street?" I smiled.

"He's the old guy I work for. A few days a week I check in on him. He's in a wheelchair. Refuses to give up his home. I take him for walks. Read to him. Listen to him complain about his nurse."

God, he was a good person, too. "That's so sweet."

"Don't tell anyone that. They'll think less of me. Still, it means I can't see you until later."

"That's okay." Later was forever from now.

"Can we meet? Do your parents lock you up on a Sunday night?"**

"We can meet," I said.

We made plans. I lay in bed for a long time just feeling delicious anticipation. Then excitement hit. I got up. I had to move a mountain or something.

..........................

* The word "languid" is one of those words that sound perfect for what it is. Like "prickly." Or "luminescence." See? Words are magical that way.

** Telling people about your dead mother is always delicate. You have to be prepared for them to spill their sympathy as if it happened yesterday. One math teacher, after telling me how much she was looking forward to meeting my mother on open house night and therefore forcing me to explain, grasped me in a long, heartfelt hug after I'd told her. This is not to say I don't feel my own grief, which can hit powerfully at unexpected times. It's just that the telling does not automatically bring on my own upset, as people assume. I deal more with their reaction than they do with mine, and so you have to choose your timing.

* * *

I told Dad that Shakti and me and our friends Kels and Cleo were all getting sushi and doing our calculus together. Dad didn't believe in sushi. He believed in meat. I didn't want to keep a secret from him, and I knew I wouldn't for long, but if love wasn't just yours first, it was like cutting up and handing out your birthday cake before you blew out the candles.

The drive in the car felt like it was miles and miles long instead of just a few. We decided to meet in front of Denny Hall on the University of Washington campus. Denny is the oldest building there, all ancient stone and chiming bells. A long walkway under elms leads up to it, with carved benches on either side marking the earliest graduating classes. There's lawn there, too, places to walk and sit and talk. I'd brought a blanket. I'd brought small containers of juice so my breath could smell like raspberries and pomegranates when we sat close.

There he was. He also had a blanket under his arm. I guess we were thinking the same thing, then. The anticipation had been so bright and sharp it almost hurt. My whole body was waiting. I knew this, because when he leaned over and kissed my cheek hello, I felt warm and electric, and the smell of him, that musky deodorant or shampoo or soap, whatever it was—it burned itself into that permanent place in my brain, the one that would make sure that I would remember that smell when I was old and had forgotten most other things.

I covered the hand he'd set on my face with my own. My face felt hot. I moved his mouth over to mine. I'd never felt anything like this, or had done anything like that, and I felt that sense again, power. He wanted me so badly, I could tell. He was trying not to go there yet, but I was leading and he could only follow and that made me feel like I could lift the sky with one hand.

The thing is, it can feel good to make someone lose all control.

I was holding a ball of fire in my hands, like a sorceress. He was pulling at my shirt, pulling me down to the grass, and I went with him. Forget the blankets. Tongues and mouths and hands doing what tongues and mouths and hands were thinking of doing from the first moment, probably.

I pulled back, then. I felt like I'd been abducted and sucked into another world. I wasn't even sure where I was for a minute. I was breathless. There was a guy walking his dog right near us. A pair of students with backpacks. But that world with Christian, the one we had ended up in when we were kissing, that place—it was the one I wanted to stay in.

He looked into my eyes, and I looked into his. I saw so much there. I always would. His eyes were a vivid blue, and so clear it seemed like I could look in there forever and never reach an end. All that feeling—it seemed like it meant something. Something huge. You're supposed to listen to yourself, right? That's what I was sure I was doing. What I was hearing—it was so *loud*.

He shot meaning into me with his eyes, and I did the same back. I looked at his face—full lips, cheekbones. They were cheekbones I could miss and miss if they went away. I could miss that voice so much if I didn't have it with me always. Sometimes this seems surprising, but people, a person, can feel that way about you, too. It's just your regular old self to you, but to them, they couldn't imagine not looking at your nose, or your chin, the daily old chin you don't even see anymore. It's hard to believe, but it's true. Your old chin can be magic like that, who would have thought.

"I don't even know what to say," he said.

"I almost didn't go to that game," I said.

"My friend Evan asked me to hang out that night," Christian said. "I almost didn't go, either."

We sat there with the enormity of that thought. As I said, our meeting felt like fate. But like my father says, fate's got a fucking sick sense of humor. Fate is a shape-shifter. It is the kindest and most generous entity imaginable, laying out more goodness than a person deserves, and then it shrinks and curls and forms into something grotesque. You think something is one thing, but then it's another.

We got back up. Christian spread out the blanket, and we sat on it this time. I circled my knees with my arms.

"You are so beautiful," he said.

I felt beautiful. I'd never felt beautiful before, not really. I didn't feel ugly, but I never saw myself like Hailey Denison or Zoe Faraone, the kind of girls with blond hair to their waists and stiff, perfect makeup, who only ate rice cakes and half a container of non-non-nonfat yogurt before throwing the rest away. You never really saw their insides. I had brown hair, and I was not thin as a rye crisp. I ate lunch and liked it. Most of the time, I said what I thought.

"*You* are a million things," I said.

"Happy?" he said.

I smiled.

"Completely blown away?" he said. "There's two. Come here."

He was stretched out, and I stretched beside him. He traced the curve of my T-shirt with one finger, along the open neck.

"Did you wear this just for me?" It was cut a little low. I laughed. "Maybe, maybe not."

"You must have guys following you all over school, wearing that," he said.

I thought it was a compliment. I was sitting there, soaking in the great ego feed of new love, where your wonderfulness merges with his wonderfulness, magic dust that creates some sky-high shiny Christmas tree sparkling with admiration and flattery and tinsel and lights and a billion, hopeful, unopened presents underneath. I just saw it as praise, falling down now like glittering snowflakes. But it was something else. A drop of poison on that gathering snow. That moment in the fairy tale when we know what just happened but the princess doesn't.

We talked. For hours, it must have been, because the sky got that sweet, tender yellow tint of a late fall afternoon turning to evening. We talked about everything—his growing up in various European cities, his parent's awful divorce, his financier father who just moved to Stockholm and who never seemed to call anymore. How his mom would leave them both for months at a time ever since he was a baby, traveling for her work, the work she'd given up now that she'd married his stepfather. The decision they all made for him to come to America to be permanently with her now that one of them was "settled." The ways he and his mother couldn't seem to get along. I was driving slowly past his own personal accident scene, taking it in with a sad, shocked heart: the crushed car, the trapped bodies. He didn't deserve anything bad that ever happened to him. My mental doctor's bag was out, ready to save him if he needed it. I held his hand.

We talked about his life now, too. Classes, his love of architecture and science and math and anything with exact outcomes. And me—how I didn't know what I wanted to study in college, how the not knowing pressed; my own dad, my mother, the ways I missed her. What I remembered—her holding me. Her voice. How I hated calculus and things with exact outcomes. Even our differences matched perfectly. We finally got up. We stretched and ached from sitting in one place, like old people. That's how long we were there.

We kicked through the layer of orange leaves on the ground, walked to our cars. We had chosen the same lot, our cars only a space away, more fate, I was sure. There were a ton of parking lots in that place, small circles upon circles between trees, and rows and rows of spaces. We leaned against his car and kissed some more until my lips were tingly and numb. He plucked a huge orange leaf from the ground and handed it to me, found another and held it carefully by its thin stem, something to remember this by. It was corny, I know. But if you've fallen in love, you've done it too, whether you want to admit it or not. You have a worn ticket stub or a paper napkin or a flower so dry it's turning to dust. You experienced magic once, and you want to have a little evidence of that. You don't want to forget it.

Of course, you never forget it. We said good-bye, our fingertips trailing away from each other. Even our fingertips were reluctant to leave.

I started the car. The radio blasted on just as it was when

Stay

I had turned the car off, and the air conditioner, too, and that seemed strange, because a million years had passed. It was like that moment in the Narnia books, where Lucy and Susan and Peter and Edmund come back through the wardrobe after conquering the White Witch and meeting Aslan and becoming kings and queens, only to find themselves children again back in the room in their uncle's house where it all began. I had to pee desperately, I realized. I was starving. All of the other human needs had been zapped away under that love spell, but now they were back. I was back.

I drove home. I was probably unsafe. Driving under a different influence. My thoughts were not with that steering wheel and those mirrors and that four-way stop. I pulled up in front of our house. When I got out, I could smell that my father had cooked something fabulous with garlic. I was so hungry. I had never been that hungry before, I was sure of it.

He was at his desk in his office when I went in. He was tapping the end of a pen against a stack of manuscript pages. He didn't keep regular hours.

"Clara Pea," he said. "You enjoy the raw fish? Man created fire to cook raw things, remember."

I was holding that leaf. I was spinning it in a circle by its stem. "I think I'm falling in love," I said.

He set his pen down, took his glasses off, leaned back in his chair. "Ah."

"I didn't meet Shakti and everyone for sushi," I said. It was time to tell him about Christian, but I also needed some of those leftovers, that was for sure.

"I see. Well, wonderful. Tell me he's nothing like Mr. Dick. I mean *Ricks.*"

"Nothing like," I said. "*Nothing.*"

"Fabulous," he said.

And it was. But if fate is a shape-shifter, then love is too. It can be, anyway, in its most dangerous form. It's your best day, and then your worst. It's your most hope and then your most despair. Lightness, darkness, it can swing between extremes at lightning speed—a boat upon the water on the most gorgeous day, and then the clouds crawl in and the sky turns black and the sea rages and the boat is lost.

# Chapter 6

The smell of coffee woke me, and so did those seagulls, insisting on whatever seagulls insist on. The coffee meant that my father was likely working. His best ideas, he said, came just after he was shot through with the glorious speeding train of caffeine.

I got up and saw that I was right. Dad had set up his laptop on the kitchen table, which had windows all around it in a half circle. He was surrounded by dunes and gray sky and yellow beach grass. His eyes were on that screen like he was watching a movie, which I guess he was, right there in his own head. He didn't notice me in there at all until I opened the refrigerator door.

"You want some coffee, C. P.?"

"You know I don't drink that stuff." To me, coffee tasted like cigarettes, with a dash of milk and sugar.

He handed me his cup to be refilled but kept his eyes on the screen. I looked at the cup. *Toronto Film Festival.*

"Hey, did you see?" I asked. I waved the cup around. "More evidence that the guy's in the film business?"

But Dad didn't answer. "What's that French word for 'boredom'? Why can't I think of it?"

I took out a box of cereal, the milk. This was the culinary decline that happened when Dad was working. "No idea."

"*Ennui.*" He typed.

"'Bored' sounds more boring," I said, but Dad didn't want to play. There was only the *tip tip tip* of his laptop keys.

I ate my cereal in silence. The spoon clanked against the side of the bowl in the quiet. The whole day could be like this. If I stayed here, I would hear each wave roll in and out and each footstep of mine and each breath. I would turn pages in my book and hear too loudly each papery flutter. I could feel the wide emptiness of where we were. Sea upon sea upon sea, endless beach upon beach, minutes dragging with nothing to do but mourn the miserable state of my life. Dad had been right.

I got ready, and then I swiped the keys off of the kitchen counter. "Going to the lighthouse in search of human beings," I said.

"Great," Dad said. He looked up. He actually saw me. He smiled. The smile was more about the writing going well, probably, than anything else, but that was okay. "You don't want to be too alone out here. Take some money. Buy some lunch."

"I'll get you some taffy."

"Perfect."

*Stay*

I got lost going to the lighthouse and had to loop back around twice to find it. They obviously didn't believe in signs around there. Finally, the right road. I could tell someone was home this time. There was a Jeep out front with the top off. I parked the Saab in the gravel lot, got out. The clouds hadn't cleared yet, and the sky was smeary white, fog whipping around fast like a pissed off ghost. It was cold. You couldn't see the top of the lighthouse. It was missing, vanished in fog.

I turned the knob of the front door and walked in to a hallway with an old wood floor. It smelled like old wood in there, too, the mustiness and echo of age. A room to the right held the gift shop. I could see a cash register with rows of gift cards in front and shelves of carved miniature lighthouses and sweatshirts and jars of local foods. To the left was a large room decorated with sepia prints of the Pigeon Head Point of long ago and glass cases that held objects—museum stuff, from what I could tell. Telescopes and maps and who knew what. Antique objects for people to stroll by and gaze at on rainy days when the beach gave a visitor nothing else to do. My father would have read every tiny, typed card. There was a long stairway in front of me, chained off. The lighthouse keeper must live up there.

I was trying to remember her name. Sounded like it belonged to a Mafia crime family. Started with an *S*? I pictured some old lady in stretchy pants. Someone who wouldn't mind selling snow globes with seagulls in them for the rest of her remaining life. A little dog came barreling down the steps. He was white, with a black spot on his back and cute, folded over ears. He was barking like he hadn't seen me in years.

"Well, hi," I said.

He was jumping up on me, a little circus dog on his hind legs. You couldn't look at him and not want to laugh. "Funny one," I said to him.

"Roger!" a woman called. A moment later, she appeared on the stairwell. She wasn't what I imagined at all. At *all*. She was maybe only thirty—black hair falling in long, loose curls down her back, deep black eyes, thick brows. She wore jeans and a white shirt, a denim jacket with the cuffs rolled up. "Roger, you are a naughty, naughty boy. Why are you always jump on the guest? You must not do that, Roger."

She had an accent. An accent that made me think of another accent.* Italian, though. Her name came to me all at once. Sylvie Genovese. She scooped up Roger the dog. She put him on her shoulder and held him there with one hand. He seemed to like it up there. He seemed used to it. He was smiling.

"Ms. Genovese?"

"*Mrs.*"

"I'm Clara Oates? I'm inquiring about the job?" She was the kind of person who made you put question marks after the things you said. And made you use words like *inquiring*. Imposing. And not because she was old and shriveled like I'd imagined, but because she was strong and beautiful.

..........................

* Sylvie Genovese is not the second person in this story with an accent, but the third. My mother was French, and although hers had mostly faded away, I remember her voice sounding different when she was angry or excited. Accents are funny in that they have this odd draw for us, yet we forget we have one, too. No one is without an accent, but the one you've got seems like oatmeal to their caviar.

"You will fill out an application, then." She walked past me, into the gift shop. Roger's little behind rode high on her shoulder. When she got to the counter, she set him back on the floor with one hand. He had calmed down now and only sniffed my sandal.

"All right."

"I need a few hours in the mornings and no more. I like to go out fishing and such then. Sometimes a tour bus stops . . ." She waved her hand to indicate what a nuisance it all was.

"That's fine," I said. She slid the paper across to me. Slapped down a pen.

"Only for the summer," she said.

"We're only here for the summer."

"We?"

"My father and I."

She fussed around the shop while I filled out the form. I could feel her watching me. I wasn't sure that I wanted to work there. It seemed as empty and isolated as home. Lonely here or lonely there, though I guess lonely here meant being paid. But then I stopped at the end of the form. I didn't know why we hadn't thought of it before. *References.*

"It asks for references . . ." I said. My voice sounded loud in there.

"Is it a problem?" She shoved her hands down into her jean pockets and looked at me in challenge.

"I worked at a bookstore every summer for three years."

"Put it down on the paper," she said.

"You can't call them," I said. I didn't know why I was telling her this. I should have just gotten out of there. I should have told Dad his mistake, made a new plan. I could read through the classics. Write some journal. Whatever.

She was back behind the counter. She held a pen in her hand. She was tapping the end just like Dad always did. "I can't call them."

"No."

"And why not I can't call them?"

"My old boyfriend got a job there," I said. "He can't know where I am."

She looked at me for a long time. Her eyes were a deep black, but suddenly kind. "Yes," she said. She thought. "I see. You need to be away from him. They will speak to him, you think."

"He finds out things," I said.

"You cannot trust anyone," she said.

"That's how it feels."

She nodded as if we suddenly understood each other. "Come back on Monday," she said. "I will teach you what you need to know. The people who come—they like a small tour sometimes. I will tell you exactly how do you do. They ask questions. I will give you a history book." She bent under the counter. "Damn it, where is it? No. Shit. One moment. Here it is." She straightened. Handed me a thin book. It looked well used. Water had spilled on it once—the pages were bunched and wavy. *Bishop Rock: History or Legend?* "Read the chapter on Pigeon Head. Head of a pigeon?" She made her eyes wide at the ridiculousness, held her hands out as if there was nothing to be done about it. "It is crazy."

"I know," I said. It *was* hard to believe. "Anyway, thank you. I'll read it." I knelt down and petted Roger. He was sitting so nicely and staring up at me. "He's so sweet."

"A little fiend," she said. But you could tell he was her baby. "True, he has some fine qualities, yes. He does not bore you with his religion beliefs. He does not speak on and on about the pain of his childhood."

I looked down at Roger. He looked so simple. He stood and wagged, as if he knew he was being discussed. He made me smile.

"Thank you," I said again. I wasn't completely sure I should be grateful. I started to head out. Something occurred to me. "Does it work? Is it a working lighthouse?"

"Of course," she said. "Standing there looking so pretty is not enough."

"And do you run it?" I was thinking of Mr. Genovese, I guess.

"Well, I am the keeper, yes?" she said. "I am the one here to make certain that the boats do not crash into the rocks."

I went back to the car. I got in and shut the door, but then I realized how early it still was. Dad wouldn't be out of his trance until later in the afternoon. I got back out of the car again, hoping she wasn't watching me. In and out—Sylvie Genovese wasn't the kind of person to be indecisive. I walked over to the lighthouse and looked up at it. The fog had moved on, and now it stood in all its glory. It couldn't just stand there and look pretty, but it was pretty. Beautiful and protective.

I walked to the edge of the bluff where my father and I had stood the day before. I noticed a trail I hadn't seen then, which wound down to the beach. It was steep, and I had on crappy sandals for steep, but I decided to go down there anyway. I did that embarrassing edging walk you do down slippery slopes, that sideways maneuver that involves clutching at clumps of grass, and then finally I was down. The beach curved left for miles, but to my right it ended not long after the lighthouse. The rocks gathered and then gathered more until passing would be impossible unless the tide was way out. I saw a motorboat up near the lighthouse cliff that must have been Sylvie's.

I went left. Took off my sandals, because that was an unbreakable Beach Rule, no matter how cold it was. I rolled up my jeans. I walked in the soft, thick sand closer to land, moved past the beach layer where all of the scary stuff collected, then headed down to the hard, wet ground closest to the water. I could walk forever there; I could even walk all the way back to the beach house if I wanted. I could see Possession Point, our house tiny but visible in the distance. I picked up a stick and dragged it behind me. I tried out the water and found it freezing. I collected a few shells, rinsed them off, and put them in my pocket. I walked past a few houses, imagining that I could choose which one was mine. Modern, with huge glass windows? Small but charming? The houses were spread out here, your own bit of the endless beach and the endless sea, and it was obvious these people lived a life that was aware of both of these elements. A statue made from driftwood decorated one deck, a string of floats likely washed ashore lined another railing. A rowboat was pulled up tight to one small house, its oars stuck up in the sand.

And then I was at that shack I had seen from the shore before.

*Stay*

Maybe people just stored their boats there, or their garden tools, or their whatevers. It was smaller than a one-car garage, made out of shingles and planks weathered gray. Maybe no one actually *lived* there. Wait—it had a chimney, though. An even smaller building stood off to the side. Wait—no. Was it an outhouse? Did people have those anymore? Because it looked like one of those outhouses you saw in the hillbilly movies.

You pictured a guy with no teeth. But then again, it had a certain charm. It had to, or it wouldn't have kept me there so long, looking at it. I started noticing things. Firewood stacked up. An *apple* tree? Could that be, there on the beach? Did this beach just grow unlikely things? I saw plants in yellow pots on the windowsill inside. A pair of orange gardening clogs.

"You're not the tax assessor," a woman said.

I startled. She came up from behind me, a woman with gray hair cut just under her chin and a face with deep wrinkles and a stern mouth. She wore jeans and a sweatshirt with short sleeves. She was small, but her arms were roped with muscles. She carried two tin buckets, one overflowing with what looked like weeds.

"No," I said.

"Not much other reason to stare, other than to assess value."

"Just curiosity," I said.

"It's a curious place, isn't it?"

"Do you live here?" I asked.

"I do. It's my full-time home now, if you can believe it. I had an apartment in New York, which I finally gave up last year. Would you believe that either? We used to come here in the summers. But now it's just me."

"New York," I said. "Wow."

"You're thinking how different it is there from here. Which is the point. There, you get what you need only with much effort. You can't collect your grittle and snips for dinner, right off of your own land." She held up the bucket. I wondered if maybe she was crazy.

"Well, thank you for letting me look," I said.

"Annabelle Aurora," she said. She set down the buckets, held out a hand.

"Clara Oates," I said. We shook.

"Summer visitor," she said.

"Yes."

"You can come by for dinner sometime. Bring your father."

I swear to God, my heart stopped. She'd shocked me, that was for sure. While I was used to being connected to my father in our own city, I hadn't expected this sudden knowledge by some unknown old lady with an outhouse on a beach. It seemed as likely she'd know my father as I'd know hers.

"Tell him I have muscles," she said.

I was sure she was crazy then. She had muscles, all right. As tiny as she was, she looked like she could kick your ass to the ground if you crossed her. But then she tapped one of the buckets with the tip of her shoe. I saw inside—a mound of curved black shells. Mussels.

"I will. Thanks," I said.

I got the hell out of there. It had taken me a long time to get down that trail, but it took me no time at all to get back up. It was stupid, but my heart was beating fast. She'd spooked me. I remembered that feeling, possible danger, how it made you both clumsy and focused in your need to flee. My hand shook as I tried to fit the car key in the lock. I got inside and locked the doors around me and I sat there and calmed down. It was so stupid, because somewhere inside I knew I had nothing to fear from some old woman who lived in a shack.

See, though? This was where I was now. An old woman, a branch scraping on glass, wind in trees that was only wind, anything at all had the ability to fling me to that place where I was so frightened, so, so frightened, and where his hand was around my ankle at the top of those stairs. It was about that hand. It was about car lights in my rearview mirror. It was about not knowing what might happen next. It was not about an old lady with orange gardening clogs.

And that was part of why we were here, I knew. Another part. So that a tree branch and the wind and strange old ladies could become only themselves again.

I bought Dad the funniest colors of taffy. The pink ones with blue stripes. Yellow with green. Purple. The really gross colors. Our mystery host with his fine taste would never think to have those colors in the smooth wood bowl on his dining table. Perfect.

I was lying to myself, though, I knew. I didn't come back to town for taffy. I came back to circle around the idea of Finn Bishop.

I knew, because I brushed my hair and checked how I looked before I got out of the car, and you didn't do that for the ladies at the taffy place. After I came out of the shop, I stopped at the food booth right by the docks. The Cove. I looked up at the menu posted on the wall behind the counter.

"Variations on a cheeseburger," the girl behind the counter said. She was a little older than me, I guessed. Long brown hair tied back, eyes that didn't take shit. Either it was just my day, or the ocean made people tough around here.

"I'll have a cheeseburger," I said.

"Good choice. Fries?"

"That's okay," I said.

"You gotta have fries. They're fantastic. On the house. Don't feed them to the seagulls, though, okay? They come around and make my life a living hell. Cove combo two," she said to the cook in the back. "Look at him." She pointed to one of the picnic tables set out front. A seagull stood on it, plucking at something under his wing.

"He doesn't seem to be going anywhere," I said.

"Gulliver. That's what I call him. I can't get rid of the guy. He's like a stray dog. He tries to follow me home."

I laughed. In a few minutes my lunch was ready, and I took the bag and carried it to the grass that overlooked the marina. *Obsession* was not moored there, but I looked out over the water. I could see it not far off, and I ate slowly and watched it move in. The girl was right. The fries were fantastic.

The boat eased to the end of the dock. It was as beautiful as I remembered. The guy who had been high up on the mast before, the one I had guessed was Finn's brother, was steering a huge silver wheel. He eased forward, backed up, and landed neatly alongside the dock, where Finn jumped off and grabbed the ropes to tie it down. I remembered my driving test, how the whole parallel parking thing seemed as complicated and frustrating as teaching cats to play Monopoly. But these two guys got this huge sailboat where it needed to be as smooth as anything.

I watched as Finn leaped down, whipped those ropes fast around the dock cleats. The boat snugged right up against a stairwell, which Finn then climbed, giving a hand from boat to stair to several passengers on board. I watched the people walk down the steps—several couples, a family with two girls, another family with a toddler in a life jacket—and they all looked relaxed and happy and windblown. One guy stopped back at the ticket booth, which today had a young woman inside of it, and took out his wallet and handed over some bills, maybe arranging another ride for another day. The passengers wandered off the dock at various times—the couple with the toddler headed for The Cove, the family with the girls stopped to take pictures.

Finn hopped back on the boat. He obviously had an ease there. You could tell it was his place. I watched him joke with the other guy, and then Finn went down below for a while before coming up again. He worked, making the boat right again after the sail. He coiled the wild ropes into neat circles. He arranged the collapsed sail into folds.

I had finished my cheeseburger, rolled up the foil into a ball. I was almost done with my drink. I'd been staring, sure. It was then that Finn must have finally felt my eyes on him. I was far away but not so far that he couldn't see me. He looked my way. He shaded his eyes with his arm as if to make sure it was me. He smiled. He waved, and I waved back.

I didn't walk over and talk to him, though, not then. If I

needed the time for a tree branch to become just a tree branch again and the wind to become just the wind, then a boy, most of all, needed some time to be only a boy.

My dad laughed so hard. "You are shitting me," he said. "You found Annabelle Aurora? On your first day?"

"You *know* her?"

"Very well. She was a professor of mine in New York. I saw her at a party there years later, and we kept in touch. She's an old friend, Pea. She stayed with us once when she came to a writers' conference in town. You were just a baby. Of course I knew she was out here. We keep in touch by e-mail. It made the place a good choice, in my opinion."

"She's a *friend* of yours."

"And a poet. A very well-known one, I might add.* I didn't tell her I arrived yet."

"I'm not sure she exactly has a *phone.*"

"What do you mean?"

"It's a shack. She's got an *outhouse.* You always said poets only got paid in magazine copies."

He laughed again. He was loving this. He sure got a kick out of that crazy old lady. "Annabelle is loaded."

"No!"

"*Loaded.* Her husband was some newspaper guy. Like in,

........................

* Three accents, two famous people, if you're keeping a tally. Dad knows tons of writers, so there may be more coming. Oh, and Christian's father was married for a short while to a woman who was married to one of the Rolling Stones, if that counts.

'owner,' not reporter. She might have even had some family money. They had this great apartment. Two daughters. Very close to the girls."

"That's surprising. She's alone in that weird place."

"Happy as a clam, I have no doubt. She always liked the outer edges. The farther, the better."

"Clams—right. She said to tell you she had mussels."

He slapped his hand on the table. "That fucking Annabelle," he said. "Good memory for an old broad." He was grinning wide. His eyes were sparkly. "When she came out to stay with us, we steamed some for dinner. You were too young to remember this, I'm guessing. Your mother—she was in some mood. She went inside. Upset . . . I can't remember. Annabelle and I ate mussels on the back deck and drank beers until we were toasted. Laughed our asses off remembering these people in our classes and those stupid parties where literary people try so hard to be literary people. Cool superiority as a mask for overflowing insecurity. 'Every time I see people in social circumstances like that, I can't help but imagine them in junior high, worrying about who they're going to eat lunch with,' Annabelle had said, and I always thought about that later. You see a person's inner thirteen-year-old and you won't look at them the same way again."

"Probably," I said. But I was thinking about Dad and old Annabelle Aurora on our deck on a summer night, and my mother in her room. I felt like maybe I *could* remember that night if I tried hard enough. I wondered what my mother had been thinking and feeling, what had upset her. Those were the times you really felt her absence—when you would never know her, didn't know her now enough to even guess what would make her leave a houseguest in the middle of dinner. You only had these words—*mood, upset*—and yet you had nothing to hang them on. You had other words, too. But a word like *French*, or *photographer*, or *sensitive*, they had a thousand meanings and pictures and your own images would be only guesses. It was all the things you could never understand and could never possess that made you ache.

"Annabelle Aurora," my father said. His eyes were still all gleamy.

"The mother you never had?" I said.*

"I wouldn't say that, exactly," he said. "Not at all, really."

"She scared me, knowing who I was like that. I thought she was some crazy old fan who knew your life history."

"She knows my life history, all right. Indeed she does."

I tried to read that book again before I went to sleep. I didn't like that book, but I kept going for all the reasons a person hangs in with something that isn't good—you feel bad about not giving it a chance, you've already come too far to give up now, you believe it's going to get better. When you're a person whose life has mostly brought good things, you believe in goodness. You believe that things will work out. Even the worst things will work out. You believe in a happy ending.

......................

* My father's own mother, Grandma Oates, was a conservative woman who lived in Iowa with her sister, my aunt Barbara. Grandma Oates made you believe it was possible for babies to be switched in hospitals.

*Stay*

But you are naive. The mostly good in your life has made you that way. You've spent so much time seeing the bright side that you don't even believe the other side exists. You are wrong about that.

I closed that book. I wouldn't open it again, I vowed. It was time I learned something.

# Chapter 7

He called that night, the night I had come home from the park and had eaten everything in the fridge. Kissing makes you hungry. *Hunger* makes you hungry. It had gotten late. I had school the next day. I was getting tired, but I just wanted more of him, too, like he wanted of me. I was downstairs in the kitchen getting something to drink, speaking softly, the phone crooked between my shoulder and my ear, when Dad came through. He was turning lights off. He tapped the place on his wrist where a watch would be, turning his eyebrows down in concern. *I know!* I mouthed. I was mad at him, because I knew he didn't get this, or even if he did in some general way, he didn't get *this*.

Christian and I talked every night after that. We were both taking AP classes and calculus and had too much homework, so we couldn't get together, and that next weekend he had plans to go to his parents' cabin. It was almost unbearable how long those weeks were. I knew if he came over to study that we wouldn't study, but we ended up spending just as much time on the phone anyway. We spent a lot of time saying *I should just come over* and *If I'd have come over we could have spent all this time together instead of on the phone*, things like that. Things you say. Maybe I was nervous for Dad to meet him, or for him to meet Dad, though I had no real reason to think they wouldn't get along terrifically. Christian was smart and well-read and Dad liked that. There was something, though, that I knew could happen, which was that Dad could see things, he was an observer, and maybe I just didn't want him seeing and observing anything that might ruin this. I needed him to like Christian and keep his mouth shut and leave it at that.

Finally, on Friday night, Christian came over to pick me up to go to a movie. I introduced him to Dad and they stood in the hall by the front door as if no one wanted to venture further in. There was this strained kind of chitchat about the number of daylight hours Copenhagen experienced in the winter or some such thing, and I kept seeing each of them through the others' eyes, and I got us out of there fast.

It was so good to see him. God. I felt so happy that we were finally at Friday. The word *Friday*—streamers could have hung from it, balloons. It was such a great word.

"I love watching you drive," I said.

"I love seeing you in the seat beside me," he said.

It felt very Mr. and Mrs., being in his car with him driving, but I also felt a little nervous. We had talked about anything and everything for hours and hours, but it was still all new; being in his car was new, that careful new that made you worry you had mascara tracks or would say something stupid, the exactly stupidest thing to make him know he didn't want to be there with you after all. You did that when you started to care a lot—you worried he was watching your every move to make sure he really wanted you. You could forget that maybe *you* were supposed to being doing that too. You forgot it wasn't just you being watched and judged and trying to pass some test.

I looked around his car for pieces of him, ways to know him better, but it was very clean—no wrappers or dust or books or empty bottles. Dylan Ricks had had a soccer ball hanging from his rearview mirror and sports equipment piled in the back, water bottles and empty PowerBar wrappers, dirt from cleats and muddy games on the carpets. Athlete leftovers everywhere. I pictured Christian vacuuming the rugs for me, catching the crumbs between the seats, making sure everything shined. Actually, he always kept his car like that, but I didn't know that then. He liked things clean.* I watched his finger adjust the radio dial. His hands were clean, too. So neat, nails trimmed. I liked that, I told myself. I wasn't sure I really did, but I told myself I did. It was different from Dylan or from any other guys I knew, even my father, with his spilled spaghetti on his shirts, or the back of his car, so messy with books and empty coffee cups.

........................

* Even if, weirdly, he could never seem to throw anything away. In his room he kept piles of papers—old tests, schoolwork, cards, photos—and stacks of old clothes folded in his closet. Obviously, he couldn't part with things easily. Maybe this should have been a warning sign.

"You'll like this song," Christian said. "I hear it and I think of you."

"The Way She Moves", by Slow Change. I'd never really liked them—Hunter Eden seemed like a dick, but that didn't matter now. I couldn't wait to go home and really listen to the lyrics. "I hear the neighbor's TV and I think of you," I said.

He didn't quite know what I meant. He looked at me sideways. "I mean, *anything* will do it," I said.

"Right," he said. "Exactly."

He took my hand. His skin on mine—it sent a zip line of energy through me. A physical hum. I rubbed the underside of his arm with my fingertips until we hit a stoplight and he had to shift gears. I squeezed his forearm—I just kept wanting to touch him. He smelled so good, even from there, that I kept sniffing the air like a dog in the back of a pickup.

We stood in the ticket line. He put his arms around me from behind and I leaned in tight. "We're stuck," I said.

"Good," he said. We inched forward in our stuck way. "It's going to make it hard to see the movie," he said.

"It's going to make it hard to drive home," I said.

"We'll have to decide whose home to live in. Which school. You'll have to tie our shoes since you're in front."

I laughed.

"You Americans laugh so loud," he said.

I had a prickle of hurt feelings, but I didn't say anything. "Us Americans like funny boyfriends," I said. The word was out before I could think. My thought-brakes were a minute too slow. It was all right, though. He kissed my neck.

"I like the sound of that. Does that mean you're mine?"

I stuck our hands in my jacket pockets. I pretended to think about it. "Yes . . ." His. I liked the sound of that too. It's strange, isn't it, how that idea of *belonging* to someone can sound so great? It can be comforting, the way it makes things decided. We like the thought of being held, until it's too tight. We like that certainty, until it means there is no way out. And we like being his, until we realize we're not *ours* anymore.

It was the first time we'd been out in public together, and the sense of *his* and *mine*, the sense of *us*, was something we were trying on, showing other people to see how it felt. It felt good. Great. It felt like a statement, though the two guys in front of us who smelled like pot couldn't have cared less, and neither did the ticket seller, with his straight, raven-black hair who didn't even look at us when he took Christian's money. Christian insisted on paying, he always would, and that felt good, too. He was taking care of me. You take care of the people you love, but it's true, too, that you take care of the things you own.

I wasn't paying attention to the movie. I was seeing how Christian looked in the seat beside me, as the lights of the film flickered, as they went from bright to dark. He looked so good in profile. He would notice me watching him and squeeze my hand but go back to watching the action. The way he looked made me want to get out of there. I couldn't wait for us to be alone. The date stuff was fine, going to the movies, whatever. But what I really wanted was to be back in that land we ended up in when we were kissing. That place we disappeared in (and it felt like an actual place, a physical space) where no one else could ever enter.

*Stay*

It was finally over. I couldn't tell you what that movie was about for anything. Two spies, that's all. I can't even remember the name of the film now, though if I tried hard enough, I might. It's not important. What's important was how urgent it all felt. This is the thing I want to say: It wasn't just him. I wanted to be with him just as much as he wanted to be with me, maybe more, a lot of the time.

We held hands as we walked out of the theater. The night was cool and welcome, the busy parking lot, cars coming and going, it was welcome, too. Things were happening and shifting, which was so much better than sitting in that seat, waiting. The night was alive again. He unlocked my door for me, and I put my hands on either side of him.

"Kiss," I said. He did, but he seemed in a hurry to be done.

"Let's go," he said.

He drove me back home. He didn't do what Dylan used to—park a few blocks away to have a few minutes alone before going back. He pulled up to my street and actually got right out. I wondered if something was wrong. We walked up to my doorstep. I knew Dad would be asleep, so I didn't even think about it—when Christian leaned in to me, I pulled the back of his head so his mouth was hard on mine, maybe because that's what I wanted from him. Maybe because I was trying to be that sexy girl he couldn't resist. But he could resist. He seemed to be somewhere else. His body felt away from me, and then it didn't. He was there again, we both were, and his hands were on me, untucking my shirt, his hands up my sides. It got a little out of control. A lot.

"See what you do?" he said. His lips were shiny in the streetlight.

"Good night," I said. I was teasing. It was fun. Christian was grinning.

"Shit," he said. "Shit."

"I guess you could say I like you. Really like you," I said.

"Yeah? I guess *you* could say I feel too much."

I didn't know what *that* meant. I wanted to ask; I felt the asking rise up with some sort of desperation, and so I kept it down. Just went on smiling. It seemed dangerous to pursue it. If I did, I thought I might uncover some doubts of his that would grow uncontrollably when exposed to light and air. I pretended everything was fine, that I missed the undercurrent. He kissed my forehead. Kissed my *forehead,* as if protecting my innocence. He headed back to the car, waved over his shoulder.

I went inside. I felt anxious, confused. I wanted to call him right then, that minute, but I didn't. I felt some ugly rush of clinging-begging-panic. I was being stupid, I told myself. This had become too important too fast.

I was wrong about Dad being asleep. He was actually in our family room, his feet up on the trunk we used as a coffee table, the remote control in his hand. He never watched TV.

I walked past the doorway, and he looked up. He looked at my untucked shirt. I'm sure my hair was a mess.

"TV?" I asked.

"Got some surfing moving at Total Vid, but I finished it. Now, 'Fifty-seven channels and nothing on.'" He was using his quoting voice, though I wasn't sure what it was he was quoting.* He was wearing his plaid PJ bottoms, some T-shirt from a concert a million years ago. "Have fun?"

"Yep," I said. "You waiting up for me?" He never waited up before.

"Making sure you're home safe. My fatherly duty."

"Why wouldn't I be safe?" I suddenly felt testy. It was the night spilling out, sure, but now here was Dad just sitting there, and everything felt weird, but it was Dad that I could get mad at.

"Driving in cars, earthquakes, boys, a million reasons. Food poisoning. Choking on a popcorn kernel."

"You didn't like him."

"I never said that." But I could tell I was right. His voice tipped up at the end.

"What? He's a great guy. Great. He treats me so well."

"Terrific. I'm glad."

"What?"

"Clara."

"What was it?"

He turned off the TV. Set the remote control down. "He seemed a little . . ."

"What?"

"Rigid."

"Rigid. Great." I was furious. "He's not some loose, loud American guy, so what? What's wrong with it anyway? He was

..........................

* "57 Channels (And 'Nothin On)," Bruce Springsteen. From the *Human Touch* album, released in 1992. I just looked it up.

being polite. Polite is a good thing. You're the only parent I know who wouldn't love polite. No one would be good enough in your mind."

Which was a lie, I knew. He wasn't all that protective about guys, not really. Not even with Dylan, when he should have been. "Untrue," he said. "Look, C.P. Rigid can be . . . controlling. Sometimes controlling. Hell, a lot of times. After the last guy, Pea, something to look out for."

"He's nothing like Dylan. All you have to do is spend five minutes with him to see that." They *were* different. Christian was courteous and mannered and got good grades and had life goals. Dylan barely passed classes and even got into it with teachers. "*Nice* is the difference," I said to Dad. Nice was protection enough.

"Nice can have an edge."

"That's ridiculous! That's the stupidest thing I ever heard."

"You got your garden variety nice, C.P., where they're just regular, fine people, and you got your goody-two-shoes nice. Underlying hostility. Self-righteousness without the balls to show its true colors."

"Jesus." I spun around to leave.

"C.P., I'm sorry. But did you not tell me to be honest after last time?"

I stopped. Actually, I'd made him promise. Shakti, too. It had been one of those situations where after you break up, everyone tells you how they knew he was a creep all along. You're mad they didn't tell you, but how could they? You wanted their honest opinion, but you wanted their support, too, and there is no such thing as a truthful lie.

"You saw him for *five minutes*," I said.

"Okay," my father said.

"I'm going to bed."

"I don't even know the guy," he said.

I went to my room. The phone rang, and it was Christian. I let it go. I had to calm down a minute. I sat on my bed until the pissed-off-ness rode away. The confusion was still there. The clawing anxiety of things maybe going wrong, possible loss. I dialed.

"Hi," I said. Oh, I sounded cheerful.

"Hi," he said.

I waited. Watched the landscape for oncoming trucks barreling my way. But Christian just started talking about something Mr. Hooper had done that day that he had forgotten to tell me. Everything was normal again, and the thought that I might lose him turned down to some dim light, a distant hum; still, it was a bad, panicked feeling I would remember. I would have avoided it in any way I could. His voice turned breathy in my ear.

"You make me so crazy," he said.*

I was worried I would lose him. Him, which was not just *him*, but some sort of new life, some hopeful excitement, a

......................

* A guy, Dr. Frank Tallis, wrote this book called *Love Sick: Love as a Mental Illness*. He talked about how falling in love made you go through many of the same things as losing your mind. Not sleeping and eating, thinking obsessively about the person, deluded thoughts . . . I read it. He's right. Think of the words: *I'm crazy about you. You make me crazy. Crazy in love.* Let's just say that maybe it's *always* a thin line.

new me, full of spells and the ability to hypnotize. That power. And the idea of that loss—the ugly rush of clinging-begging-panic . . . I had felt it, *I* had. It's important to be honest about that. I had danced there, too.

After we hung up, I found that song, "The Way She Moves", and I listened to every word carefully, looking for meaning. *Your eyes are on her and you want her. Your eyes have her. She's yours* . . . I decided I would put it on a CD for him, with a bunch of other songs I felt summed us up perfectly. All kinds of music suddenly seemed to make sense. All of the lyrics and movies and fuss about love . . . This was what it was about. *This.*

I met his parents. His mom and his stepfather. Sandy was sweet, small and blond, kind. Elliot was a little cynical and sharp, I thought, the thoughtless kind of cruel. Where your own humorous jab meant more than someone else's feelings. But I couldn't see what the problem was with his mom. I really couldn't. She'd left him a lot when he was young, I guess. But she always seemed to be trying hard. It felt complicated there.

October turned to November. We did everything together. We'd bundle up and walk to the Rose Garden at the zoo, make out in the gazebo. I'd go with him to Mr. Hooper's house; we would sit in the room with the French doors and the fireplace as Christian read from novels he'd bring from the Seattle library. Mr. Hooper wore his jogging suit and his scuffers. He didn't care if the plot was slow or if the book took place in the 1700s or now or if there was romance or war. I think he just liked the sound of

Christian's voice, which I understood. Christian would make Mr. Hooper grilled cheese and tea.

I went to Sandy and Elliot's cabin east of the mountains with all of them once, rode in the back with Christian like we were little kids, eating red licorice and playing I Spy. We made a fort in the snow, tucked ourselves inside and tried to kiss, but our lips were too cold to work very well. He told me about winter in Copenhagen when he was a boy, how he and his parents would rent skates at the outdoor rink in the center of the city, set picturesquely in front of the snowy Royal Danish Theatre.

In early December, a guy in Christian's class, Jason Patricks, jumped from the ledge of Snoqualmie Falls, and we went to his funeral together, joining all the others, our hands tight together. The casket was set in the front of the church, and even though I had not known Jason, he was alive and now not and inside that box. I didn't remember my mother's funeral, and I could feel it then, the grief and the loss and the thorny mess that life was, sitting there in front of us in the shine of that wood and the waxy smell of flowers, and I felt so close to Christian there beside me, then. It felt like we had gone through something together, or at least stood witness together to something huge that now bound us.

We'd known each other for a few months when he told me he loved me. We had talked around the idea, we had used all the not-quite-there expressions of love, the appetizers and the desserts and the salad, but not the main meal. *I think I'm falling in love. I love that about you. You're a person I could seriously love.* Still, it was the direct three words that you wanted; those were the ones that meant something. He had picked me up after school. We were in his car. We were parked near the gym where we had met. That basketball game seemed like a long time ago. He'd become such a daily presence in my life, it seemed weird that there had been a time when he wasn't in it. Shakti complained she never saw me anymore. All my friends did. I tried to make sure I wasn't one of those girls who dropped all their friends when a guy came into her life, but I guess I was, and I'm telling the truth here, so the truth was that I didn't mind.

"I've said this to you a million times already in my head," Christian had said.

I was quiet. An old-fashioned word comes to mind: *coy*. It was like he was on bended knee with a velvet box, with me waiting primly in some Victorian outfit. And the truth again—I wasn't going to be the one to say it first. What's that about? Love must be more about power than we think, if even in its most intimate moment of expression we think about not being the one who risks the most.

"I love you," he said. He was glad to have it out, I guess, because he said it two more times, relieved, and then he rolled down his window and shouted it out, which was so unlike him that I laughed and grabbed his arm.

"Christian!" I said. Two senior girls were looking at us like we were the star performers in the idiot circus. "Roll that up!" I was laughing, and I was so happy. He put the window up. I held his hands. His eyes were bright. "I love you, too," I said.

And I did. That was the thing you should understand. Bad things happened. It was like seeing something great on the beach, something you ran toward because it looked special and different, and when you got close, you saw it was something that

*Stay*

made you look away, a syringe, a condom, a dead seagull buzzing with flies. But I did love him. Very much.

We'd gotten so close by then. It embarrasses me now, but we used those words: *soul mates*. Hard to admit that. Hard to admit, too, that I felt some future was actually possible. At least, I couldn't imagine life without him in it. We couldn't keep our hands off each other, either. There were *I want yous* and more *I want yous* but that's as far as it went. He took those things seriously. For someone who spent years of his childhood in a city where women went topless in the parks on summer afternoons, he was surprisingly, staunchly prudish. He judged people who had sex too soon. They were loose and stupid and had no morals, and I said I agreed but didn't know how I really felt. It could be complicated, I thought. Okay, truth *again*. He had used the word *slut*. About girls who had sex.

That night we had gone out with his friends—Jake and his girlfriend Olivia and Zach. We went to Neumo's. A band I can't remember. We were dancing. I wondered if Zach had had a few beers or something beforehand. He was loose and kept making dumb jokes. It was the first time we'd gone out with Christian's friends. I'd met them. Hung out a little. But we'd never gone somewhere.

After the concert everyone was laughing and having the kind of good feeling that comes after dancing to loud music in a small place. You felt happy. Or you did usually. But things were weird. I'd tried to hold Christian's hand in there, but he kept snatching it away. He was barely talking. But when we got back into our own car, he snapped on the engine. His face had a tight look. He almost looked like someone else.

*  83  *

I didn't say anything. I just held my purse. I wanted a mint, but I didn't want to unzip my purse and get one out. I wanted things to be in that still place *before* a fight, not in that other, upsetting one after a fight starts.

"*You* had fun," he said finally.

I thought that was the idea, you know, to have fun. I wondered what his problem was. I didn't know. I made my best guess. Christian didn't drink. He was straight that way, too, actually. I was guessing he was pissed at Zach and pissed at me for joking with him. He had no right to accuse me of anything, but I couldn't stand the thought of us arguing. We never argued. The thought made me remember that time we'd gone to the movies. That terrible, anxious feeling that I might lose him.

"Zach seemed drunk," I said. "He was acting like an asshole." I didn't really think so.

Christian was silent. The muscle in his jaw just kept working. I concentrated on the view outside. Streetlights, a McDonald's, a bus stop where an old lady sat holding her purse like I was. She was up very late for someone so old. I felt worried for her. I watched a guy walking his dog past an empty bank parking lot. We wound around by Lake Union. Sailboats, lively restaurants. The Space Needle already decorated for Christmas with the tree at the top.

"I saw you looking at that guy," he said.

I had no idea what he was talking about.

"What guy?"

"Come on, Clara. You were looking at him the whole night."

"Who?"

"By the stage? Long hair? Oh come on." A car tried to pass into our lane, but Christian wouldn't let him in. It looked rejected, driving so slowly there beside us with its blinker on.

"I have no idea what you're talking about. I didn't even see the guy by the stage. Christian, for God's sake, I was there with you. You were the only one I was looking at. Christian, pull over. Just, stop, and let's talk."

He did. He swerved right there onto Fairview, which was the street directly next to the lake. He pulled over, parked on a gravel strip in front of a boatyard. I felt panicky. I wanted to make this right. It was ridiculous. The strange thing was, if he'd complained about Zach, I might have understood. But I didn't even see the person he meant. I tried to think. Guy by the stage? There were a million guys by the stage. I was looking at the *stage*, probably. The *musicians*.

I wasn't mad, though, about being accused. More, I felt bad. Did he really not know how much I cared? It was only him I wanted to look at. He was more than enough for my eyes. I told him so. I was pleading. Part of me was pleading, and another part of me was wondering why in the hell I was pleading. I was wondering why I was sitting in front of a boatyard convincing someone I hadn't looked at a guy I hadn't looked at.

He softened. "I'm sorry," he said. "I don't want to lose you." It was funny, but he could be insecure. I'd noticed that. He would make these comments about his looks or his abilities, but he had no reason to be insecure, none. He was this gorgeous blond, blue-eyed Dane and he was smart and nice and girls were crazy for his accent, but the person he was and the person he thought he was didn't know each other and could never even be friends. It made me sad. I thought it was part of my girlfriend job to set him straight about how great he was. The insecurity—it seemed like a small thing. Ridiculous enough that it could easily be fixed with my reassurance.

"Why would you lose me?" I said.

We started to kiss. After a while, I had said *I want everything with you.* And so we had everything. For the first time. After that fight. In the car, a cliché.

But the important thing at this part of the story, another part I've never told, is that he whispered something to me then. *You're sure you've never done this?* It was something he'd asked me before. I shook my head into his bare shoulder, but it was a lie. I didn't tell him about that one time with Dylan, that one fast, strange time. I didn't tell him the truth then, or whenever we'd talked about this. He'd never been with a girl before. I knew this would matter to him. But what I knew even more than that was that he was the *jealous type.* That's how I thought of it. As if the words were small print, equal to other qualities a person might have—the athletic type. The creative type. The type to get easily lost, or be late, or didn't like food that was too different. It meant you made accommodations, you got directions beforehand or told him the concert was earlier or picked a place to eat that had hamburgers or didn't say things that would hurt him. You didn't even tell him the truth about who you were or what you had done. You protected him, kept things from him he couldn't handle. Or else protected yourself from what he couldn't handle. You managed it all, like

*Stay*

someone who works in an office and who types and answers the phone at the same time.

*Why would you lose me?* I had asked. And you can see, can't you, better than I could, that the answer to that question was right there in the car with us as my knee rested against the gear shift and my elbow against glass? The answer was not a small human quality, a minor trait or a quiet one, but a loud twisting force moving between and around and through, gathering, the way a cloud gathers darkness, the way the clouds did right then over that car and the single streetlight and the sign that read LAKE UNION BOAT REPAIR. VALUE AND SATISFACTION. WE CARE.

# Chapter 8

I returned that book to the Bishop Rock Library the next morning. I had a few more days to fill before I started work at Pigeon Head Point. I wandered around in the stacks of fiction. I tipped out the spines, read the covers and first pages. I did what I could to make sure I had a few books right enough to devote myself to.

Afterward I went to the docks. The wind was whipping pretty good, and the sailboats were clanging, and the dock was groaning and squeaking. The boats bobbed and sloshed, and it all seemed happy, if a little deranged. *Obsession* was gone from her spot. I sat on the end of a nearby dock, took my sandals off, dangled my feet in the water. I couldn't see the boat anywhere, and then I could, and it seemed her arrival was very fast. She got larger and larger and more in focus, and suddenly they were close enough that I could see the faces of the individual passengers, and I could hear Finn shout something and the others laugh, and the big sail came down, tumbling into messy folds.

I watched everyone get off the boat and saw Finn return again to coil the ropes. There was a familiarity to it that made it all feel good, and so I got up, carrying my sandals by their straps, and walked over.

"You going out again?" I shouted.

"Hey," he said. His brother stood at the tip of the boat* smoking a cigarette, looking out. He turned when he heard my voice. "Shy girl."

"Clara," I said.

"Finn," he said, though his name had traveled through my mind on a million different paths already. "My brother Jack. Don't mind him; he's trying to quit."

"Don't mind him; he's an idiot," Jack said, blowing smoke up into the air. You could tell they got along just fine, though. They both were thin and fit and had unshaven scruff, but Jack's hair was longer and wilder and Finn had those sweet eyes. Finn hopped off the boat. There he was, next to me, in his tight T-shirt and loose jeans, black hair messed up from a windy, windy ride.

........................

* Called the bow. The back, called the stern. I knew this only in some vague way before, and might have failed the quiz if there had been one. The left is *port*, the right is *starboard*. Sailing has its own language. Colorful, too. *Bowsprits* and *breeches*, *buoys* and *battening down hatches*, language from another time. Nothing like all the icy tech words we have now—HTML and CD-ROM and CPUs—no romance. And then there's the jib sheet and the spinnaker, the luffing and the jibing, lively, cheery words. And of course, the stays. The stays: the wire that supports the mast. Thin and hardly noticeable, but the only thing keeping the mast from toppling.

"Come on out," he said. He seemed shy himself. But not so shy that he couldn't say what he wanted. "It's *fast*. It's *fantastic*." His eyes danced.

I must have shivered. It was a little cold out there. "Scared?" he said.

"No," I said. "My father's afraid, not me."

"The whole ghost thing?" he asked.

"Ghost thing?"

"I thought maybe you were staying at the Captain Bishop Inn. They love that stuff. Shove it at the folks that go there. People eat it up. They make *pamphlets*, even." I shook my head. I didn't know what he meant. "Deception Pass? Used to have a lot of sailing vessels. The big old ships . . . But—high winds, narrow channel . . . The waters were, *are*, so treacherous there that most of the ships sailed around the whole island rather than go through that pass. They had to lose a few for sailors to know that, though, right? So, supposedly, you know. Old dead sailors haunting the waters. Captain Bishop's young widowed wife throwing herself off of the lighthouse in despair. Blah blah blah."

"Some TV show came out here and filmed the lighthouse and now we have every bored, middle-aged kook who is hoping to be freaked out," Jack said.

"I know the shows," I said. "Old ship on choppy sea? Guy with a pocket watch and a telescope? Filmy white images?"

"You got it," Finn said.

"I didn't even know," I said. "My father just hates the water."

"Ah," Finn nodded. He shrugged his shoulders, to each his

own. "Anyway, you wouldn't believe how many people ask about the ships down under there. Number one question."

"Tell me about the ships down under there," I said.

He laughed. Someone called Jack's name. It was the girl from The Cove, yesterday's hamburger place. She was waving at him madly.

"Our sister," Finn said.

"Pretend I never saw," Jack said. "I'm not chasing that fucking seagull for her."

"There's this seagull . . ." Finn said. I nodded. I knew about him. "She claims to hate that seagull, but I have my doubts. You coming?"

"I can't," I said. "I've got to—"

"Work at the lighthouse?" he grinned. "Did she hire you?"

"Starting on Monday," I said. The brothers looked at each other. Knowing glance. "What? Come on. Tell me."

"Maybe you ought to start job hunting," Finn said.

Jack cracked up. "She'll fire you by . . ." He looked at his brother. "I say Friday."

"Next Monday," Finn said. "She hates the weekend tourists more than she hates the workers."

"True," Jack said. He thought. "Can I change my bet?"

I groaned. "Really? That bad?"

"She chased this one guy with her Jeep," Finn said. "Remember that?"

They both were chuckling away. I crossed my arms. "I'm proving you both wrong," I said. I'd suddenly decided. I'd charm the skin off that snake and show these guys. "I'm lasting the summer."

"No fucking way," Jack said. He'd finished his cigarette. Turned his back on his sister, who had given up and gone back into the shack. The seagull still sat on that table. He looked pretty comfy.

"You last the summer and I'll sail you over to the San Juan Islands and back. Private charter."

"You idiot," Jack said. "You gotta make that a bet you can *win*. Jesus, I haven't taught you anything."

I was having so much fun there. I wondered about Finn and Jack and their sister and their life in that place. *This* would be their life during the summers. There would be no driving to Neumo's or out to eat in various parts of the city. No concerts or shows or the pierced people at Total Vid or traffic or city buses. No jobs at vintage music stores or comedy places. Just the beach and water and this salty air and working with your hands until you were so tired that maybe you actually slept at night.

"How about next week?" I said. "After work? After I *don't* get fired? I'll come out then,"

"That's so great," Finn said. "Cool." He was grinning. "Very cool."

"Only if you promise to tell me all about the drowned sailors," I said.

"And *I'll* tell you about what happened the first time Finn heard about the drowned sailors." Jack put his hands on Finn's shoulders.

"Shut up, idiot," Finn warned.

"It was the middle of the night . . ."

"God damn it, Jack." Finn lunged for his brother and missed.

"Awake all night, scared shitless." Finn lunged again, and this time he caught Jack by the waist and then tucked him under one arm, his knuckles against his scalp. I'd forgotten how physical guys could be. Jack and Finn did not have careful movements and clean hands. They didn't seem like they would flinch when they heard loud noises like Christian did. They didn't seem sensitive, in all ways that sensitive made a person require careful handling.

"Our father's white T-shirt in the kitchen, okay, okay!" Jack pleaded. Finn let go. Jack was laughing and so was I.

"I was *seven*," Finn said.

"You never heard anyone of any age scream like that," Jack said.

"You rat bastard," Finn said. "Your breath smells like a fucking *ash tray*." But he wasn't really bothered. I waited for it, thinking there might be that moment where you saw his hurt or humiliation or shame. When you live for a while with a sensitive person, you are always anticipating. You're two steps ahead, knowing what the reaction will be to that comment or that film moment or that song. You start trying to steer you both clear of any of the places he could fall into and stay. After that night at the concert I tried to keep my eyes from wandering accidentally somewhere that might upset him. Movies with cheating girlfriends made him sullen, and so I would read the reviews before we chose one, suggesting safe plots with exploding buses and car crashes. His friend, Evan, was teasing him about his *girlie silky hair* once, just giving him a bad time, and you could see how hurt he got. Really hurt. More than friend-kidding-around hurt. You anticipate, and when you do that for a long while, it's hard to shake. You get edgy. Like men back from the war who jump when a car backfires.

But Jack's story just rolled right off of Finn. He didn't care. I realized he could take jokes and small blows to the ego without it destroying him. I guess it was the sturdiness of confidence. And that was the first thing I really liked about Finn Bishop.

"I got a surprise for you tonight, Clara Bella," my father said that late afternoon. He was sitting out on the deck, an open book on his knee. The tide was inching in. You could see where his foot-steps had been a way off, now half covered.

"Why does that worry me?" I said. "Except there's not much to do out here but the fried clam special at Butch's Harbor Bar. That guy Butch gets around. There's a flyer in every window. Actually, it sounds kind of good."

"I'm not telling," my father said. He looked pleased with himself. You could tell he hadn't showered all day—his hair was unwashed and his beard was growing, and he had the same shorts on he'd been wearing for the past four days. Hopefully, wherever we were going, he wasn't going out like that. "Better dress warm."

I factored that through the Potential Disaster department of my brain, and all the alarms went off. I was thinking sunset sail with Finn Bishop, me and my dad. I was thinking Dad was going for some bold move (he liked bold moves), face your fear and do it anyway, fear is the biggest bullshitter romantic night for three merged with book research and intrusive questions. "We're not sailing with the Bishop brothers," I said.

His eyebrows shot up. He smiled. "Glad to hear you're mak-ing friends, C.P."

"No comment."

"Rightly so. No, you know you couldn't get me to go on that thing. Something else. Come on. Let's get out of here in, say, twenty minutes?"

When we met back up, Dad was showered, wearing jeans and a white shirt with the tails out, a bottle of wine tucked under one arm. We got in the car and drove toward the lighthouse and parked.

"Oh, no," I said.

"Come on. You'll love this old broad."

"She's weird, Dad. I got the creeps."

"That was your own deal. Had nothing to do with her."

We inched our way down the steep trail. "How'd you even get a hold of her? Does she even have *electricity*?"

"I sent her an e-mail. I was guessing she'd be as addicted to it as she ever was. She goes to the Captain Bishop Inn every morning and uses their computer. I wasn't expecting to hear back from her so soon."

"Lucky us," I said. Dad was ahead of me. He did the sideways dance down. "Don't break your ankle or anything. I'd never get you out of here."

"You forget I played football."

"One lousy season."

He landed there nicely on his feet. I decided I'd better shut my mouth, because it was me who was slipping and skittering. The lighthouse stood above us, and the keeper's house (with Sylvie Genovese inside, I was guessing, due to the Jeep out front) was lit and cozy on that cliff. She was probably watching, ready to fire me for my lack of climbing skills. My mood, high and happy after the docks that day, was also slipping.

Part of me wanted my own bed in my own room back home, my friends, my life, or rather, my old-old life. But I was here, sliding down some cliff, my just-washed hair already turning stringy from salt air, my "surprise" a dinner with a crazy lady who lived in a shack with an outhouse. We'd better not stay late, because I couldn't hold it that long, and there was no way I was peeing in that place.

"I'm in a baked potato mood," Dad said. "Butter. You know, Pea, I love butter. I really do love it. My heart even swells a little when I think of it. Wonder what we'll have. Where is her place anyway?"

I landed. Dad was taking off his sandals, and I did too. So much for showering. So much for Butch's Harbor Bar. I wouldn't have minded it. Red-and-white-checked plastic tablecloths with cigarette burns in them sounded kind of nice right then. Hot fried clams served in paper rectangle boats, I imagined. A Budweiser sign in back of the bar with a waterfall that looked like it was moving. "Believe me, you'll know her house when you see it," I said. We walked. "Nope, that's not it. That place has indoor plumbing," I said.

My father gave me a look. "I'm expecting your best," he said. I was two steps behind him, dragging the way I used to when I was a kid and didn't want to go somewhere. "How often do you get to have dinner with an esteemed poet? I'm talking National Book Award."

He waited for me to catch up. "Fine," I said. I saw the shack up ahead at the same time he did. Maybe my mind moved over a bit when I did, the way a mind can when you get more information. Because Annabelle Aurora had lit the place up for our welcome. Candles big and small lined the railing of the small deck and the steps to the front door, and there were candles on the windowsills and on pieces of driftwood and set upon rocks out front. Little flickering lights were everywhere. Firefly magic.

"It's beautiful," I said.

"One of the hardest tasks as a human being is knowing when to keep an open mind," my father said. "And when not to."

I took that hit. I had it coming. Annabelle Aurora emerged from her door and took my father up into a great hug. "Bobby. Look at you!" she said. "My eyes are so happy right this minute. So happy." She took my hands. "Clara. We meet again."

Annabelle Aurora's stern mouth had relaxed into a smile and her eyes were glittery. She wore a long caftan of a bright magenta. "This is beautiful," Dad said. He felt the fabric with his fingers.

"India," she said. "Come in, come in."

It was not at all what I had imagined. I pictured cat food bowls and the smell of tomato soup and a couch with worrisome stains. But the house was clean and warm, with wood paneling and tiny paintings and books in piles used as end tables. It was a cozy, sheltered cave, and it smelled like garlic and wine. From inside, mostly what you saw was the sea out before you. The lighthouse. The sun resting on the horizon.

They chatted while she steamed the mussels and tossed the "grittle and snips," the edible plantings she found on the beach, into a salad. She unfolded a little table and set it out on the deck. She draped a cloth over the top.

"So pretty," I said. The cloth was blue and soft, swoops of

shapes. It looked more like something you'd wear than spill food on.

"Thailand," she said.

We brought out the dishes. Melted butter to dip the mussels in, warm baked bread, the mysterious salad. The sun dipped, and the lights from the candles lit the night like earth stars. Dad and Annabelle Aurora talked books and old friends, though Annabelle remembered to include me. *Did you know your father almost failed my class?* she would ask. Or, *Have you ever been to New York in the winter? Well, your father hadn't either.* We laughed and they drank wine. The salad was strange and tasted like grass and herbs and seaweed. Annabelle told us how she tried to live mostly from the land. She was worried about the mark she'd made in this life. What was wasted. She could manage to eat and survive with most everything from her garden and the beach.

"No more capers in cut glass jars?" my father said. She leaned over and pinched his arm. We watched the candles flicker.

"Did you hear that Daniella Morgan married that violinist?" she asked.

"I heard," he said.

"She was in our class," Annabelle Aurora explained. "Your father followed her around like a puppy. And . . . what was her name? *Summer of the Gray Swan?* That story. I haven't forgotten it."

"You haven't forgotten her name, either, you old bitch," my father said. Annabelle laughed. "You have a mind like a steel trap."

"Listen to us and our clichés," she said. "Someone should pummel us with a red pencil. Fiona Husted."

My father looked down at his bread.

"She dumped him," Annabelle said to me. "And then she became very successful."

"She regretted it," he said. "Not the success, of course."

"Ha!"

"I know she did." His voice was quiet.

"Yes, well," Annabelle Aurora said. She poured more wine. I thought about my mother, then. The thought came suddenly, a memory, maybe, sparked by this conversation, that name, *Fiona Husted*. A door slamming—the night she'd had a "mood" when Annabelle visited for dinner. These kinds of stories, maybe, were funny for only a while. Maybe after a while they just made you feel bad. I wondered about the rocky territory of love and security, the ways a known person can suddenly seem unknown enough to threaten our sense of safety. Past loves were never past, Christian had said. I had argued that this was stupid. We could never be part of every corner of a person's life, and you just lived with that. You didn't go delving around in those corners in ways that made you feel weird. That was just asking for trouble. You had to separate the real threats from the ones that lived only in your imagination.

"Ah. All in the sordid past," my father said.

"Still," Annabelle said. "You should maybe start living again. Fiona Husted never married."

He was looking at her, and she was looking at him, and they were saying things that only they understood. "'Love's tangled branches'" he quoted.*

........................

* Annabelle Aurora, *Green Pastures, Selected Poems.*

"It was a different time in my life. And yours."

"'Deep scratches on bare arms to those who risk passing . . .'"

"'To those who *brave* passing,' smart-ass." She threw her napkin at him. It was sort of flirtatious.*

I helped Annabelle cut thick slices of raspberry pie. We came inside. It was getting cold, and there were mosquitoes. Annabelle started to yawn. Her old eyes looked tired. My father noticed, too, and we cleared the dishes and got ready to leave. He went outside to fold up the table for her.

Annabelle Aurora took my hands. Hers were small and warm, but she gripped me tightly. "Adrienne Rich wrote about this, what you're doing," she said to me. "Primitive tribes send their women away 'to go down into herself, to introvert, in order to evoke her instincts and intuitions.'** Yes? You, here? Think of it as a natural process. You find yourself by finding your instinct. By listening. By seeing what *is*."

"Dad told you why we're here," I said.

"Well, we all come to the ends of the earth for our own reasons," she said. She shrugged, as if to say it were a simple matter of fact.

"What are your reasons?" I asked.

"To lick my wounds. By the time a person's my age, they have quite a number of those, I suppose."

---

* If she'd slept with him or something, I didn't want to know. She hadn't *always* been that old. Still. I'd die.

** Adrienne Rich, *Of Woman Born*. I'd insert the proper footnote form here, but that's one of those things I never could get to stick in my mind. Footnote form, roman numerals, common denominators. Trash bin of the brain.

*Stay*

Dad returned. Annabelle dropped my hands and hugged him good-bye. "Annabelle, it was lovely," he said.

And it *had* been lovely. My father and I trudged back up the narrow piece of sand that was all that was left of the beach now that the tide had come in. We climbed our way back up the steep slope. My father reached the top and held his hand out to me. The lighthouse shot out its intermittent beam in that deep darkness. Sylvie Genovese's own lights were out. You could only hear the intermittent *chshsh* of waves unfurling on sand and the *threep threep* of crickets. The sea was endless-dark except for the glowing tips of the waves in the moonlight.

We were quiet. My father was deep in his own thoughts. And I was thinking about the women of primitive tribes and a hundred drowned sailors and closing my eyes in my bed at the ends of the earth.

# Chapter 9

I was not a girl who felt so free and comfortable with my own body that it was easy for me to share it. I was shy. In my bathing suit, I was shy. I remember being scared to start middle school because we thought we were going to have to take showers in P.E. That was the rumor. The image I had was straight out of a prison movie. Naked, exposed me, huddled, arms clutching for cover, as the other girls stood under the water, free and fearless. I still have dreams about that—some sleep-brain P.E. class where I can't find the hook I left my clothes on. In the dream I am Holocaust thin, as if even my usual protective fat has left me to fend for myself. Of course, they never made us take showers. Still, I am not one of those women you see in gym locker rooms strutting around with their bare droopy breasts and pocked thighs. They don't even seem to know it might be a good idea to undress in the bathroom stall. Then again, who's the one with the problem.

I was self-conscious when Dylan Ricks first kissed me, when he touched me. To me, my body seemed only good enough, something you'd buy if it were 60 percent off, but not at full price. I didn't know what men liked in a body. From what I could tell, it wasn't what I had. We were told to be thin, but it seemed to me it was girls who wanted that, not boys. Boys liked breasts and asses and thin girls didn't have those. I was neither thin enough to be admired by girls, nor lush enough to be admired by boys, so my body just seemed . . . serviceable. A toaster. A bicycle. A thing capable enough, I guessed, of carrying my spirit around. I couldn't understand the worth it might have to Dylan. Dylan had said I was inhibited, but I wasn't inhibited, I was sixteen.

When I first leaned in to kiss Christian on those bleachers, the momentum of the night picked me up and set me down into another way of being. A new person in your life gives the rest of it a chance to be new, too. Your life can be whatever you want it to, from there on out. I leaned in and kissed and that is who I was to him, not shy, but bold. Not inhibited, but brave. I was that to him and so I kept being that. It was what I thought he wanted and what he was attracted to, and yet it was this, this exact thing I wasn't even really, that made him the most insecure.

I got to the point, later, where I didn't know who I was. I didn't know which one of those people was me. I just couldn't tell.

We didn't make love often after that time in the car, but when we did, there was an intensity that made me feel too much—I was glass, transparent and breakable. It bound us closer together. It was the one thing we alone had with each other, with no one else, and to me that made it feel like it was brick set tight against more brick, another layer to our own private wall, but that's not how Christian saw it. For him, it was as if he'd had a nice object, a painting, say, or some vase, and then he suddenly found out it was rare and valuable, so valuable it made him nervous. He needed to guard it. He needed to make sure no one would steal it. It was perfect, so he also needed to make sure it stayed perfect, with the help of his constant, small corrections. When summer came and I started my bookstore job again, he'd ask too many questions about who came in. He worried about my coworker, Mark, even though Mark was a graduate student and had a girl-friend. I learned what not to say.

My father noticed. Christian and he always stayed their polite distance, but Dad would catch me in the hall sometimes, stop me on the way to my room. *What's with all his questions, C. P.?*, he'd ask. *You in jail or something? You the princess in the tower?* I'd get pissed, and he'd back off. He learned what not to say, too.

Still, if it was just *that* all the time, just insecurities and jeal-ousies, I would have left. It wasn't just that all the time. Not at all. We went swimming a lot that summer. He'd come by Armchair Books when I was done working, and we'd head across the street to Greenlake. We'd lay our towels out on the dock; our hair slicked back, that clean, tired, swimming happiness just soaking up the late afternoon sun. We sometimes laughed so hard, my stomach hurt. We would drive. We'd ride the ferries back and forth from Seattle to the islands just to feel the strong wind on the decks. I wasn't a princess in a tower when we stood at the front end of the ferry watching the city zoom toward us across the water, Christian's arms around me from behind.

"Unforgettable," he would say.

"I know," I would agree.

It was just after school started again, senior year, when my dad went to this literary event. Wait, I remember. Book party at Third Place Books, for . . . What was his name. The guy that does the literary courtroom novels.* Christian and I were alone in the house. I'd made a fire. We'd ordered a pizza, and we were sitting on the couch, the pizza in the box in front of us on the coffee table. The fire snapped and popped and made my face hot. We were using paper towels on the backs of Dad's magazines for plates.

"Cheese chin," I said to Christian. I pointed.

"You're the cheese chin," he said. "Maybe you'd like to use a fork."

"Fork you," I said, and he laughed.

We kissed a tomato sauce and sausage kiss and it was delicious. Just as delicious as past kisses like the orange juice kiss and the ice cream sandwich one. We ate and tried to remember every time we'd ever had a pizza. "Round Table," I'd said. "I was on a T-ball team. End of season party. I was maybe six. They gave us little statues."

"I can't picture you playing sports," he said.

"One season," I said. "Your turn."

......................

* Jeff David Farley. Friend of my father's. There, I told you there might be another famous person.

"We're not counting every night my father ordered it in instead of cooking, right? So . . . Okay. Classroom holiday party when I was twelve. Mrs. Bonnevier, that year we spent in France. She paid for it with her own money. I saw her take the bills from her purse. It seemed sad."

I nodded. I thought. "My father said we used to go to someplace called Pizza and Pipes when I was a baby. Him and my mom and me. They thought it was hilarious. It had some enormous pipe organ in the place. Like, two stories tall. It's not there anymore."

"And you'd think pizza plus enormous musical instruments would really bring in the crowds," Christian said.

"Exactly. Okay. Pagliacchi Pizza. In the car, with . . . Wait. It's not my turn."

Christian chewed, swallowed. He looked at me. His face glowed in the orange light of the fire. I thought he was beautiful. God, I thought. My eyes would be a hundred years old and still want to keep looking and looking at him. "With who?"

I felt it, some stone drop inside. I could hear the way his voice changed. He was still smiling. But I knew I could take some wrong turn here and he wouldn't be smiling anymore. The whole night could be ruined right there. I practically saw the street sign in front of me. DANGEROUS CURVES AHEAD.

"My *father*. We ate it in the front seat of the car as we drove home from Portland. Don't remember why we were there. Just him trying to shift and eat a big messy all-meat number and worrying about getting in an accident."

"I thought you were going to say you had it with Dylan."

Stay

"Nope," I said. The bad feeling shouted louder. It grew badder and bigger, but my insides were shrinking, shriveling.

"Well, I'm sure you did. Ate pizza. Did lots of things. You guys were together six months."

Of course we had. I'd eaten pizza in the car with Dylan, too, once. After a football game, and he was starved, but we wanted to be alone. And other times. Once right on that same couch. He'd been sitting right where Christian was, and we'd used magazines for plates. I wouldn't have told Christian that, though. I wouldn't have mentioned any of those things. "Not even," I said. "Dylan didn't like pizza. If I'd have eaten pizza with him, it would have been the worst pizza ever. I'd have thrown it right up. I'd have had to put pepperonis over my eyes just to look at it."

He didn't laugh. He got quiet. It was very quiet except for the fire. A log cracked and snapped in half, showing its secret inner kryptonite. "Christian . . ." I moaned. "Let's not do this?"

"Do what?"

I took his magazine from him, set it down. I climbed on his lap. "You're the only one I ever want to eat pizza with forevermore," I said. I plastered a bunch of kisses on his face. "Pizza is your food from now on. Cornflakes are. Oranges are."

He turned his mouth away.

"If I ever have to eat pizza with anyone but you, I'll refuse. I'll do like this." I clasped my mouth shut. I pretended to talk through it. "I hant bleet hanyflung ike at."

"Stop," he said.

"What?" I said. I was pleading a little.

"I just can't stand the thought of your mouth on someone else's. Let alone anything *else*."

I got off his lap. "Yeah? I can't stand the thought of yours on Angelie what's-her-face's. Or that other girl." But I was lying. I didn't really think about it much. I couldn't even remember the one girl's name.

"But you see him all the time," Christian said.

"What do you mean? I never see him," I said. Another lie. Dylan was in my Spanish class.

"You probably wish you did."

"Aaargh!" I pretended to strangle him. Nothing. He just sat there, wearing his mood like a cape, drawn around himself. We finished the pizza. We lay down next to each other and kissed, but it was all layered with hurt and distance, some weird emotional parfait. I kept trying and trying to reach him. See, I got deep into it with him. I was right there, too. I didn't stop it or step out of it. I felt as desperate to make him stay close, to keep him close, as he did—love, if that's what you could call it, was bound up with some bottomless, clutching need. Tightly bound, so that you couldn't tell the need from the love. It got late and Christian went home. I watched the taillights of his car disappear down the street. Even the taillights seemed hurt.

That night I lay in bed, listened to my father's car come into the garage, listened to him brush his teeth in the bathroom. Usually I might get up to see him, but I pretended to be asleep. All at once, my head was busy counting up my lies. I had never been a liar, but now they rolled off my tongue like lies were a second language I was suddenly fluent in.

*Stay*

I was only right there, where the path has turned and you think you might be lost but aren't even sure of it yet. The place in those creepy movies with the couple in the car on a dark night, a secluded road, where they pull off and they're making out and she first hears the twig branch break.

Those lies. I didn't realize it fully yet, but I guess you could say I was already in hiding from Christian Nilsson.

# Chapter 10

By the third day of my new job, I knew I would not be going to Friday Harbor with Finn Bishop. Some snakes couldn't be charmed, and Sylvie Genovese was one of them.

She toured me around the grounds. She took me inside the lighthouse, up its narrow, endless flight of winding stairs to the top where the lantern was. But she made it clear she would only take people up there who she felt were smart enough to be safe. *It is not a play area*, she said to me, wagging her finger as if I had already used the upper balcony like a jungle gym. She taught me how to use the cash register, and when I made a mistake, she'd snap: *Have you been listening? What did I say about this?* She quizzed me on the reading material. Silly me, I hadn't remembered the exact date of Captain Bishop's marriage to Eliza Bishop. I smiled and chatted with the visitors who came in, but I hadn't moved the tour on quickly enough, and I'd let the children touch things in the store without watching them. I couldn't understand if we were trying to welcome people or drive them away.

I complimented her hair. *This nest?* I praised Roger. *Ah, he is just a little* demone. I didn't take lunch. *You have to eat.* I took lunch. *I like to see devotion to the task.* The only time she seemed happy was when she'd come in from fishing, after bringing her little boat out to sea, or working in her garden with Roger sleeping in a spot of sun nearby. You saw her smile then, when she was alone or had just been alone. I guessed snakes weren't much for company. It was so different from Armchair Books, where the owner, Derek, with his kind eyes and beard, would laugh and have parties for us and his favorite customers after the store closed on Thursdays, for no reason. Armchair Books had a fireplace and posters of Parisian book stalls on the walls, a picture of an armchair painted on the front window.

I was glad for the moment when Sylvie took her boat keys off the hook by the door, the ones attached to a foam key chain so they could float if dropped in water. I'd have an hour's peace. If no one came in, I'd dust the cases in the museum that were filled with old paraffin containers and navigational instruments, or refill the shelves, or fold the sweatshirts and T-shirts that were always getting unfolded. I'd make sure there were lots of choices of sizes available in all styles: the simple lighthouse image with its name underneath, the lighthouse with *Bishop Rock Rocks!* in crazy letters, the pigeon head (he was actually a seagull) with a small lighthouse in the background, *Pigeon Head Point Lighthouse* written in script. I was glad she didn't make me wear one. Those T-shirts with the flat slabs of rubbery images always felt unbearably scratchy and uncomfortable to me.

When all of that was done, and if there were no visitors anywhere on the premises, I was allowed to sit by the counter and read, which is what I would do, taking my bookmark from my latest find from the Bishop Rock Library. I would wonder what the upstairs of the house was like, where Sylvie Genovese lived. I could hear her on the phone sometimes, speaking Italian, and I wondered what brought her here, if she, too, were licking her wounds. You could see her boat zipping along or bobbing in the waters out front, her small figure capably steering that motor, her chin tipped to the sun.

That's what I was doing, reading, wondering about Sylvie Genovese as Roger kept guard by the door nearby, when I heard Sylvie shouting outside. She was agitated and yelling about something, and Roger leaped up and started to bark, and I got up too and ran out, seeing if I could be of help. She'd probably get pissed at me for trying to help if I did, or for not helping if I didn't, I thought, but her voice was too excited not to wonder what was going on.

I wasn't prepared for what I saw.

"Dad?"

My father was sprawled out along the grass on the top of the cliff. His mouth was twisted in pain and he had twigs and grass in his hair and a swipe of sand stuck to his face and along one leg. Sylvie was kneeling beside him sweating madly, her own leg scratched and bleeding a bit. Roger barked and turned in circles, doing another badly timed circus trick.

"You know him? He belongs to you?" Sylvie said in that beautiful voice.

"I wouldn't exactly say that," I said.

"Clara," he said.

"What are you doing?" I asked. *Asked* sounds like I was calm and reasonable. It was actually sort of a high shriek. Like I didn't have enough problems with Sylvie Genovese.

"Visiting Annabelle." He winced. "I think I broke my ankle."

"He fell. I had to haul him up."

I wanted to laugh, but I wasn't that stupid. I wished I could have seen *that*—gorgeous, small Sylvie Genovese manhandling poor broken Pops. He had *sand* stuck to the side of his *face*. A bubble of hysteria rose up, and I tried to swallow it down. I clapped my hands so that Roger would stop the jumping around and the barking.

"Roger!" Sylvie said, and he was immediately still. He sat his little butt right down and looked at her with eager attention, as if he were a student about to be asked a question he was sure he knew the answer to. "Go in my bathroom upstairs and get the medical kit. Under the counter," she said.

Okay, I'm an idiot, because for a second I thought she was talking to Roger until I realized she meant me. I ran back inside. I crossed the rope that was strung between the banisters. I made a wrong turn and ended up in Sylvie's bedroom. I saw her unmade bed filled with white pillows and a plump white comforter and a soft saffron-colored quilt, books all around, a room to love. Her jeans were tossed on the floor, a pair of black undies, too. I backed out, found the bathroom. It smelled good, and there was an array of bottles and lotions on the counter, a picture in a frame facedown.

I had no time to snoop, but I did have time to lift the frame and set it back down again, time enough to see the picture of Sylvie Genovese standing next to a man holding a basket of lemons in front of an orange house. I looked under the counter. A box of tampons, toilet paper, cleaning supplies. Wait. A blue plastic container with a handle. I yanked it out, opened the clasps. Bingo. An Ace bandage, iodine, cotton swabs, all that stuff. I ran back down the stairs.

Sylvie Genovese's sweater was bundled up under my father's head. He was laughing, and so was she. She was looking right down at him, and her teeth were so white against her olive skin, and his hair was so black against his own. She plucked a strand of grass from his shirt. I stopped suddenly, holding that kit, causing Roger, who I didn't realize had been following so closely, to run into the back of my legs. Sylvie had not yet wrapped my father's ankle in the tight, tan cloth. She had not yet cleaned her own wound.

But I knew right then I might be making it to Friday Harbor after all.


"I was beginning to think you weren't coming," Finn Bishop said.

"Just busy at work." I smiled. I had waited for a long time for the boat to come in; finally I saw the tip of the mast in the sharp blue sky and there it was, *Obsession*, returning to the dock and getting bigger and bigger as it neared. Finn had helped the passengers off, extending his hand and all the while looking over at me and beaming. Finally they had all disembarked, and Jack had headed over to get some food at The Cove. We were standing there alone, alone if you didn't count the fisherman and the tourists and the knobby-kneed seagulls and a single pelican standing on a piling.

"Not fired yet?"

"No," I said smugly. I was feeling smug.

"Ready to come on board?" He had his hands in his jeans pockets. He was rocking a bit on his heels.

I was ready. "I've heard the ghosts of drowned sailors are haunting these waters," I said.

"Yes, ma'am. You never want to be in a boat after dark. They'll grab you by the ankles and pull you down, trying to save themselves."

He hopped on the boat, reached over and took my hand, and I came on too. I shivered in spite of myself. The image of a hand around an ankle. "Cold?" he asked.

"Fine," I said. Great, actually. I was filling up with great. Funny, but it was so different being on the dock versus being on the boat, and we hadn't even left yet. Maybe it was the thrill of what was coming—the about-to-leave before the leaving. The boat rocked. I realized you needed special footing to keep your balance.

"Careful," Finn said.

"Where should I be?" There were bench seats by the big steering that Jack used, and there was the huge deck-nose of the boat, lined with complicated rows of ropes. It would be easy to be in the way here.

"The best seat—way up front. I won't worry about you being hit with the boom." He slapped the huge metal rail at the bottom of the big sail. "You've got to hold on. The boat will heel, right?"

He tilted his hand. "You won't fall. No one ever has. You got these lifelines." He pushed against the thin wires stretched along-side the boat, a railing of sorts, but not one you could imagine holding up anything, let alone a slipping body.

He waited. "If you're nervous about that, you can sit back here and listen to Jack bullshit the customers."

"I'm not nervous," I said. I could see Finn's sure footing. I climbed up, made my way over ropes and pulleys to the very tip of the boat. "Here?"

Finn nodded, pleased. "That's right."

We talked for a bit. He asked where I was from and where we were staying and for how long. I told him the *what* but not the *why*. Something occurred to me. Maybe Dad would consider it cheating, but I asked anyway. "The house we're staying in? The one at the very tip of Possession Point?"

"I know it. We go right past there, what, six times a day?"

"Do you know who lives there?"

"Nope. Someone who's gone a lot. It always seems empty."

"So you don't know if the guy's a movie director."

Finn laughed. "I don't think so. Nope. We'd know it. Some cousin of Kurt Cobain's was out here for a while and everyone knew the poor sucker's every move. 'He's a vegetarian.' 'He bought fifty pounds of concrete at the hardware store.'"

"We're just trying to figure out about our host," I said. "Lame personal mystery. "

"I can find out for you."

"That's okay. Dad would probably rather keep guessing," I said.

He looked at me. "I like to guess about someone. But then, it's even better when you know more." He was sitting beside me with his legs stretched out. "I'd like to know more," he said to me. "You know, about you."

My stomach flipped. His eyes really were sweet, if you could believe eyes. It's hard to trust those kinds of observations when they'd been so wrong before. I thought about Annabelle's word, *instinct*. I worried mine had been lost at sea like those drowned sailors, the ways it had gone wrong haunting me forevermore.

"I'd like to know more about you, too."

We had that pleased moment between us, where you both just sit there and smile and don't dare say anything to interrupt it. And then there was the thud of shoes on deck, and a shout.

"Break it up, love birds," Jack said.

Finn blushed. "Oh my God, I'm sorry. I'm going to kill him," he said. "Jack, shut your fucking mouth," he called.

"It's okay." I laughed.

"You got ten minutes to clean those toilets before we take off again," Jack shouted.

"I hate him," Finn said. "You're a rat bastard," he called.

Jack was in a fine mood. He cracked open the cap of a bottle of root beer and took a long swig. "Ahh, not quite the real thing, but it'll do."

"He's got a new girlfriend," Finn said. "He's going to be impossible. He's been taking her out on the boat at night. Got in at three a.m. Looks wide awake, too."

"He does," I said. Jack was about as happy as a guy could get.

The swing of his arms looked happy. The curve of his back did, as he bent over and untangled a line.

"That fucking seagull followed Cleo home again," Jack shouted to us. "And he was there on the table again at eleven a.m. like he was ready to start work. Cleo's finally got a steady guy."

"Better looking than the last one. Probably smarter, too," Finn shouted back. "I better get going," he said to me.

"Do what you need to," I said. "I'm happy here."

"This boat hasn't been this lucky in a long while," Finn said.

He leaped to his feet. I watched his ass in those jeans. I was guilty of all the things Christian accused me of. I admired how his belt sat on his hips. The braid of leather around his wrist. That black shaggy hair that curled around his face. I watched the dock move up and down, leaned back on my palms and breathed in the good air. In a few minutes a middle-aged couple came aboard, wearing matching sweatshirts. I might have seen them around the grounds of the lighthouse. They sat in the seats back by the wheel. He took her picture with the camera around his neck.

And then another couple. Matching blonds with blond children. A boy and a girl. She was pouting about something, and the boy went over to the wheel and was going to steer until his mother told him to quit. Two guys in baseball caps came aboard as their wives stayed behind snapping photos. We waited awhile, but that was everyone for this trip. Finn got busy. He was undoing lines from the dock and hopping back on again. Uncinching ropes and cinching others. Jack was motoring, steering the boat out toward the wide water, shaking his head at Finn and Finn shaking his head back at him when a small motorboat crossed in front of them. Jack turned off their own motor, made a little speech to the passengers, safety talk, a few jokes that made the people laugh. I could only hear every few words where I was. The wind was picking up. Finn began to hoist the huge sail. He grabbed the rope with two hands and pulled down, crouching all the way to the ground, one long movement that involved his whole body. He did it again and again, until the grand white sail began to lift and lift and then it was there, all the way up, and it was enormous and majestic. You could see how hard it was to raise that sail, how strong Finn had to be.

The boat took over from there. We sailed out, and it was fast, and as the boat slanted, I held on as Finn had told me to, my feet anchored hard against the floor. There was the speed, and the holding on, and the thrill of the incline, yet it was relaxing, too. The gliding along the water, the repetition of motion—it almost made me sleepy. A second sail was hoisted, and then there was only forward motion again. Calm speed. And then, a flurry—the warning that they were "coming about," the swing of the huge boom, lines skittering on deck, the clatter of the rings and ropes against metal, the tilt, the other way this time, and then, smooth, fast sailing again.

"You okay?" Finn, on his quick feet. Standing above me. He was brave to walk around like that.

"Great," I said. "This is fantastic."

"Right?" he said. He breathed. He stretched his arms behind his head. I didn't realize how much work sailing took, or how much strength. You could see he was an athlete. Not just for a season—you could see that this sport was a way of living. A connection to water and sky and rhythms of earth and atmosphere. "Now you'll come again?"

"Absolutely."

Finn scooted off. He worked hard. I watched him. Maybe it was just his ease here, or his physical strength, but he looked *healthy.* He looked like he was happy, even. I looked for angst in his jawline. I looked for the possibility of dark thoughts there, across his forehead. But he was just moving about that boat like he and it were one, the way you see a cowboy ride his horse, the way you see old people who know how to dance together.

The guy with the camera pointed one finger and everyone stood and looked—there was the smooth black head of a sea lion in the distance. A fishing boat we passed pulled up a huge trap of crab. The sun, the waves. The sense of possibility. The creatures doing the things creatures have been doing for centuries. It seemed possible to find instinct here.

We docked. I felt so satisfied. It was as if I'd eaten a big meal of fresh air and sun. I wanted to take a nap. I could have slept for days. I hadn't felt that relaxed in a long time.

I waited on the dock until Finn was done with his duties. The couple asked me to take a picture of them, and the man showed me how to use his camera. They looked great in the tiny square with their matching shirts. Finn showed up. He'd snuck a mint— I could smell the sweet puff of his breath.

"Thank you so much," I said. "This was fantastic."

"You free later?" he said. Casual. Easy. It all felt like that. "Get some food or something?"

"Butch's Harbor Bar? Fried clam special, one week only?" I said.

"One week only since, what, the 1970s? Excellent choice, Miss Clara."

We made a plan, said good-bye. I felt sleepy and rested and happy, too, like my insides were having their own little party. I couldn't wait for Butch's Harbor Bar. I felt so pleased and full of regular life that I reached for my phone. I had my hand on it, just like I always did—I was going to call Shakti and tell her about this. I had it in my palm and looked down. My whole life was sitting there, it seemed. But I just wanted to hear her voice. I missed my friend so much right then. I missed the normal thing you do, which is to call your best friend and share the good things that might be happening. I put my phone back in my pocket. I couldn't take that risk. The only way to truly be safe was if no one knew where we were.

I stopped to get us some groceries, and then I drove home. On the street by our house on Possession Point, I saw my father, riding in circles on a bicycle. I rolled my window down.

"Where'd you get that?" I asked.

"Look at this thing. I found it in the shed out back. He's got to be one successful bastard. You don't leave a bike like this out in sea air where it can rust, unless you can replace it like nothing."

"You taking up biking?" He looked a little wobbly on it. That ankle, probably. "And, what, did you have some sort of miracle cure after your fall?"

He ignored that. "I figure we could use a way for us both to get around." He was smiling. He looked happier than I'd seen him in maybe forever.

"I see," I said. And I did. I felt both nervous and glad. Dad had never even dated much, for all the attention he got from women. Annabelle Aurora had said he should start living again, but it never seemed to me that he *hadn't* been living. He worked and had his friends and every now and then he might go out and come home late but it would end before I ever met anyone. I guess I figured he was still in love with my mother.

I drove the car the rest of the way to the house and parked, and he rode that bike and set it against the porch. I got out, locked the car door, though there wasn't exactly anyone around to break into it. He looked like he was walking funny. "You okay?" I asked.

"Fucking ankle."

"Just like the old nursery rhyme. 'Asses, asses, we all fall down.'"

"Hilarious."

"Maybe you shouldn't be riding that bike."

"It's fine. I was an *athlete*."

"One lousy season," I said. "She said she was married."

He turned. "What?"

"*Mrs.* Genovese."

He thought about this.

"There's probably an explanation," I said. Who knew.

"I'm sure there is," he said. "Because she agreed to go out with me tonight." I opened the trunk to get the groceries. He put his hands on his hips, looked out to the sea. His shirtsleeves were rolled up, and I could see scratches from where he had fallen.

"At least it's not Fiona Husted," I said to his back. I just hadn't liked the sound of her name when Annabelle had said it. Sylvie Genovese was maybe a snake my father could charm, but Fiona Husted was a big unknown.

My father swung around and stared at me. I swear, his mouth dropped open. He looked spooked. "Jesus," he said.

"What?" I said. I had a plastic bag full of lettuce and bananas and yogurt on my arm.

"You just sounded . . ."

"Sounded what?"

"Like your mother. I swear to God. Exactly."

I didn't know how to take this. It could have been a good thing, couldn't it, except for that look on his face? That look—it was troubled. He actually took a step back from me. I wasn't my mother. I was me. I wanted to move past that moment, fast. What I saw disturbed me—a flash of the complicated feelings he'd had about her. It was the first time I'd witnessed it in such a large way. Then again, maybe I was just at that point where you suddenly see your parents clearly. I held the bag out to him. "Here." I flung it his direction, and he caught it. I took out the other bag and slammed the trunk. I tried to sound casual. "I've got a date tonight myself," I said.

"Really." His face returned to normal. He even looked pleased. He nodded. "I see."

We walked inside. Rather, he *hobbled* inside. He went to the bathroom, rummaged around for what I was guessing was the aspirin bottle. "The dating thing . . . I'll go slow," I called to him. "I don't want you to worry."

"Clara, you learned more with all of this . . . I don't worry." He came back out, two white tablets in his palm. "You learned *too* much. Your problem is going to be letting go of this experience, not holding on to it."

He was probably right. Everything that had happened with Christian—it took up so much space, it was like another person inside of me. That's how heavy it felt. The guilt, the responsibility. The weight of memory and decisions. I wanted to be as far away from Christian as I could, and yet I still worried about him every day. I still thought about him endlessly. It was my fault, what happened. I was sure. But Dad was right—nothing like this would ever happen again. That was the only thing in all this that gave me any rest.

He took out a glass, filled it with water, and swallowed the pills. He turned back to face me. He was smiling again. "Look at us," he said. "Who would have thought?" I felt good, too. My father's eyes looked bright, and my heart speeded along at the thought of Finn and me at Butch's Harbor Bar.

"Wouldn't it be weird? We come here when things are so awful . . ." I said. "Can a whole lot of good come from that much bad?"

"Phoenix rising from the ashes!" Dad twanged like a Southern preacher.

"We are reborn," I said, like a Southern preacher, too.

"Hal-le-lu-jah," he said. And then, he did something very un-Dad-like. My literary father with his writerly wild hair and black glasses raised up his arm, slapped me a sports-father high five as I slapped him one back.

*Stay*

\* \* \*

Dad insisted on riding that bike to Sylvie Genovese's in spite of his ankle, and so I took the car to Butch's Harbor Bar. The place was crowded, spilling people and music, but when I got to the doorway I could see Finn at a table, waving his arm at me.

"Nothing like someplace quiet and romantic," he shouted.

It suited me just fine. I liked it there. Country music blared; you could see Butch with his huge belly and gray beard behind the bar. The waitresses wore red aprons. The food was served in red plastic baskets with checked paper inside. It was a place where people laughed loud.

I slid into the seat across from Finn. We joked about his brother and sister and that seagull. I asked him about the rest of his family. His mother owned and ran the boat and restaurant business since his father died.

"My mother," I shouted. "She died, too." It was a funny thing to shout.

He nodded. We could have said more to each other about this, but we didn't.\* We ate our fried clam special and passed the napkins and sipped icy cold Cokes in red plastic cups. Every time someone came through the door, especially if it was a guy our age, I tried to make sure I kept my eyes on Finn's. I watched my words when we talked about school. I didn't mention anyone

......................

\* We didn't need to. You share an experience like that, and you both know you have a whole planet of connection and understanding between you. I knew more about Finn right then and he knew more about me than we could have if we'd spent six months talking nonstop.

from my past, unless it was a girl. But when our waitress finished her shift only to be replaced by a friend of Finn's, he introduced him to me. I was well-trained, you know? And so I didn't joke with them at first. I was aware of what I was doing, but I couldn't stop myself. I felt like I'd been in one of those cults where the women wear long dresses and are forbidden to watch television. Once out in the world, television was still a thing to fear. But Finn looked only relaxed and happy. And so I joked with them, and I remembered how good it felt to do that, and Finn's face never changed. It seemed possible but also impossible that he might not see threats everywhere. It seemed possible but impossible that I might be able to relax, too.

"We done here?" Finn said. I really liked those sweet eyes. Really liked. I would never again be attracted to anyone who wasn't entirely and completely kind. Down to their cells kind. The garden variety of nice, as my dad said, not the sort that was righteousness in hiding. Being attracted to anything else—to badness or darkness or trouble—it seemed not only immature but slightly twisted. You might as well say you were drawn to car crashes, or burning buildings, or cancer. I was scared to see Finn's goodness (I'd been wrong about that before), but I *did* see it. There was something uncomplicated about him, and I had come to know that "complicated" was something to distrust.

We shoved our empty baskets away. Those clams had been fantastic. You saw why the place was so crowded. Butch was telling some story and sliding beers down the bar, like you see in Western movies. "How about some quiet?" Finn said.

"Quiet sounds good," I said.

I went to the bathroom and checked that I didn't have anything embarrassing in my teeth. I looked like me, but a different me, in the mirror. It was funny, because I felt like myself, but I also wondered where exactly I was and how I got here. In that bathroom, with cowboy music playing outside the door and a guy waiting for me on the sidewalk outside, I was someone I needed to get to know.

He'd snuck a mint again, but so had I. Our mutual mint breath meant we hoped to stand closer. The street seemed so quiet after that restaurant. Finn took my fingers, ran with me across the street to where the water was. His hands were rough and callused from those ropes. He did not have Christian's smooth, protected hands.

"Want to go to the beach?" he asked.

"Sure." I didn't know where people here went on a weekend night. At home we would have gone to a coffee place. Maybe one of the parks by one of the lakes.

He kept hold of my fingers. I didn't mind. We stood at the top of the breaker wall, looked down at the stretch of sand going in both directions. Bonfires dotted the shoreline. *This* is where people went on weekends; I could tell. They gathered in groups, small orange-lit parties. A guy called Finn's name and Finn waved, and a girl gestured for him to join them. There was laughter, beer bottles tilted for a drink in the moonlight. I felt a little shy. I would be the tourist girl people looked at with curiosity.

"Friday night," he apologized. "Maybe somewhere more quiet? We can see if Jack's hijacked *Obsession*."

"Okay."

We walked down the main street to a now familiar place, the docks. *Obsession* was in its place. The lapping and sloshing water sounded different and more insistent in the dark. A few of the boats were glowing from inside, looking like snug hideaways. Finn climbed up on the boat, held his hand out, and helped me over. He opened the hatch below, called out Jack's name. Finn disappeared for a second. I imagined Jack popping out, hitching up his pants with his shirt off, but the boat was empty. I wondered what it was like down there, what it would be like to be with Finn in his own snug hideaway. A boat seemed like the best kind of secret place—better than a treehouse or a fort tucked into a forest. You could hide, but you could flee, too.

"Just us," Finn said. He had some thick blankets under his arm, which he set on the deck for us to sit on. "You warm enough? I'd take you out, but it really takes two of us, and that idiot never remembers to leave the keys, anyway."

"This is great." I sat down, looking out onto the sea, where the moon had dipped the waves into gold light. You could hear someone's radio. The waves lapped and sloshed against the side of the boat. "Hidden."

Finn sat down next to me. He stretched out his long legs. I wondered how that word would sound, *hidden*. Would he think I meant something by it? That this was something I regularly did?

"I love being hidden sometimes. Do you ever just love that? When no one knows where you are?" He hadn't misinterpreted. I decided to try letting all of that go, the weighing and the measuring. I would say what I wanted, slip off the chains.

# Stay

It seemed strange how at ease I felt. You could be comfortable with Finn Bishop, and yet, the space between us still felt charged.*

"We aren't supposed to be on a boat after dark, remember?" I said. "The ghosts will grab our ankles trying to save themselves?"

"You have more ghost action right where you work," Finn said.

"Sylvie Genovese?" I guess in some ways she did seem haunted.

Finn laughed. "Eliza Bishop. The Captain's wife? People really *have* seen her. My mother, and she doesn't even believe in that shit. Lots of other people. They hear her in the house. They see her up on the tower. She flung herself off of there after the old guy drowned at sea."

"I read about it. I was practically *quizzed* on it. Guess I better keep my eyes open for her."

"The sailors down there . . ." He gestured out toward the black waters. "People say they hear them moaning. Wind and a little imagination, right? There's this guy. Randy Vishner. Fisherman? He claims they overturned his boat, grabbed his legs, and yanked him down. But Randy Vishner . . ." He tipped his hand up as if drinking from a bottle.

"'This is your brain. This is your brain on booze,'" I said.

"Exactly. Alcohol hauntings."

"We have a ghost near us, supposedly, at home," I said. "Greenlake. This lake in the middle of the city? A girl was

........................

* Shakti always said we should have a guy we *wanted* to keep shaving our legs for. I knew what she meant.

murdered there, by her boyfriend. You're supposed to see her at night when you go there to make out."*

"That'll kill the mood. Pardon the pun," Finn said.

Finn had found my hand again. I was glad. It was stupid, I know, but all that talk gave me the creeps. Especially sitting there in the darkness, where the night's black sea looked capable of different things than the day's blue one. There were bodies under that water, drowned ships. I felt little prickles of nerves. That tingle that goes up your back, even when there's no good reason for it. I squeezed his hand, and he squeezed mine back.

We talked about my plans now that I'd graduated, plans I was still unsure about. I'd gotten off track last year with everything that happened. I'd missed acceptance deadlines. But all I told Finn was that I was taking a year off before I went to school. He had gone away for two years himself but was back home again. He was thinking about staying. He loved being with his family and running the business. We talked about other things. Music. Learning to drive. Being an only child. Loving fried foods and orange juice and the crunchy layer of frosting that a cupcake gets. I told him about my second grade teacher, Miss Spelling. How much I loved that name.**

The radio that had been playing was off now. It was quiet between us, too. Finn was looking in my eyes like he'd found

* My father would mention Jennifer Riley to me, because she was a real girl with a real boyfriend (who was still in jail somewhere in California). She'd tried to break it off. He used a knife. One of the synonyms for "obsession," after all, is "to haunt."

** Okay, I'm lame, but I still like it. Especially how Miss Spelling is a misspelling.

something good there, and I was looking back in his. His face had started to look familiar to me. I wanted to kiss him so bad, and you could feel that space where you knew it was going to happen. I looked at his mouth. I wanted to lean in to it. Instead, my own voice surprised me.

"I want to kiss you, but I want to look forward to the thought of kissing you for a while first."

"I know exactly what you mean," he said. "Exactly."

We were whispering. It might have been one of those rare, perfect moments. We sat there in it, taking it in, until he stood up. "Come on," he said. "It's getting late."

He walked me back to my car. He kissed my hair good-bye. He said something into it very quietly. "Shy girl."

I had been a shy girl, a cautious, mostly quiet one, but I had been renamed and renamed again, redefined until I couldn't see myself anymore. I had been bold and then I had been *forward*, and then, when things got worse and I had been twisted into the unrecognizable, I had been only lost. But with that word, "shy"— I was returned to myself again.

My father wasn't home yet when I got there. We'd forgotten to leave a light on, and the house was all gray shadows and emptiness. I let myself in. I felt nervous out there all alone. I could hear the wind whistling around the roof, the thrash of the waves. I undressed, with that silly, strange feeling that someone was watching. I thought about ghosts and the rest of those who can't let go. I tried to fall asleep, but I only lay awake with my eyes open. I thought about that huge, heavy paperweight under my father's bed, wishing it were under my own. I had that same old feeling you had when you were a kid, when you needed to get up to pee but were too afraid. I used to think those robbers were in the hall, waiting, but now I thought of the widows of sea captains and dead girls.

I told myself how stupid I was being, and I got up, and the floor was cold under my feet, and my long T-shirt made me feel too exposed. My ankles were bare. My legs. I crept down the hall. I was actually creeping, so I might not disturb whatever—whomever—might be disturbed. I reached the bathroom and that's when I screamed. I actually screamed, stupid, stupid—it was my father in his white T-shirt, heading the same direction with the quietest of steps.

"Clara!" he said.

"Oh, God, Dad, I'm sorry." I had my hand to my chest.

"*I'm* sorry. I didn't mean to startle you."

"I didn't hear you come in."

"Jesus, honey. Next time I'll make more noise."

"I guess I got a little creeped out here on my own." We faced each other in the hall. My heart was still doing this mad *babamp babamp*. Something was different, though. I squinted in the darkness. I took a good look at him for the first time. "Are you okay?"

"She's not married," he said. "Never has been. She only uses 'Mrs.' so people will keep their distance."

"Well, that's good, isn't it?" He flipped the bathroom light on, and we both blinked in the sudden brightness. Maybe it was the shock of instant illumination, but it looked like his olive skin had turned pale. He searched around for that aspirin bottle again, as if he'd forgotten where he'd put it.

He turned to me, stared. "It's just that . . ."

He looked ill. "What? Are you going to be sick?"

"I could maybe love this woman," he said.

I didn't know what to say or what to think. In the hall, I had been scared enough to scream, but right then, as he stood there holding that bottle, his eyes hollow, he was the one who looked like he'd seen a ghost.

# Chapter 11

Christian and I were the kind of couple people start thinking of as one person. Our names came together when anyone spoke about either of us. Christian and Clara. *ChristianandClara.* We saw all of the seasons and the holidays and were going on our second view of them together. We had our second Christmas. He gave me this necklace with intertwined *C*'s. I gave him a leather wristband* he never took off as long as I knew him. It wasn't really his type, but he wore it anyway. I was with him when Mr. Hooper got sick. We visited him in the hospital in that blue and white gown, and then he was back home again in his jogging suit and scuffers, more thin and quiet than before. Christian and I made plans to go to college together. I was there for him after

..........................

* Funny how we don't call these bracelets even though they are bracelets.

he had this big blowout with his stepfather. We had history. That leaf he had given me had long ago turned brown and crunchy and layered with meaning. We had daily *routine.*

Routine is cement for some people, coziness made solid, certainty building more certainty. For others, routine cracks surfaces with its weight, creating a boredom that presses down and down until something breaks. You'd understand either of those things, wouldn't you? The settling in or the boredom of settling in? But what I didn't understand was this thing that happened—when routine caused a person more fear. Because the more Christian came to rely on me, to feel I was the "perfect" person for him, the more convinced he became that he would lose me. And the more he was afraid of losing me, the more paranoid he got and the more he made sure that what would happen next was what he feared most.

And what a shame it was. It was all so *needless.* I loved him. The only one who changed that was Christian himself.

*Are you wearing that?*

*I guess I am, since I have it on.*

*I can practically see your nipples.*

It's hard to stand up for yourself when you are burning with shame.

I've heard that people stay in bad situations because a relationship like that gets turned up by degrees. It is said that a frog will jump out of a pot of boiling water. But place him in a pot and turn it up a little at a time, and he will stay until he is boiled to death. Us frogs understand this.

*Why you didn't tell me you were going to the library?* he asked me once.

*I didn't know. I just decided.*

*You just decided as you were driving past? When it's ten minutes out of your way?*

*It's not logical, Christian. It's not some sort of math equation you can find a flaw in. I decided, I went.*

*A person doesn't mention a plan they have, it makes you wonder if they have something to hide.*

*Christian, listen. You've got to stop this. You've got to knock this off. All this jealous stuff, distrust—it doesn't look good on you. It's unattractive. You're wrecking things.* It wasn't the first time I said it. I said it all the time. The anger, though, it was just another ineffective tool in the box with the other ways I dealt with Christian's jealousy. It lay there uselessly along with the reassurance and the joking and the diversion, the ways I kept my eyes down, the clothes I wore or didn't wear anymore.

*I'm sorry, Clara. You're right. You are. I am so sorry. I don't deserve you.*

It was sometime around February. Cold enough that everything was white with frost, even in the afternoon. I was glad Christian was coming to pick me up from school. I hate the cold. I feel it deep in my bones in a way I'm not sure everyone does. The bell had rung and there was the slamming of locker doors and the mix of people lingering to stay and people hurrying to go. I was heading out the main entrance of school. A few guys were ahead of me, and I saw him there. Dylan Ricks. His friend, Jake McNeal, stopped to tie his shoe, and they all stopped and Dylan saw me.

"Hey," he said.

The whole scene suddenly played out in my mind. Christian would be waiting at the curb in his car. He would remember Dylan from the time I'd pointed him out long ago, before I knew not to. Christian would see Dylan talking to me and would watch my own lips move, and I would have to look at Dylan, and I knew what that would mean. So I just brushed past Dylan like I didn't notice him there right in front of me, which was stupid and embarrassing. And when I got to the car, I understood that I was right; Christian's face was tight and hard, and that tightness made me mad in a way it hadn't before. I had guessed it and now that's what was happening, and when you start predicting things like that, you realize you've reached some end point of knowing. This is how it will always be and will always be and will always be. It's the dark side of knowing how he'll order his coffee and that he'll get stressed when he's late because he always gets stressed when he's late.

"I thought you said you never saw Dylan." The car was idling. Christian flicked off the heat with an angry hand even though it was freezing. "You lied to me."

Which was true. I saw Dylan every day in Spanish. I borrowed a pen from him when mine started leaking ink. He told me when his dog died, because I'd really liked that dog.

"You probably lied about sleeping with him, too," Christian said. "You're the kind of person that *would* sleep with him."

Also true.

I started to realize that anything I did, any way I could have handled this—well, I couldn't win. No matter what. Each way I turned, there "it" was. The realization changed something. But, see, the problem was, other things had changed, too. I had started to wonder if maybe Christian was right about me. I wondered if maybe I *was* that someone he always accused me of being. Maybe I'd been her all along.

The lying got worse. More and more, he thought I was trying to hide things from him because I *was* hiding things from him. I *wanted* to hide things from him. I wanted space to breathe. I went with Shakti and Nick to Red Robin and told him I went with Dad. I did that all the time. I had a roast beef sandwich once and told him I had a salad. I really did. I think I just wanted pieces of me he couldn't see or find or judge somehow.

I started to think a lot about going away to school. We had both planned to go to the University of Washington so we could be together, but instead I dreamed about foreign cities that were farther away and full of strangers. I went with my father to check out a university in Vancouver, Canada, and Christian called so many times that my father got pissed and took my phone and stuck it in the pocket of his jacket. I wasn't sure I minded. I avoided looking at that pocket.

Christian could always feel my lies and sense my secret retreat. We went to visit Mr. Hooper. I read to him, a Chekhov book of stories Christian had gotten from the library. *The proposal embarrassed her with its suddenness, by the fact that the word* wife *had been spoken, and by the necessity of refusing it. She could not even remember what she had said to Laptev, but she continued to feel traces of the violent, disagreeable emotion with which she had rejected him* . . . Mr. Hooper had fallen asleep. His wispy white hair stood up straight against the back of the chair where his head lay and made me feel sad.

"I love you," Christian said. He took the book from me. Kissed me softly.

"I love you too," I said. I meant it.

"You won't ever leave me, will you?" he said.

*If you go to school in Vancouver, it's over,* he said.

*Why? It's not that far away,* I said.

*You'd take up with someone else.*

*No.*

*You were the one,* he said, *who came on to me. You came right up to me. You threw yourself at me.*

*You wish,* I'd said. The anger—it was my favorite tool now. He'd used up my patience.

*That other guy had his hands all over you that day.*

*Who?*

*You know who. Nick. I saw him.*

*He's my* friend.

*And are you always so forward with guys? You kissed me. You were the one who pushed for sex. Angelie would never have done that. She had morals. She respected herself.*

Angelie was the girl at the basketball game. The one he'd been seeing before me. For, maybe, a month. He'd brought her up often. She'd become the Virgin Mary, I swear. *Go ahead and be with Angelie, then,* I said. *Go for it.*

*You wouldn't even care, would you?*

I sighed. *Of course I'd care, Christian.*

*You'd just go with some other guy.*

*Well, probably I would, eventually.* The phrase, *some other guy*—I was getting tired of it. Those words grated on me. He said those three words as often than any. More often than "I love you."

*You'd tell everyone what an asshole I'd been.* He was afraid of this. Really afraid. Of people knowing the kinds of things he said when we were alone.

*No. I wouldn't do that.*

*All you'd have to do is call up Jake Ritchee. I'm sure he'd have sex with you, too.*

We were in his room. Sandy and Elliot were gone. Shopping. Costco, or something. It was a regular weekend day. The tree outside his room was empty of all leaves. Stark. The street was messy and windblown. We'd probably had a small storm the night before. One of their garbage cans was knocked over. I'd been staring out his window, because I didn't want to see his face when he got like this. His words pissed me off, but confused me, too. I turned away from the window. I looked at him.

*Who is Jake Ritchee? I don't even know a Jake Ritchee.*

*Right,* he said. He looked disgusted. He started pacing in his room. The space felt too small. I wanted out of there.

*I've never heard of Jake Ritchee. I don't know what you're even talking about.*

*He gave you his card. His fucking phone number.*

I had no idea what he meant. None. He searched around on his desk. Shoving books and papers. *Calculus Concepts* landed on the floor with a smack. *You never heard of him?* His voice dripped sarcasm. He handed me a business card. I looked down. I saw my own writing there on the back. My name and phone number. My e-mail address. I turned the card over. *Jake Ritchee*, it read. *Smith and Gray Auto.*

I remembered. I remembered bringing my father's car in to be repaired. I remembered Jake Ritchee, too, in his blue coveralls, a guy about twenty-something, who explained our diseased transmission to me so that I could explain it to my father. I had plucked one of his cards from the plastic tray on the counter, next to some shiny pamphlets advertising radial tires. My father always had questions.

I opened my mouth to explain, because explaining was what I always did with Christian, another tool in that box. But I stopped. I had another realization then as I held that card, a way too late realization: I was tired of explaining. I had jumped right into this game and played it along with him, and that had been my fault. But I had reached the sudden point where I didn't want to do it anymore. No explanation would be good enough, ever. If he had kept this card since that night, if he chose that meaning over the one the card really had—his truths would never, could never, be what the truth really was.

I tossed the card at him. It spun like a little paper boomerang and fell, hitting the top of Christian's shoe. I walked to the door.

*You're not going to leave,* he said.

*Yep,* I said.

*So you dated this guy.*

*Jake Ritchee fixed my father's car.*

*I know how you like dark-haired guys,* he said.

I brushed past him. I walked down the stairs. Christian's mother had just gotten a cat, and it slipped out the front door when I opened it. I went down the driveway and remembered that Christian had driven me over. I didn't have Dad's car. And it was raining now, hard. It didn't matter. I walked to the bus stop nearby. I knew the route from coming here so many times. I waited about twenty minutes for the 259. I sat behind an old woman in a red crocheted hat. It had a green fringy ball on top. Very Christmas-y.

The rain dripped down the large windows of the bus. The huge wipers were going fast. My pant legs were wet, and I was cold. And then his words sank in. They sank in, and I sat there in some sort of shock. Christian had gone to Smith and Gray Auto to check out Jake Ritchee. It would be the only way he'd know that Jake Ritchee had black hair.

The seat had a rip in it, and foam was coming out. The brakes screeched when the bus stopped. I got up to get out. The floor was slick with water from people's shoes. I brushed past the seated passengers in their bulky coats. I knew something I didn't know before. Knew, but didn't want to know.

It was possible that Christian was crazy.

# Chapter 12

So, Dad was an idiot for riding that bike to Sylvie's with his bad ankle. A love idiot. He spent the next few days wincing and holding on to furniture when he walked. I thought he needed to see a doctor, but he refused.* Each night he'd drink more of our mystery host's scotch, which seemed to numb the pain enough for him to hobble around and do the dishes and other jobs I insist he not do but he did anyway.

At work, I asked Sylvie Genovese about doctors on the island, and that night there was a knock at the door and Sylvie Genovese was there with this older guy with a long gray ponytail and a black doctor's bag, just like the kind you see doctors carrying in old

........................

* I don't know why we insist on pain when pain is so often easy to eliminate. It's funny the ways we try to punish ourselves when we feel we've committed some crime.

movies. He didn't look like a real doctor. *Watch him be Roger's vet or something,* I said to myself, but I was wrong. Lately I'd been wrong a lot. The one thing I was figuring out good and well was that you needed information about people, more information, to really know for sure. First impressions were tricky. They could be so sharply on target that they were an instant bulls-eye, or they could be that humorous dart that hits a tree, or worse, the dangerous dart that injures. There was only one way to know and that was time. With the doctor, it took very little time at all—Sylvie Genovese introduced him as Dr. Leroy Vicci, who had a practice there in Bishop Rock. It turned out that Sylvie and Dr. Vicci were cousins, and he and his family were part of the reason she came to the island.

Dr. Vicci sat my father down and moved his ankle in careful circles. It took him seconds to determine it wasn't broken. It needed more ice and less activity and a strong anti-inflammatory.

*Sometimes that's all you need,* Dr. Vicci said. *To know it's not broken. To know you're still whole and that you'll heal.*

It sounded like a metaphor. I looked at my father, thinking he'd catch my eye then, but he'd missed it. He was watching Sylvie Genovese's long fingers on the back of that kitchen chair.

I wondered if Sylvie and I would become friends now, but that didn't happen. She was less snappish with me, though, and didn't listen in anymore when I gave tours of the lighthouse. I would catch her looking at me, in some way that meant she was taking in the details and trying to understand the whole picture. I guessed she was someone who felt the need for slow gathering of information, too.

For one day we lost the bright warmth of summer—clouds

lay low on the beach and then moved fast as they pelted us with rain, the kind of summer rain that brings up all of the smells of the earth. Gloominess that means a day inside. Fog was everywhere—circling the lighthouse, hanging low in the trees. I wondered what Finn and Jack did on days like this.

Not a single soul came into the lighthouse. Even the tourists were staying dry in their B and B's. The rain came down hard, the white-wet sort that looks like snow. Sylvie did something unusual. She brought me a cup of tea, mint, like I like. She set it down on the counter where I sat. She had a cup, too. Roger followed behind like a little butler.

"Too cold not to have tea," she said. She warmed her hands on the cup. Stuck her nose toward the steam and breathed in.

"Thank you," I said.

The wind picked up. Her garden wind chimes were going crazy, and you could hear the flapping of the plastic that covered her dirt pile, a corner slipping loose and taking advantage of the wild ride.

"Miserable beach weather," she said.

"I bet it makes you wish you were home," I said. Dad had told me she'd lived in Italy as a child, then in Southern California, then back to Italy. By "home" I meant either of those places. Sunny and warm ones.

"I am home," she said.

She didn't say anything more. It was quiet between us. You could hear the wind whistling a bit. The sea was getting rough out there. "Do you ever see the ghost that's supposed to be here?" I asked. "The captain's wife or whatever she is?"

Sylvie surprised me. She laughed. Roger liked this and hopped up on his back legs, jumping on Sylvie's knees. He was always game for going along with whatever feeling was in the room. She gave him a small push down and then set her hand on his butt so he sat nicely. "I do not believe in ghosts, so they do not believe in me."

"So, you don't see her, walking up the lighthouse stairwell? She isn't in your kitchen making Kraft macaroni and cheese?"

"That is what a ghost would come back for, true? No, we are the ones who haunt ourselves. I am sure of it."

Sylvie Genovese let me go home early. When I was gathering my things, she appeared again, this time with a large orange pot with foil stretched over the top. "So he stays off of that leg," she said. The pot was warm. It smelled delicious.

"It's not Kraft macaroni and cheese," I said. Sylvie Genovese laughed.

Twice in one day. It was a new record.

The orange pot sat on the seat beside me as I drove to the docks. *Obsession* seemed shut down and closed up. The Cove was open, though. Finn's sister was sitting inside, reading *Jane Eyre* as rain dripped down from the awning. That seagull was out there, too, the rain dripping off his wings. Cleo didn't seem the *Jane Eyre* type. I'd have guessed something tougher, true crime, one of Dad's books, even.

"That Darby is a pansy," she said. "The shit they make you read for school. Online class at the community college. It's a frilly romance! You can't tell me it's not." I was glad to know I wasn't always wrong about people.

"You like mysteries? Bobby Oates?"

"Love. *Love. The Paring Knife.* Let's talk classic."

"He's my dad," I said.

"You're fucking kidding me," she said. "No way." I realized all at once how stupid it was, what I had just done. What was I thinking? Bragging to get in good with Finn's sister? As if some twisted need to be special hadn't gotten me into enough trouble? I remembered too late what Finn had said about the cousin of Kurt Cobain. How the whole town knew his every move. Stupid, stupid. All we needed was one newspaper article on the web, and he could find us.*

"You won't say anything to anyone? His privacy is important to him."

"No, no, of course. Sure. You bring him down sometime. I'll make him the best cheeseburger he's had in his life."

"I'll tell him," I said.

"You looking for Finn?" she said.

"Kind of," I said. Yes.

She flipped her phone out of her pocket, punched a few buttons, and within seconds, I swear, the hatch opened on *Obsession* and Finn stuck his head out and called my name, waving.

"Thanks," I said to Cleo.

"No problem."

"I'll let you get back to the pansy," I said.

..................

* Which only shows how nervous I still was. Skittish. No one cares too much about authors, unless you're Stephen King or J. K. Rowling. My father had a lot of fans. Still, an author is not a rock star, or even a rock star's cousin.

"Tell your dad he's awesome."

I smiled, headed down the dock to the boat. I was glad I had my jacket. I stuck my hands deep into my pockets. Finn helped me up on board, and then I followed him down the few stairs into the boat's cabin. It was as warm as I had imagined—teak wood benches with cushioned seats and teak wood cabinets in a small kitchen. Through a narrow doorway I could see a triangular berth up front, and through another, a small bathroom. It was a little messy down there, too, but in a comfortable way. A few coats piled up, a box of crackers on the sink, some mail. A life jacket, some rigging. Two pieces of something metal being repaired on a paper towel. Charts, and a radio. A book opened to keep its place. A thick paperback with a picture of an iceberg on it. Finn read, which was great. He read adventure, even better. Christian didn't approve of too many American books. Or much of anything American, really.

I wondered when I would stop looking at everything in comparison to what Christian was or wasn't or did or didn't. It had become a weird kind of map, a way of maneuvering.

"It's nice down here," I said.

"Shelter from the storm. No one's going out today," he said. "Hot chocolate?"

"That'd be great."

He put a pot on the stove, made it the old-fashioned way with milk and chocolate. He poured us two steaming cups. My cup said VICTORIA TO MAUI RACE, 2004, and his said PACIFIC CUP, 1998. "Did the boat do these races?" I pointed to the cups. I knew he himself would have been pretty young during those.

"Yep. My father and some other guys."

I nodded. He told me a story about how his father took off on his own boat when he was just twenty-two. How he met Finn's mom in Key West, at the gathering the town has every night to celebrate the setting of the sun. We were sitting across from each other, him on one bench and me on the other, our feet propped on the opposite side across. He grabbed my foot and gave it a little shake, and I did the same back. We were grinning at each other. I liked it there in the warm bottom of that boat. You could hear the water sloshing against the sides.

I was just having a nice rest in those sweet eyes when my phone rang in my pocket. "That's got to be my father, spoiling the moment," I said to Finn.

"Parents are so good at that."

"I'm guessing he did something stupid, like go for a walk on his bad ankle, and now he's marooned on a driftwood log somewhere."

"Parents can be such children," Finn said. "We ought to raise them better."

I smiled, pulled the phone from my pocket, and looked at the screen. I stopped smiling. I suddenly froze. The kind of suddenly like screeching brakes, or when you all at once realize you can't breathe after falling on your back off the monkey bars. I felt like gasping. Drowned sailors under water, deeper and deeper, until that moment when your chest grips for a single chance at air.

"Clara?" Finn leaned forward. I just looked at the phone. I hadn't seen that number in a while, not since I had changed mine and had only given the new one out to my closest friends. It's funny how a number can be as familiar as your own home, as weighted with meaning. The number leaped out and told me a hundred things. It zipped me right through our history—the first time I saw it, the last time. It was a memory all on its own.

"Are you okay? You're, like . . . white." Finn had put down his cup. He swapped benches to sit beside me.

I shoved the phone in my pocket. I didn't want him to see that number and all it meant. If he saw that number, it would tell him all the ways I was horrible and ugly and heartless.

"I guess it wasn't your dad," Finn tried again.

"No."

It was as if Christian had come out from the place I'd hidden him to slap me again with his presence. It wasn't fair for a person to shove himself at you again and again when you wanted them gone. We should have the right to have someone leave when we want, to only allow those in who we want in. But the truth is, people can force their way into your life whenever they choose. If they want to remind you forevermore that they exist, they will. They can reappear in a card or a call or a "chance" meeting, they can remember your birthday or the day you met with some innocuous small note. No matter how little they matter in your new life, they can insist on being seen and recognized and remembered. A restraining order, those pieces of paper we think could/should protect us from such things, only we in this situation understand the complexities of that. How that paper is an invitation for more contact, for more binding ties and communications, even through other people.

And, of course, those weren't the only ways a person could be held hostage forever. Christian had inked his phone number on my palm that night long ago, but his mark on me was permanent. What had happened—forgetting would be impossible. I would never forget, and he would never be forgotten. Even if he only resurfaced in a song or in my thoughts or in the colors of a fall day or in a chunk of broken glass, what was between us was forever. He'd made sure of that.

"Hmm," Finn said. He looked at me gently. "You have secrets." It wasn't an accusation, just a statement of fact. Finn did not talk in layers—his words were fact just like wind was fact and water was fact.

"Everyone has secrets," I said. I was thinking about me, but also about my father. Sylvie Genovese for sure. Annabelle Aurora maybe. The mailman. The women who sold taffy. Butch, from Butch's Harbor Bar. Cleo. Finn, likely.

"Everyone? I don't have secrets," Finn said. "I'm all right here. This is where I work and where I live. This is who I am. Okay, one secret. My mother once showed us that old movie *To Catch a Thief*? Cary Grant and Grace Kelly? I had a crush on Grace Kelly. That's weird for a ten-year-old. I imagined we were married. I thought about it all through the fourth grade."

I smiled, but my heart felt sick and heavy. That phone seemed hot in my pocket. I didn't want to ever touch it again. Christian had found my number, and it was as if he had located me right there in Bishop Rock, right there in Finn's boat with Finn beside me, holding my hand now. I was furious and anxious. Christian didn't know where I was, I told myself. He had my number, that was all. A number could be anywhere. He wasn't in the room, looking at me, but that's what it felt like. He felt that near.

I told Finn about Christian. Or, at least, I told him that I'd broken it off and that Christian couldn't let go. I told him that a policeman friend of my father's* had been advising us. Don't expect some restraining order to protect you, he'd said. They often make a bad situation a dangerous one. No contact, period. It wouldn't be a bad idea to leave town for a while. He'll go away eventually if you don't reward him with a response. I told Finn that I couldn't let anyone know where I was. But I didn't tell him everything. It's a simple truth that a secret is something you're ashamed of.

Finn let out a long exhale after I told him. "Wow," he said. I waited for what might come next. Some distancing maneuver on his part. I didn't come without complications. I fought some weird urge to apologize.

"I'm sorry this happened to you," Finn said finally.

A lump started in my throat. I wanted to say something, but I didn't dare. I thought I might cry, the way you do when someone gives you some kindness when you most need it but when it seems the most surprising thing.

..........................

* Wayne Branson. The Captain Branson that is often thanked in the acknowledgment page of my father's books. A long-time resource of his, and also his old friend. My father is the godparent to Wayne and Jody's oldest girl. Bad choice. What my father knows about religion could be held in the ashtray of his car, along with that one cigarette he's carried there since he quit smoking years ago.

Finn's eyes were intent. "I just want to say—if that guy comes around here, Jack and I will take turns knocking some sense into his fucking head."

We're supposed to hate violence, and we do hate violence. An act of violence is the worst and most shocking thing a human being does. And yet the truth is, the absolute honest truth, is that words like Finn's . . . When you feel small and there is someone large and brave standing beside you, baring his teeth, ready to protect . . . Even when you know you wouldn't want him to, and even though you know he's not even that type . . . Well, here's what you do, then. You squeeze his hands. You look into his eyes. You let yourself, for a moment, anyway, feel safe.

I brought the orange pot from Sylvie Genovese inside the house. I was surprised to find old Annabelle Aurora sitting at our table with Dad, sharing a pot of green tea. There was a crab sitting in newspaper in the kitchen sink. His laptop* was open on the table, meaning he'd been working. I was glad. Ever since his ankle and Sylvie Genovese, he'd been too distracted to work. He'd stare off and answered different questions than the one you'd asked.

"You make us dinner on the drive home?" he joked.

"My boss thought she'd save you some hobbling around."

I couldn't believe what happened next. I just couldn't. He blushed. I'd never seen him blush in his entire life.

......................

* Dad's, not the crab's.

"I've never seen you blush in your entire life," Annabelle Aurora said.

See? "He's red as that crab," I said.

"I am not blushing," he said. Annabelle and I looked at each other and laughed. "It's hot in here is all."

"A sudden rise in temperature," Annabelle said. She wore her jeans and a loose red shirt and a gorgeous orange scarf. Her blue eyes glittered.

"And only his face seems to feel it," I said.

He shut his eyes for a moment, shook his head, as if summoning the great patience putting up with us required. I brought him the pot, and he lifted the lid. The dish had cooled, but even so, all kinds of smells danced out—onions and wine and cheese and twirling bunches of herbs.

"Stunning." Annabelle said.

"Look at this. You'll have to stay for dinner," my father said to Annabelle.

"No, Bobby, I can't. I have to get back to my scribbling. The impatient muse . . ."

"Reminds me. Did you read that article by Charles Whitney?" my father said. "The muse, the spark of inspiration . . . *New York Times?*"

"Dad," I interrupted. This could go on all day. One line from him and off they'd go on another conversation. I knew this from that one night at dinner. But I didn't have time for that. My father must have heard something in my voice. He finally stopped and looked at me.

"What happened?" he said.

*Stay*

"He called."

Annabelle sighed. My father slammed his palm on the table. "God damn it. All right. Clara Pea, we'll get the number changed this afternoon. Did he leave a message?"

"I didn't want to listen."

"Give the phone to me."

I took it out of my pocket. I wished I could have put a Kleenex around it to handle it, like some crime scene knife. My father punched the buttons to retrieve the message—his eyes were black, a lock of hair fell over his face. He was pissed. I heard Christian's voice. Not the actual words, but the murmuring rhythms, his own self alive and speaking just a while before.

My father saved the message. "Same old bullshit," he said.

I put my head in my hands. Arms came around me. The soft, thin arms of Annabelle. It was like being held by a mother. It was something I remembered. It made me want to weep. I put my face into her shoulder. She was thin, but solid. Firmly planted.

"I'm sorry," I said. "I'm sorry, I'm sorry."

My father set the phone down and sighed. "Clara, *I'm* sorry." He had misunderstood me. He thought my apology was because of his anger. But my apology was a thousand apologies.

I felt another set of arms around both Annabelle and me. Dad's more familiar ones. It was funny, but as we stood there in that house on the endless beach of Possession Point, the wind whispering around us, the waves chopping and churning, the smells of Sylvie Genovese's amazing concoction lingering in our midst, we felt like a small family.

* 155 *

"Three out of the four of us in this room need to seriously embrace self-forgiveness," Annabelle said.

I separated from her, showed her the question with my eyes. *Four?*

But my father was ahead of me. "The crab," he said, and smiled.

# Chapter 13

By the time I got home that day after the Jake Ritchie fight, Christian had called sixteen times.

People can attach themselves to something—an idea, another person, a desire—with an impossibly strong grip, and in the case of restless ghosts, a grip stronger than death. *Will* is a powerful thing. *Will*—it's supposed to be a good trait, a more determined and persistent version of determination and persistence. But *will* and *obsession*—they sit right next to each other. They pretend to be strangers and all the while meet secretly at midnight.

This is what happens. You don't even know it. You can be choosing Milk Duds versus Junior Mints at the movies, you can be ordering the chicken sandwich versus the veggie, you can be joking and laughing on a long car ride or talking for hours on the phone and it can already be in motion. In their mind, you are theirs and will always be theirs and your own choice about that matters very little. I can't tell you how to avoid this. I've been there, and still I can't. A person shows signs—of clutching on too fast, of being needy, of not hearing the word "no," of jealousy, of guarding you and your freedom. But the signs can be so small they skitter right past you. Sometimes they *dance* past, looking satiny, something you should applaud. Someone's jealousy can make you feel good. Special. But it's not even about you. It's about a hand that is already gripping. It's about their need, circling around your throat.

The signs, anyway—they aren't enough to make you understand what is really going to happen.

We made up. We made up, but I knew I had already decided something. I didn't know when I would break things off, just that I would. A small piece clicks into place, and it's done in your mind. You can put up with a lot of shit and then just be finished all at once. A decision can seem to make itself, quiet but firm. But the thing was, he knew it somehow. Like he always knew. I swear, he could read my mind. As soon as I had decided it, he started asking me if I was planning to break up. Maybe his paranoia gave him a sixth sense to emotional danger, same as a hurt animal knows when the coyote is near, or when the eagle is flying above him with his talons out.

We were in my bedroom doing homework. It was stupid. Another stupid thing, but they were all that way, little things that wouldn't even cross another person's mind. My blinds were open. I walked past the window and handed Christian a glass full of ice and sparkling water. He was sitting on my bed with his legs crossed, back against the wall.

"Do you ever shut those?" he said.

"These?" I thought he meant my eyes. I blinked them at him. I was being silly. I had stayed up late studying for a midterm the night before, and I thought that's what he was talking about. Maybe I looked tired, or something.

"Your *blinds*."

I could feel things start to get weird, the usual wave of panic, the searching to make sense of what was happening. I couldn't figure out where he was headed about the blinds. My mind tumbled in an attempt to figure it out—what could be bothering him, how I could explain so that he would be okay. And then I remembered something else—I didn't really care anymore. The panic flattened out. Anger and impatience stepped in its place. I really used to care whether I lost him. That long ago night when I thought he might leave me had stayed and done its work. But now I wished he *would* leave. It changed everything.

"What about the blinds?" I turned the lever so that they went one way and then the other. I swear, my patience had gotten on a bus and left town and I doubted I would ever see it again.

"You're so flip. Every time I come in here, they're open. Do you ever *close* them? Or do you just keep them like that so whoever walks past can see you undress?"

"That's exactly what I do," I said. "You should see the crowds gather around ten o'clock. I charge them ticket prices. No, actually. I pay *them* for the chance to watch me undress."

"I don't doubt it," he said. He was spinning the glass in his palm. His eyes got hard.

"You know me," I said. "Any chance I get to attract other

guys, I just go for it. Lots of times I don't even wait for night. I just do it right here in the daylight." I unbuttoned the first button of my shirt, then the second. I looked out onto the street. It was still and silent. Rain dripped from a neighbor's roof. A spider had built a web from the gutter to my window ledge, and it glittered with white raindrops.

The glass hit the wall by my desk. It didn't shatter, but broke apart into three neat pieces. Water dripped down the wall. Water was soaking the sheets from last year's paper on *Tess of the d'Urbervilles*. It was dripping down my chemistry textbook, and down my cup of pens and pencils and the legs of the desk. I gave a little scream. It felt so sudden. We were in one place, and then all at once there was water dripping and things getting wrecked and broken glass, and Christian was on his feet and I was scared.

He was walking to me. His arms were out. His face was twisted up like he might cry.

"Get out of here," I said.

He did start to cry then. Big, noisy, gushing tears. I felt embarrassed and horrified and frightened all at once. My hand was out, I saw. Out in front of me like a stop sign. "Don't. Get out."

"You're going to leave me, aren't you? You're going to leave me." He sunk down to the floor. He folded and fell, as if whatever kept a body standing was gone.

"Christian," I said. His head was in his hands. He was sobbing. I didn't know what to do. He had gone from menacing to falling apart in seconds, and it was too fast and confusing for me to catch up. I was scared. Now the sobbing was scaring me as much as the throwing of the glass. The emotions seemed to be spinning and gathering into some great ball that was somehow in my hands.

"I knew you would," he cried.

I had to manage this, and now Christian seemed so small and vulnerable that I knelt beside him and put my arms around him. He clung to me. He cried and said he was sorry over and over. My heart ached—I felt bad for him, but I was also repulsed. I hated how his arms felt on me. I felt like I was being buried under a fallen building.

We sat there for a long time. He stopped crying, and there was only that heavy, heavy silence of things gone wrong. That terrible place you sit in when he's done something awful and so have you, and you now are looking at the mess of regret all around. One thing different and you wouldn't be where you are, but it's too late. There's nothing to be done except sit there until the pain lessens and you can move again, though the pain of that regret will stay with you for days. You carry it on you like an open wound.

"I think maybe you should go," I said. Very carefully. It still seemed like there was a bomb in the building that might go off.

"Don't tell anyone about this, please? Please don't tell."

"I won't."

"Stay with me. Promise me you won't leave," he said. He gripped my arms. He locked my eyes. I didn't want to look in those eyes. They were not a safe place to be.

"Okay," I said.

"Look at me. Promise."

I looked. I hated doing it. "I promise," I lied. I pictured it to soothe myself: The minute he was gone, I would bolt the door, except we didn't have a bolt. I would shove some heavy piece of furniture in front of it, like they did in the movies.

He kissed me. I hated those lips. I didn't want them on mine. I hated the feel of them. But even more, I didn't want the bomb to go off. So I kissed an awful kiss.

He got up. I was so glad he was out of my room and then so glad he was down the stairs, and then he hugged me at the door. I had drawn so far into myself I could barely breathe. I felt squeezed by my own self fleeing him inside. He was out the door finally. I was smiling at him, saying soft words. I waved. He was far enough away that I could shut the door. I waited a long, impossible moment, and then I turned the lock ever so slowly so he wouldn't hear it.

It still felt like the bomb was in the house. I hid myself away from the window and stood still until his car drove off. I walked slowly up the stairs and shut my door and sat with my back against it and my phone in my hand. This was someone I had loved. We had lain together, skin on skin, been as close as two people could, and he was a stranger. He was that someone who you are afraid of as a child, *stranger*. They never told you that *stranger* might be someone you knew. Light came in the window, and you could see the dark blotches on the wall where the water hadn't dried yet. The ink on the papers had smeared. It was good that the ink was black and blotchy. I could look down and see it, that glass, too. It seemed possible that none of it actually happened—that's how surreal it was. The ink made it true.

\* \* \*

*Stay*

After a while my father came home, carrying bags of groceries. I could hear him rustling and putting things away. It was getting close to dinnertime. I heard the clatter of pans. I knew he'd be coming up soon to say hello, to ask me about rice versus pasta, white sauce versus red. I needed to clean up that glass. I didn't want him to see. But I also *did* want him to see. I was alone with something too big to be alone with. I couldn't even seem to make a decision about that—whether to talk to my father. My head was both so numb and so full that nothing felt clear.

I scooped up the glass onto a file folder on my desk. I walked downstairs. Our house was a hundred years old, and the kitchen was all tall glass cabinets to the ceiling, which was rimmed in thick, dark molding. The floors were deep, old wood—you could see the tiny nails that anchored each piece into place. There was a round, sturdy table in there, too, curved legs, a soft African blanket used as a rug underneath that gave a shot of color to the room. My father's back was to me as he put dishes from the dishwasher into the cupboards. He was in his jeans and a chunky gray sweater, his hair wavy and loose, wearing those leather scuffers he loved. I might have gotten away with dumping the glass without being seen, but he whipped around when he heard me come in.

"Jesus, Clara, what's the matter?"

So much for hiding anything from him. He could read the slightest change in mood on my face; he always could. Something this big, then—it was an emotional billboard. I opened my mouth, but nothing came out. He looked down at the glass. He took the folder from me and dumped it in the garbage.

"You guys break up?" he said.

"Fight," I said.

"Where a glass got broken? C. P., not good, not good. What happened." It wasn't a question, which I was glad about. I needed someone to tell me what to do. Most of the time I hate people telling me what to do.* Whenever my dad told me to vacuum or clean out the garage, or whatever, I'd even wait for a while to do it so it would feel like my own idea. But I needed that now. Direction. I needed something certain.

I told him everything. I had barely begun when he started to make tea. Dad was like an old lady when it came to tea—he thought it was necessary in a crisis. I told him about the fight, yes. But I also told him about Christian and "other guys," the way he watched what I wore, the time he asked me to cut Dylan's picture out of the yearbook. Dad was doing really good for a while, just listening. But finally he shoved his chair back in anger.

"C. P., this guy is dangerous. He's a fucking freak."**

"Dad! Christian? You know him. You know how nice he is. He wouldn't hurt a *fly*." Really, he wouldn't hurt one. He would only catch them and send them back outside.

"God damn C. P. Do you know how often you say that about him? Do you ever hear yourself? Nice isn't the same as *good*," he said. "People are 'nice' for a million reasons. 'Nice' is the outside.

......................

* This may seem ironic, given what I've described about my relationship with Christian. This is not irony. Or some discrepancy in the story. It is, instead, one of its major points.

** Leave it to Dad to tell it like it is.

What people get to *see*. What you *want* people to see. 'Good' is the inside. And this is a bad person, C. He's making you a fucking prisoner. You're letting him."

"I know," I said. I did know.

"*Why* are you letting him?"

"He's hurt. He's sometimes just so hurt."

"Hurt people are very powerful people, C. Hurt is a weapon. Better weapon than most because it doesn't look like one."

"I don't want to lose what we have. I love him. It was so good. I can't imagine not having him in my life."

"Yeah, but you also *can* imagine it. And it sounds freeing."

I hated that he was right so often. I didn't know how it was that he knew all this. It's like he experienced it himself. Maybe that was just his writer-insides. But, yeah. Freeing. A terrible push-pull of loss and gain. "It felt . . . true. I mean, like he was the *one*. I don't know how to give that up. I don't want to lose the good part."

"You already did lose it, the minute it was gone. A guy doesn't hear your voice? Controls you? You're nervous around him, Clara. I see it. You're not a mouse. When have you ever been a mouse? You weren't even a mouse with Dylan. You dumped his ass when he got like that."

"Like that? It's not the same thing."

"It's exactly the same thing. One uses his strength to get what he wants, the other uses his weakness."

I didn't say anything. I looked at my hands. They were mine, but they felt separate from me. All of me felt separate from me. He was right. I was lost. I'd gotten separated from my own self somewhere on a dark, huge, and endless mountain, and who knew whether we could find each other again.

"You gotta get away from this guy, C. Immediately. He can open every goddamn door for you and kiss the ass of every teacher, I don't care. The stuff he's doing behind closed doors where he thinks no one is looking—it's dangerous. The distraught, pathetic manipulators are the most lethal. You're going to get hurt. Remember that girl who got killed at Greenlake?"

I didn't answer. But I was paying attention. It was like my insides were suddenly sitting up. Some piece of me could still hear reason, and it was taking notes, making the other, emotional part stop for a second and listen.

"Jennifer Riley. I can see her picture now. Young. High school. One of those kind of guys, Clara. Crazy jealous is nothing to mess with. Slashed her throat with a knife. True love. Soul mates. Meant to be together for-evah."

"Okay," I said.

"Okay? You gotta ditch this guy."

"Yes," I said.

"I'm taking you at your word, right?" He studied me.

I nodded.

"Okay. We've got to eat. I'm going to make us something," he said. He was upset, though. He stood in front of the open refrigerator for a long time, just looking.

I played with the string of my tea bag in my cup. I looped it around the cup handle. I made all the little rows completely even. I knew what I had to do, but I could tell by the look in my father's eyes over dinner that he and I both understood that it was now not as simple as it sounded. It was clear I was standing beside Christian on the highest ledge of a building. I was looking down. I could see the street way, way below and the tiny people and the tiny cars honking; I could feel the cement wall under my hands and the sick feeling in my stomach. Doing what I needed to do to get off safely—it surely meant Christian would jump.

# Chapter 14

I drove with Dad that next Saturday to Anacortes, the closest large town from Bishop Rock. We drove back over Deception Pass, and one more time again on the return trip. I had a new phone number now. My phone felt okay again to me, fresh, like a second-chance phone. But the eerie question still lingered: How did Christian get that number? And how long until he would somehow get this one? We ate lunch in a café called Mama's Kitchen, and my father talked with Captain Branson as I ate a turkey sandwich on rye. It's a weird thing, how something crazy and unimaginable can fold into your life to the point that you can listen to your father talk about restraining orders and eat a turkey sandwich at the same time. The most insane things can become normal if you have them around you long enough. A mind can't seem to hold anything too crazy for too long without finding a way to make it seem normal.*

"Branson suggests holding the line," my father said when he hung up. He agreed to a refill of his coffee cup with a nod, and the waitress poured it. "That's what he says, 'Hold the line.' 'Hang tough.' 'Ride it out.' The man speaks in rugged scraps of machismo. Wait, I like that." He looked around. I knew what he wanted. I got him a pen out of my purse, and he wrote the phrase on a napkin.

"No restraining order?"

"He still thinks it's best not to engage. The guy didn't threaten, and that's when you do something different. Contact is what he's after, and even legal contact is contact. 'You respond after the fiftieth time, and he learns it takes fifty times to get what he wants.' Stay away for a while until things calm down."

"We'll end up living here."

"I like it here," he said.

"I know what you like," I said. "*Who.*"

"Nope. Not true. It's not about Sylvie Genovese. I'm not going down that path, I've decided," he said. "I've changed my mind about that. I'm holding the line. I'm hanging tough."

"Whatever," I said.

He meant it, though. Over the next two weeks while I saw Finn when I could (out sailing, grabbing coffee, getting food

......................

* I guess that goes for soldiers during a war, too. People during funerals. Long illnesses. All of high school, for that matter.

at Butch's and sitting out on the beach) Dad stayed at home. He worked on his book. He would rub his neck from so much time bent down over a screen. He got another stack of books from the library and was reading and tossing the finished ones onto a pile by the leather chair in the living room. He was spending too much time by himself, as far as I could see it. His ankle had healed, and he was back to taking long walks on the beach. He sat there with that scotch in the evening. Swirled it in the glass in some morose way. I didn't understand what his problem was. It was the kind of alone that could gather you up and keep you. The kind that needs to be stopped or else it might become something permanent. It looked a little like depression. At least, he was thinking too much and doing too little. Wearing the same clothes too often. Leaving the room when I nagged him about any of it. He was becoming one of those people who spilled cereal on their shirt in the morning and didn't care about wearing the stain all day. It was pissing me off. *You don't want to be too alone out here*, he had told me. And yet *too alone* was exactly what he was.

Sylvie took back her empty, clean orange pot and read the note that Dad had tucked inside. I don't know what it said, but whatever it was, Sylvie turned bitchy again. Sometimes she made me stay late when there was nothing to do. Her eyebrows were always down, and she'd take that boat out on the water and rev the motor—I could hear it. I could see her zipping around on the ocean like she was trying to outrun whatever was behind her.

They *both* were pissing me off. I didn't get the giddy love-stuff and then the complete withdrawal. I guess he still loved my mother and always would. Fine—but he was driving me up a wall. Living with someone like that—it's like you're both stuck in some house with boarded-up windows. You start feeling depressed even though you're not depressed. You can catch a mood like the flu, and that sort of mood was easy to pass on to someone else. Joy is not nearly as contagious as despair.

So imagine how angry I was when one morning I was leaving for work and he was smoking that stupid cigarette he'd gotten out of the ashtray of the car. That thing had been sitting in there for years. *Years.* I couldn't even imagine it would still have in it what he needed from it, nicotine or whatever, but there he was. He was wearing this sick-looking T-shirt from a thousand years ago and his baggy pajama bottoms, and he was sucking on that thing, and I just had enough. I started yelling at him, and he was telling me it was none of my business, and I slammed out the door and went to work, which was the same thing as saving yourself from a sinking ship by jumping into the mouth of a shark.

Sylvie made me count the cash in the drawer three times, even though I kept coming up with the same number. She got several new boxes of merchandise for the store but just let them sit there where the UPS guy had dropped them, unopened. She snapped at Roger, who looked like he had his feelings hurt, I swear. His eyes got sad. I wanted to scoop him up, because I knew he was going through the same thing I was.

I decided to go see Annabelle Aurora. It was kind of like telling on Dad, but fine. He was responsible for me, sure, but I was responsible for him too. Right or not, that's how it was.

The air felt so good outside. I breathed deeply. It was a blue sky day and the ocean just kept on being the ocean—wide and consistent, in and out, in and out, bringing its little presents to the shore and taking them back again. I made my way down the trail, grasping at sea grass to keep me upright and doing the last bit in an embarrassing half slide, hands up surfer style. That part wasn't on purpose.

I hoped Annabelle was home. I walked down the beach to her place and was happy to see her gray head bent over in her garden, checking on her plants. She was holding a fistful of weeds and had a bucket of clams.

"Clara!" she said. She had an old T-shirt on, her jeans. Her eyes revved up into that twinkle. I swear, her twinkle went from zero to sixty in one second. She was happy to see me. "Where the Christ has your father been? Is he mad at me?"

"I was hoping you could explain him to *me*," I said.

"Let me make you something. A ginger drink."

I followed her inside, and she bustled around the small space. A minute later we were outside again, sitting at that folding table. She set two tomatoes in a bowl in front of us, along with a salt shaker and two tall glasses filled with a light brown liquid.

She sat down. She propped her feet up on the extra chair. The sea in front of her place had a few huge rocks in it—one shaped like the curved back of a whale, another like the sharp triangle of a fin. Waves broke around them in white froth. I sipped my drink. It was cold, but with the heat of ginger and the sharp breath of cinnamon.

"This is delicious," I said.

*Stay*

"Good," she said. She took a tomato, chomped into it like an apple, sprinkled a little salt on it, and had another bite. She gestured for me to do the same. I did. I didn't even like tomatoes all that much, but eating one that way made the tomato taste different. Sort of like its real self. Annabelle set it down on a napkin and folded her hands. A patient Buddha in the guise of an old lady, or the other way around.

I listened to the roar and crash of waves, the *chshsh* of water rolling over sand. It was sunny, and the sand looked shimmery. "Do you believe in ghosts?" I asked. It was funny how you could talk about some things in the daylight without a problem. Light is good protection.

"Ghosts," she said. She thought about this. "I think we make our own ghosts."

"That's pretty much what Sylvie Genovese said."

"Then again, the day after my brother died . . . I went out to the beach. It was filled with sand dollars. *Filled.* Not one or two, but hundreds." She pointed to a glass jar that held a few of them. "I'd never seen anything like it. He loved sand dollars. I had to wonder."

"Wow."

"Yes, indeed. How ready is one to believe in coincidence? Or that everything has an explanation? My brother himself would have said there had been a certain tide . . . Why do you ask?" She sipped her own drink.

"There's supposed to be a lot of ghosts around here. The lighthouse is haunted."

"That's what they say."

* 173 *

"You don't think it's possible? For people who are dead to stay here with us?"

"Oh, they stay here with us, all right."

"I guess so." I thought about my mother. It was strange how often I was thinking about my mother lately. She seemed more real and present to me than she had in a long time.

"Then again, I'm not one who thinks many things are *impossible*. My brother and I were different. A scientist, an artist. Who knows what to believe? We can't sit on our own island and assume we know all there is."

"I think Dad is still in love with Mom," I said.

"Really." She swirled her ice cubes.

"He's sitting around morose all the time. He can't seem to move on."

Annabelle made a little *hmmph* sound, thought about this. "Love." She looked at me with those blue eyes. "Isn't it astonishing how confused and complicated such a small, simple word is? It attracts so many other things, doesn't it, that stick to it like barnacles on rock . . . fear, guilt. Need. You can't even see the rock anymore. I imagine love in its purest form is a rare thing."

"Are you saying he's *not* still in love with my mother?"

"I'm just saying it's probably hard for him being here, right by the sea. Can you imagine how hard? But, then again, we do that, don't we? We put ourselves in the worst places in order to travel through them. We don't even realize it. It's some need we have. Inner drive . . ."

I didn't even hear the last of what she'd said. I got stuck there, on the part about him being by the sea. I didn't know what she meant. Did she mean because he'd taken a trip to the beach after my mother died? Is that what she was talking about? But I felt something at her words. A tug, like the start of a thread being pulled. The alarm of things starting to unravel. The sea. My mother and father. Something else there, too. Fiona Husted? Annabelle herself? A memory that wasn't quite a memory, more like something you saw in a photograph and thought you remembered but probably didn't.

I interrupted her philosophical rambling. "What do you mean?"

"I mean, it's purposeful, even if we don't realize it. The desire to put things in our path to figure out how to finally leave them behind . . ." She didn't understand what I was asking.

"No. The sea. What about the sea? Why would it be hard for him to be here?"

Annabelle Aurora stopped. She started to speak and then changed her mind. She looked at me, blinking. She took in a breath. An *oh!* The kind of painful surprise you get when you suddenly see that you're bleeding.

"Why would it be hard?" I asked again. My alarm was growing. She knew something. And behind that something was a whole other world beyond that island I lived on. I didn't want to know, but I needed to know. A part of you understands when it's time for that.

"Clara," she said. The wattage in her eyes dimmed. She looked sad. No, she looked crushed.

"Tell me."

"No," she said. "I'm an old woman, and I can't always keep everything straight."

I knew that wasn't true. I could ask her anything, I'd bet, what those weeds were called out there, the medicinal properties of ginger, the National Book Award winner of 1976, and she would know it. "Please," I said.

"No, Clara," she said. She was old and small enough for her wrists to be broken like twigs, but I could tell, too, that she could stand immovable as a tree trunk.

I sat there and looked at her and she at me. We were two forces. "Why are *you* here?" I asked.

"I came one summer, after I divorced my husband of thirty-five years. It was more honest here than the city. Salt grass doesn't lie, and neither do thorny urchins or sea lettuce. I'm getting too old for anything but the truth. My friends think I'm crazy. My daughters haven't forgiven me. They've tried to come and fetch me more than once. People like their own free will more than anyone else's."

"Annabelle," I tried again.

"No, Clara."

"You said you believe in the truth."

"I love your father. And this is not mine to tell."

I pushed away from the table. I wanted to get away from here. This old woman knew things about my father I didn't know. Maybe even things about me. I thought we were here to get away from Christian. But maybe there was another reason. I needed to get home to my father and find out what the hell was really going on.

"I need to go," I said.

"I'm sorry, Clara. I'm so very sorry," Annabelle said. But

when she reached her hand out to me, I turned away. I left that little house where Annabelle found truth.

By the time I had gotten back to the car, my brain had done a nifty trick, one of its best, something it was really good at. Already, several stories and excuses and reasons for what just happened had popped in to calm me down. Annabelle knew something, okay, but there were a million possible somethings that would not change my life. Maybe my dad and my mother had met by the ocean. He had a love affair, maybe, a long time ago. Some tragic happening that made him hate the water. No wonder he didn't want to talk about it. Shakti's father had been involved with some violent political protests in India, and he wouldn't say anything about that. It didn't affect Shakti's everyday life. It was her father's own private business.

The feeling I had, that I was pressing up against something huge, a sense of gathering panic—it was just me, probably. After what had happened with Christian, all of me felt fragile, that was all. I had started seeing tragedy everywhere I looked. I'd stand on a street ready to cross and would be sure I'd get hit by a car. I was sure, too, at other moments, that my father had cancer. Or that a cinder from the fire Dad had built would rise and catch and set us both ablaze. My terror had been turned on and now it couldn't be shut off, like those stupid car alarms you hear on the street that keep blaring long past any danger.

We're as good at talking ourselves out of fear as into it, aren't we? Maybe better.

I ate a Snickers bar Dad had on the seat of the car, and I

turned the key, and those two normal acts made me quite sure everything else was normal, too. The lighthouse was still the lighthouse and the road was still the road and my hands were on the wheel and there was a scrunched up chocolate bar wrapper beside me, and it was all normal enough that nothing could really be going wrong. I decided not to drive straight home and confront Dad, who would likely think I'd lost my mind. So, big deal. Annabelle knew why he was afraid of the water. So what.

I calmed down. I drove to the Bishop Rock docks. I could see *Obsession* out on the water, its tall mast looking old and regal as a king. I waved to Cleo, smelled the reassuring smell of ocean and piers and Cleo's cheeseburgers. I felt comfort at the solid sound of my shoes against the dock wood, and at the racket of those seagulls—swooping and arcing and whining seagull complaints.

Finn put his hand to his mouth and called. "Clara!" The passengers were still aboard, and a few laughed.

"Lovestruck baby," Jack sang, and tossed the rope to Finn as he hopped off. It was like watching acrobats—their sure and quick-footed moves.

I relaxed again, in spite of the strange thing that had happened back there with Annabelle Aurora. I realized this was also true in a larger way—even with my past and the sudden bouts of irrational panic it brought, it was relaxing here. It was the foreverness of the water, the ancient art of those huge white sails, the old rocks; it was the Bishop brothers with their family history that named this island. And Finn's firm grip, and Jack's cocky scrubble on his face, and Cleo's seagull that stayed and stayed every single day.

# Stay

Finn helped the passengers off the boat, lending each his hand. He trotted over to me when he was finished. Every time I saw him it was the same. *He* was the same. He was his same, easygoing self with his wide smile and shy eyes. He didn't become other, surprising things. I had realized what a great thing sameness was. You wouldn't think it, but it was true. There was a shelter in certain rhythms—seasons and tides and boats that went out and came back in, people who were steady, who kept steady hands on rudders.

I guess that's what safety is. Sameness you can count on.

And sameness was something we should be grateful for, who knew? He wrapped his arms around me. He had never given me such a big, wide open hug before. He smelled like the cold air of outside, and I loved that. Maybe we had come to a similar feeling by our own path, because it felt like we were both somewhere new and large with each other. Or maybe it was just so good to see him. It was as good a definition of love as any—the feeling of *just so good to see you* that happened to stay.

"I had a great idea," I said.

I was looking at his mouth. He had a terrific mouth.

"I wonder if it's the same great idea that I had," he said.

"You think—" But I was interrupted. He kissed me then, finally. A sweet, sweet kiss. A delicious, perfect kiss that made me think of peaches and summer and days you got to sleep late.

The kiss ended. His arms were looped around my waist. I felt so happy. "I guess we did have the same great idea," I said.

We looked at each other and smiled like we just discovered

something wonderful, maybe kissing itself, something no one else ever figured out. It seemed like ours, a terrific secret.

"Think we should tell anyone about this?" he said, reading my mind.

"No way," I said.

"Ha, look at you two, sucking face," Jack said.

If I had managed to get myself most of the way to *There's a Reasonable Explanation* after my visit with Annabelle Aurora, my afternoon with Finn completed that particular voyage. *There's a Reasonable Explanation* is definitely a place you can go, a destination. Sometimes it's a fast trip, a quick, five minute train ride, and other times it's that kind of travel that involves buses and cars and long waits in airports and heavy bags slung over your shoulder, like the time Dad and I went to Australia. You somehow get there. Tired, questioning why you ever left, but still there. You collapse into *There's a Reasonable Explanation* like some hotel bed with great sheets. Or even not great sheets. The arrival is such a relief that the bedspread could be scratchy and it wouldn't matter all that much. You're just so glad to be there.

After that kiss, I hardly noticed the small voice, the static of anxiety somewhere way back that said something was wrong. I felt happy. I felt happy and like I deserved to be that happy and that the happiness deserved "normal." I wanted all the best things for that happiness, the way you want all the best things for someone you really care about, and normal was the least it deserved.

*Stay*

So, I did something normal. I did it to spite *abnormal*, I think. It was sort of defiant. Same as all those people who said they wouldn't give in to terrorists but would just go on doing their usual thing.

I called Shakti.

Yes, I did. On purpose. I was bursting with happiness, and when I'd been bursting with happiness before, I would pick up the phone and call my best friend. I'd been doing that for years, ever since we met in the sixth grade. This time I made her promise, I made her swear, and then I spilled it all. Where we were. What had happened since. *You could have told me!* she said. *I would never, ever in a million years tell Christian where you were!* I knew that. I did. And I was so glad to have her know the truth. It felt terrible to keep my real life from her. But now she knew, and now my old life and my new one came together. As it should be.

Normal.*

..........................

* And yet, normal, too, is often a destination. A contortionist act, a yoga position. The kind where you have to put one leg over your head and balance. You can reach it. But I promise you one thing. You aren't going to stay that way forever.

# Chapter 15

Breaking up with Christian was not as easy as it should have been. Not even for me. There were things about Christian I would miss.* His voice. I was sure I would never meet anyone again with a voice like that, the way it played, up and down, like music in my ear. But then again, terrible things had been said in that voice. The way he looked—but then again, a person could turn ugly. Their actual *look* could change when their actions were repulsive. The way he made me feel—that strength and attraction. And then again, those were the things I started to

..........................

\* You're groaning at me here, I know. *I* would be. I would say, *You should have dumped that asshole and never looked back.* But if you've gone through a breakup, you know it's true, don't you? Admit it. Even if he was a creep and you are glad you're out of there, there's something you miss. His car, even. His mother. The way he rubbed your neck.

feel ashamed of. He could make me feel as hideous as he made me feel beautiful, as small as he made me feel big, as burdened as he made me feel lucky.

Breaking up could sit in front of you for a while. It was a ring of fire you had to at last decide to run through. You finally got tired of standing there and looking at it, feeling the heat, tired enough to finally just go. Getting burned at last seemed better than the *waiting* to get burned.

"Did you do it yet, C. P.?" my father asked. It was the same thing Shakti had been asking me every day. Now that she knew I intended to break it off with Christian, she'd stopped the gentle hints and questions: *Does it ever bother you when he . . . I've noticed that Christian always . . .* Instead, she came at me full force. She was talking to me like the coach of the prize fighter. *You waited too long already, Champ. You gotta get in there and do it. One fast punch, no hesitation. Take him down, Champ.* If you heard this coming out of her, you'd know how funny it was. You'd know why I cherished that girl.

"I'll *do it*, Dad."

"You wait around for it to get easier, and he'll have that knife at your throat."

I should say, too, how hard it was for words like that to actually reach the part of my brain that truly *gets* it. I was resisting the idea of any actual danger. It seemed overly dramatic in some bad-television way. The things you believed could happen if you watched soap operas, maybe, not if you read books and went to school and had a regular life. Parts of me, big parts, thought that Dad was overreacting. He was taking it too far. I tried to convince myself that what Dad said could be true, but it seemed like I was trying to manufacture fear. The times I *had* felt fear, the day of the fight about Jake Ritchee, the day Christian threw the glass—I had numbed those things in my brain with *compassion* and *understanding*, which worked on me the same way drugs and alcohol worked on other people. I understood Christian. I felt sorry for him. He was just afraid. Empathy took the edge off, and the truth is, we need our edge. Our edge is trying to speak to us, and we are too, too good at shutting it up.

The thing is, though, a person keeps being who they are. They keep doing whatever it is they've always done. And this is a huge help when you're trying to break up.

I was in Fred Meyer, buying some poster board for a senior year A.P. English assignment. The visual aid part of my presentation. I threw a sandwich in the cart, too. A mascara. Some lotion I like that was on sale. Stuff for my poster. I was cruising around the music aisle, just seeing if there was something I couldn't live without.

I looked up and there was Christian. I had one of those stupid moments where the thought flash was that I knew him from somewhere, and then, of course, all his familiarity came rushing in.

"Clara," he said. "There you are."

"What are you doing here?" I thought he was over at his friend Evan's house. Group project. Evan and some girl.

"We're finished."

My heart dropped. I thought he meant him and me. It was surprising how bad it felt when it was his idea. But then I realized he just meant they were done with their project. He was looking down into my basket. Looking in a way he thought there might be something incriminating in there. Like what? Condoms? A lacy black thong? Something other than roast beef on a kaiser and colored pencils?

And then things came together in my mind. I realized what was happening. I had told him when we last talked that I had planned on coming here after school.

He was checking on me. He was making sure I was doing what I had said I was going to. I knew that as sure as I'd known anything before.

"You're checking on me," I said. I couldn't believe it. I really couldn't. I had seen him looking at my phone before, true. I'd actually caught him with it in his hand. I wondered sometimes if he'd looked at my e-mail. I'd go downstairs or something, and come back to find the computer screen changed. But he had actually come to *Fred Meyer*. This seemed somehow more damning than if he'd checked up on me at a Starbucks or some restaurant. It was freaking *Fred Meyer*. Where they sold weed whackers and groceries and tube socks in fat packages and knockoffs of knockoffs of designer clothes.

"You said you'd be here after school."

"And I *am* here."

We were standing by the rows of CDs, by the videos, the cameras behind glass cases. A guy in a yellow Fred Meyer vest was watching us. I used to love those shoulders of Christian's, that mouth, the way his hair fell over his eye. Funny, but I realized that most of the time I didn't even hear his accent anymore.

"What are you buying?"

"I'm going to the hardware department to buy some rope to hang myself because I can't stand this anymore," I said. It was a terrible thing to say. Awful, but I couldn't stop myself. "I'm done. Christian, we're done. This is over."

He stood there staring at me. He was wearing a plaid shirt I had given him last Christmas. I loved that shirt. I had unbuttoned that shirt countless times. "Clara, you can't do this. No. Please."

"We're finished," I said.

He was right by the seasonal aisle, the place where time speeds past in candy minutes, Halloween to Christmas, Christmas to Valentine's Day, Valentine's Day to Easter. And then he turned and fled. I watched the automatic doors shut behind him. I watched them open again, letting in a mom with a toddler girl in a grocery cart. I looked over at the Fred Meyer guy in the yellow vest. He was not much older than me. Wheat-Thin thin, with glasses and pink-white skin. He shrugged at me, as if to say *That's how it goes*, though I guessed these were scenes he usually only saw in those artsy independent films. Music was playing. An old Culture Club song from the eighties. "Karma Chameleon" in cheery, *buy-me!* instrumentals.

I had done it. I'd walked through the ring of fire. I had broken up with Christian. I wanted to feel some relief, but instead I only felt some sick twist of emotion in my chest and some ache in my throat that was too big to swallow. I thought about calling Shakti or my dad, but I felt too stunned. My hands were shaking. Instead, I went to the housewares department.

*Stay*

I walked in the aisles of sheets. I stuck my arms deep down in the folds of the cool cotton blankets.

It felt different right away. There was silence from him at first. For an entire day. I got scared. My dad made me soup. Shakti offered to come over, but I said no. Nick, too. He said he was making me a CD with breakup songs on his iPod. Annie said she was taking me shopping that weekend. We'd buy *new life* shoes. But I couldn't think of soup or music or shoes. I could only hear how loud that silence was and wonder what was happening in it. I was worried about Christian. I thought about texting his friends to make sure he was okay, but I knew I shouldn't. He suddenly seemed a million miles away, like some astronaut that got his cord to the spaceship severed, and now he was floating God knew where in the blackness.

I heard from him two days later. I'd been wishing he would call, praying to whoever might be listening that he would, just to know that he was all right. Once he actually did call, though? I was wishing as badly that he'd go away and stay away. You can want someone gone and still care. You just want to care from a great distance.

I answered. He was sobbing. Pleading. I used my softest voice and said the words again. He hung up on me, then called back, angry. I had to break up with him several more times, that's what it felt like. He sent e-mails of apology and promises to change and accusations and memories of the times we'd said it was forever. I explained my reasons again and again. I started to sound like those people who answer the phones at stores.

*Thank you for calling Vibe my name is Missy how can I help you today?* As if it were all one sentence they'd stopped caring about several hundred phone calls before. It started to hurt to see his name in my e-mail box or on my phone. Not hurt like heart-hurt, but hurt like those sounds you hear at the dentist's office you just want to stop.

"I don't think a relationship is something a person should have to talk you into," Shakti said. She was sitting at our kitchen table, having one of Dad's homemade pizzas with us.*

"You shouldn't have to defend yourself about your choice, either. You don't want to be there. That's enough. That's it. That's all you need," my father said.

"He's right," Shakti said.

"She's right," he said. They grinned at each other. My dad loved Shakti. She was what he called *a solid person, no bullshit*. It was his own bullshit *she* liked. This was on any regular day. But, right then, they were a pair of deprogrammers having a lovefest while their cult member squirmed.

"Can't we change the subject? I'm sick of this one," I said.

"Not if you keep talking to the guy," my father said. He leaned back in his chair. He had eaten half of that pizza by himself.

"This is an emergency," Shakti said.

More mutual grinning and nodding.

"Don't answer his calls. Stay off the fucking computer. And for God's sake, promise you won't ever see him again."

........................

* Artichoke hearts and orange and yellow peppers. Onions and bubbly crust. Thick cheese that you could stretch as long as the strings of a bass. Too bad I felt too sick to eat.

*Stay*

"Okay," I said.

"She didn't promise," Shakti said to Dad.

"I noticed that," he said. His smile was gone. His voice was getting testy. He ran his hand through his hair in frustration. "This isn't a game, Clara. We're not kidding around here. You can't give this guy any room."

"I *promise*."

"If you don't handle this, I will."

"*No*, Dad. I told you before, no."

The house phone rang. Dad shoved his chair back. He pushed the button to answer and just as quickly pushed the button to hang up. Who knew who just got cut off—maybe one of his friends. Maybe some telemarketer asking for money for Seattle schools. Maybe Christian. Still, the point had been made.

I told Christian not to call anymore, but I kept giving in. He'd send five e-mails I'd ignore, but then that sixth would sound so sad and pathetic, I'd have to respond.* This could all end up okay, I thought, if I managed him right. I was used to managing him. I knew how to keep my eyes focused on him when we went out together. I knew how flattery could make him forget his jealousy. I knew how to play up both my own purity and my own desire for only him. It was manipulative. I didn't think I was manipulative in the rest of my life, but it seemed crucial with Christian. People who dated diabetics likely had to learn

...................

* You're groaning again. What you need to understand is how desperate he was. Here. Think of a watching a drowning kitten. Imagine walking past and doing nothing.

to give shots, and people who were with epileptics had to know when a seizure was coming. I had to do both of those things in my own way—I gave shots of reassurance and kept watch for an all-out disaster. I was his emotional nurse. I managed the crisis. Maybe I could get both of us to the other side of this in one piece. Stitched up, maybe, but still whole.

It was my responsibility. It was the least I could do. I had made this happen.

*It's been two weeks since you left me. If you really wish the best for me, you'd know the best thing would be to come back. I would treat you better than anyone you could ever find. I give you my word about that. I know why I acted like I did. I was horrible to you. I'm a different person now, I swear. Please give me another chance. I want to go to the park with you and swim to the dock like we did, remember? I want to wrap you in your scarf in the winter and unwrap you until I find your face to kiss. Remember when we bought those cherries at that stand? You are so perfect. We are perfect together. Please—we deserve another chance.*

And then, anger.

*You say you will always love me, but that's not true. That will go away when you meet the next guy. You have the ability to just go on and forget people and how much they meant, but I don't. You can put people in their own little boxes and leave them there. So much for love. So much for soul mates. I'm sorry you don't want to believe the best of me or how I can change. You put a stake through my heart. I'm the only one who cared enough to suffer like this.*

And then:

*I would wait an eternity for you. I will wait. I know I can never find someone as right for me as you are . . .*

My father had said that the only way to stop it would be silence on my part, but silence only revved things up more. How could I explain, though, what a delicate balance it all was? How his ability to be okay or not okay was in my hands, dependent on how I responded? When I didn't, his e-mails would become anxious and pages long. I would ask him again not to write or call, saying it was too hard on both of us. I leaned on the fact that it would be better for him, and that it hurt me too much to hear from him. Gentleness seemed to calm him down. So did my own "pain" which was a different pain than I was demonstrating to him. I told him I would always love him, but love was dripping out of me same as blood from a critical wound. The truth is, I played up how much it all hurt me when the hurt had stopped being hurt and was becoming a desperate desire to be free. I felt like I had a pillow over my face. Or that we were one of those couples in a dance contest, the only ones left standing, draped over each other in terrible fatigue while the seasons changed outside the ballroom window.

He begged me to see him. I had once wanted to see him so badly that I'd snuck out of the house in the middle of the night. I did. We met at a park. We made out like crazy, and I went back home feeling full and satisfied and dangerous. I had grass stains all over my body when I woke up and saw myself in the daylight. When I was about to meet him, it didn't seem like my car could get there fast enough. I would be mentally urging it and the traffic and the stop lights to *go*. Each lost minute hurt. But now

I could only feel the pull and the drag. The opposite of desire—obligation mixed with dread.

He needed some kind of closure, he said. Just one more meeting. Just once, was that too much to ask? After all we were to each other? To see each other face-to-face and say good-bye?

After all that had happened, I still believed he meant it. That it was *one last time*. I actually *believed* it. I was that naive—a trait so deep inside of me that even when I was aware of it, I was continually fooled by it.

I told Dad I was going with Nick and Akello to the movies. He told me it was good for me to get out. I tried to act casual so he wouldn't see the lie in my eyes. I was lucky, because he was having his friends Teddy and Liza over for dinner, a couple of writers he knew. He was bent down over some delicate sauce meant for halibut, and that's why he didn't notice.

In the car driving over, I tried to feel the wrongness of what I was doing. I tried to imagine the girl at Greenlake, tried to make her face my own. But I didn't feel actually *afraid*. I felt uneasy. I was nervous to see Christian again. I felt this huge, weighty block I'd been feeling for weeks, but I didn't think it was fear. I was just an exhausted nurse, weeks on the job with no break, no time to even wash the uniform, called back in to work. Another situation to manage. One more thing, and then I'd be closer to freedom.

Naive. And plain stupid. But the truth is, when you can't imagine committing evil or crazy acts, you can't imagine other people committing them either.

It was dark, and the dashboard was lit up all spaceship-like. Do you know how you can be just going along and see something and then you flash on the fact that you had dreamt that very thing? It gives you a small hole to break open, and then you remember the rest. That's what happened. The dashboard. I had dreamt it. The rest came forward—I was in a car. I was trying to get away. It had been terrifying. He was chasing me. My heart was pounding. One of those awful, real dreams, where your heart actually seems to pound in your sleep. I was outside, too, running along the banks of a dark, murky lake. Sliding in mud. It was impossible to get my footing.

What is *uneasy* when you are awake in the daylight is *terror* in the dark honesty of your dreams.

# Chapter 16

"I found this," my father said. He slapped something down on the table as I walked into the beach house that day I'd seen Annabelle. I went over to look at it. A Christmas card, the photo kind, a paper frame decorated with gold holly. It was a young couple and their new baby. A really beautiful couple. The baby had a red velvet dress on. The woman had long, blond hair and a sleek black skirt and a too-perfect smile that meant she'd had braces. I opened it. *Adam. I thought you'd like to see something I finally accomplished. Thinking of you. Amy.*

"Our film producer has a complicated romantic history," my father said. He was wearing clean clothes; I was glad of that. Something was cooking on the stove in a pot. A tomato sauce. I could smell it.

"Cool," I said. I didn't want to play.

"Amy. I'm thinking Amy didn't finish college and disappointed our Adam," he said. "And now she's popped out a baby . . ."

I walked past him. I went to my room. I tossed my purse on the bed. I wished I could be alone. Me and Finn's kiss. Me and the way things were moving forward. I wanted the happiness to have a land of its own, a valley of flowers and flowing hills and sunshine, minus any clouds coming in.

"What's wrong with *you?*" I heard him say from the living room.

Irritation shoved all that good feeling away. Good feeling can leave you so fast. "Great. You're feeling better for five minutes and *I'm* the one with the problem?"

"If you're going to take that tone with me, it would be in your best interests to stay in there," he said. "Work on reapplying to college, which we seem to have forgotten. We won't be staying here forever." I heard him moving around the kitchen. I heard the pop of a cork being slid from a wine bottle. I folded my arms and looked out my window. Irritation was turning to anger, and I wished it wouldn't. I wanted more time with that happiness. The actual, real-life clouds outside were hurrying across the sky, the evening rush; they would come in fast and then drop and hover like phantoms, low and white, waiting. Already the lighthouse was fuzzing with fog. I could see only the tip of it, and soon—wait, now—the light was on, the slow spin beginning.

I turned away from the window. I came back out of my room. In the kitchen, Dad's back was to me. It seemed like a complex back. It had years of experiences I would never know. He was a man who went to bed at night with his own thoughts. I don't know why the idea of that made him feel like a complete stranger.

"What happened with you and Mom and the ocean?" I asked. He flung around so suddenly that the lid of the pot that was on the counter fell to the floor with a clatter, along with a wooden spoon, which splattered dots of red sauce on the floor.

His mouth was open, but no words came out.

"I saw Annabelle today. She said it must be hard for you to be here."

He just kept staring at me. "Fuck," he said. He ran one hand through his hair. "Fuck."

"Why would it be hard for you to be here?"

He thought. He moved his head back and forth a little with the effort of it. "It's . . . Your mother loved the water. We had our honeymoon . . ."

He was lying, it was so obvious. Searching around for words, grasping and frantic, like when you've lost your car keys. "Did it have to do with Fiona Husted?" It came out like an accusation. I don't even know why I said it. Her name just seemed bad-familiar, like when you run across someone you'd met before, couldn't recall it, but still had a sense if the experience had been a good one or not. Maybe I'd heard that name a long time ago when I should have been sleeping. While I lay awake in my bed with my pink blanket and my plastic horses, words winding their way up through the heater vents of our old house.

"Jesus, Clara," he said.

"What happened? What?"

"Clara, stop this. Nothing happened." His face was blazing red. His eyes—we caught a raccoon once, eating the grapes on Dad's vine. We saw him in the glare of our porch light that we'd suddenly turned on. My father's eyes looked like his. Caught.

"You had some stupid fling with Fiona Husted. Mom got so upset she made herself sick?"

"You can't make someone have an aneurysm, for Christ's sake." He stepped to me. "Clara, come on. Stop this."

"Wait. You were gone. She was sick and you weren't there. You were off with someone else."

"I was right there. I did everything I could. Everyone did. They even said at the hospital—there was nothing more that could have been done."

His voice caught. He put his palms to his eyes. "Jesus, please."

"I'm sorry," I said. "Dad. I'm sorry."

"Let it alone, Clara."

The little blue flame under the sauce was still going. Red sauce started to boil and rise, threatening to spill over the sides. He grabbed the handle and shoved it off the stove, burning his hand. "Fuck!" He flung the faucet handle up, stuck his hand under the cold water.

"Are you okay?" I asked.

He didn't respond. Just kept moving his hand slowly under that water. I picked my shoes back up. I grabbed my sweatshirt out of the closet. I left through the deck door, went down the steps and out to the beach. I was done with him right then.

The sun was setting. There were streaks of an artist's pink brush in the far-off parts of the sky. They wouldn't last long. It got cold at night on the beach. I walked toward town, away from the lighthouse and Annabelle Aurora's shack. If I kept walking and walking, I could end up near the docks where *Obsession* was, and the small house that Finn had pointed out to me, the one where his family lived.

I looked down; my eyes picked amongst the shell chips and rocks and seaweed bits for something worth keeping. I didn't understand what was happening. My father had always been clear and whole and present to me. He was there for me in any way I needed, and I was there for him, too. We were on the same side. But something felt changed about that now—a dividing line had been drawn. I was the sand, and I could see where it started and ended. But he was the sea, and it went on and on, to places I didn't know or couldn't imagine.

Still, I had places of me he couldn't see, right? So there was no good reason it couldn't work the other way, too. I wondered if parents had an easier time with the secrets their children kept than children did with the secrets of their parents. A parent's secrets seemed like some sort of betrayal, where my own just seemed like a fact of life and growing up and away. I was supposed to be independent, but he was supposed to be available. Him having his own life seemed selfish, where me having my own was the right order of things.

I thought about Annabelle Aurora's daughters. They must have felt that, too, when she moved across the country, away from them, to this beach. I kept walking until I was too cold.

Until I realized that we complain about our parents acting like they own us, and yet maybe we're worse at that than they are.

I headed back home. I thought I'd come to some conclusion in my mind, that I would just let things be. He could have his secrets if they meant that much to him. Fine. But then I saw the car gone. Inside, that pan was back on the stove, the blue flame flicking low, the sauce burned down to a black crust. He could have burned our house down.

The Christmas card of our mystery host sat on the kitchen table where he'd left it. I wished this was something my mother could do—send a card after all these years to tell us how she was doing wherever she was. Funny, she had always been *my mother* and not *Mom* in my mind, as if we didn't quite know each other well enough yet to drop the formality.

God, I know that's not how she ever would have wanted it, though. It was my one comforting thought, how she'd never have left if she could have helped it. It gave me some weird reassurance, like her arms were around me still. She would have wanted to be with me always, to know my favorite music, to know I hated scratchy tags and green peppers and that my allergies got bad when the Scotch broom bloomed. That's what a mother would always want, right? See, we had a complicated relationship, my mother and I.* I wondered what she would say to me now. It was strange how near she felt lately.

The house was too quiet. I thought about starting dinner

.........................

* I guess even death doesn't make your relationship with your mother less complicated.

all over again so that it would be fixed when he returned, but I decided I wasn't even that hungry. I ate a bowl of cereal in the name of dinner-duty, and the pouring of the milk sounded loud, and so did the spoon against the bowl and the sound of my own crunching in my head.

Sometimes maybe you should let someone you love travel great distances away from you. You shouldn't think you needed to set out to retrieve them and put them back where they belonged. Sometimes they were only safe and happy, like Annabelle Aurora. And then other times, it was just possible they were lost at sea. It would be your duty, then, to get out into the boat and search, even if the waves were choppy and the wind was howling the protests of the dead.

My father didn't come back that night. At least, not until the very early hours of the morning, just before my own alarm went off. I knew, because I was sleeping the 60 percent sleep of worried people, where part of your mind is listening from the shallow depths of a dream. I woke up when I heard the car's engine and the crunch of tires driving up. He was trying to be quiet, but I knew how that went. I had snuck out before to see Christian. I understood the near-silent turning of door handles.

I let Dad sleep and went to work. I was surprised to see Roger trotting around freely in front of the visitors' center, sniffing and digging, his little butt sticking up and his nose down in a hole he'd made.

"Roger!" I called. He looked up. I might as well have just caught him with a bag of loot in front of the bank. Anyone who says dogs don't feel human feelings are wrong, if you ask me. You see guilt and shame and disappointment and hope right on their sweet furry faces. They've got everything but words.*

"What are you doing out here?" I asked.

I would have liked to hear the answer to that one. You wonder if dogs would lie, too, if they could talk. But Roger was too shocked to do the dog lie of slinking off. He was still standing there being the stunned perpetrator.

I scooped him up and went inside. The air smelled like frying butter and vanilla. A familiar smell I couldn't place at first. Then I realized. French toast. Sylvie came downstairs when she heard the door.

"Oh!" she said. She wore a soft lavender blouse I'd never seen before and the same expression Roger had had when I'd walked up.

"Roger was out front," I said.

"Oh, no! I did not even see him escape," she said.

Sure, because love or sex or whatever it was could make you careless about the other people around you. It could make you careless about everything, even the love and sex itself, that's how powerful it was. I knew about this. I put my nose in Roger's fur. He smelled like he'd been gardening—that aroma of cool, fresh dirt. "Lucky he didn't go far," I said. I set him down. He started hopping around on his back legs near Sylvie, but she didn't pick him up.

"What do you want me to do here today?" I asked. My voice was sharp.

..........................

* And, you know, the ability to drive a car and go to college.

"Just the usual, Clara." Sylvie opened the cash register with her tiny keys.

"All right," I said. "Fine."

"You're angry with me," she said.

She was right. I guess I was. I didn't know why, exactly. I took my seat behind the register. Sylvie had now become someone my father had turned to, someone who could be important to him, and I had to decide how I felt about that. My feelings were jumbled up. You could have Feeling A and Feeling B and Feeling C, but once you got to D and E, it was all too much and they smashed together in a big mess.*

I didn't have time to sort anything out, though, because just then a couple poked their heads around the door—a bookish man with a white beard and a small, sparrowlike lady. They whispered, the way you do in quiet places, like you might awaken the place itself with your voice. They asked if they could see the lighthouse, and instead of leading them outside toward the small narrow lighthouse door or telling them sharply that the lighthouse itself was not open to the public, Sylvie tossed me her keys. She handed over three sets of the gloves visitors wore inside to protect the highly polished brass of the upper floors.

"Go," she said.

I guess sleeping with my father earned me some increased responsibilities on the job. I hoped it meant a pay raise, too.

...................

* Some people can keep going through F and G and H, and some reach their limit at A. I'm sure this ties right into mental illness somehow. You know, how soon you reach the tipping point.

*Stay*

I'd never opened the small lighthouse door on my own before, and I had trouble with the key. Finally we were inside, looking up the long curve of metal stairs. The stairs wound around the cement center pole, which housed the clockwork. Long ago the clockwork used to rotate the shade around the lamp so that the beam of light would appear to go on and off.

It was freezing in there. And there was good reason Sylvie didn't usually let people go up. First, the long climb on steep, narrow steps. Then, once you finally got to the uppermost floor where the lamp was, there was the shock of where you stood. The lamp was in the center, and you stood on the deck around it. Around that deck was the old crystal casing you could see when you were outside, the glass that acted as a giant lens, making the light visible for miles. Meaning that when you stood there and looked through that glass, you saw only the hundred-foot drop down to the rocks below. There was the vast stretch of ocean, the cliffs, the most amazing view around, but the visual fact of how high up you were was impossible not to notice. The first time I went up with Sylvie, my stomach dropped and my heart squeezed in warning. You knew that the old glass has been there forever. You knew you wouldn't suddenly drop through. But, obviously, certain pieces of you didn't quite believe that.

Of course, we never took anyone out to the outside deck, where the brave keepers (and now a special service) used to go to clean that glass. The deck where The Lovely Mrs. Bishop leaped to her death.

Our feet clanged loudly on the steps, a long rhythmic march. On the way up, the couple (who'd introduced themselves as Hal and Sharon) stopped to gaze out of the long rectangular windows, though it was probably just a sneak move to catch their breaths. It was beautiful in there in a cold, silent way—the white walls made of large rectangular stones, the paned windows, the upper floors of mahogany and brass high above your head. It made you think of medieval towers and long-ago fortresses, places meant to keep you safe with their serious, straight spines.

I explained that there used to be four keepers who switched off their watch duties. I told the couple what Sylvie had told me and what I had read about in the white comfort of my room: that the lamps used to be lit with paraffin rather than the lightbulb that was there now; that a bell would have to be rung in times of danger, rather than the foghorn of today. Everything was automatic now, I said, as we reached those top floors, as Sharon's gloved hand reached out to touch the brass rails for safety and as Hal cleared his throat at first sight of the drop down.

Hal snapped a few pictures, but Sharon was ready to take the stairs back. I didn't blame her. I felt the same way. I decided I didn't mind that Sylvie took this as her duty only. It was gorgeous up there, where you could touch sky and stand above the sea, but the silence inside was so great that you could hear a hundred old stories spoken all at once. Endless hours of desperate waiting. Storms and panic and battering, crashing waves. Clattering bells and shouting voices. The turn of that brass latch of the uppermost deck. The winds howling or stilled, who knew, when Mrs. Bishop lifted her skirts and climbed that rail.

*Stay*

Maybe this is how you felt the presence of ghosts in the daylight.

I locked the door behind me; I was sure I did. The couple went into the shop and bought a snow globe and two children's T-shirts for their grandkids, and Sylvie rang them up. Hal pressed a ten dollar bill into my palm and thanked me for being a "super tour guide." Sylvie rose from her seat, left the visitors' center to me. I heard her rattling dishes upstairs, cleaning up. I dusted and straightened and then sat down again and read through one of the display books about Captain Bishop. He had weathered more than one storm before the wreck of *Glory*. His men talked about what a great leader he was. Eliza was said to be a difficult woman. She was "quarrelsome"* when he was home, but despondent when he would leave. Sailors' wives would take turns sitting with her in the first days after he set out, bringing her food she wouldn't eat.

Sylvie stood in the doorway, startling me. I slammed the book closed. She held two cups of tea again. She had changed out of that blouse and was back in a blue work shirt I had seen lots of times.

I wasn't really in the mood for tea. It was a sunny day, and although you never really felt the heat by the sea, I could tell it was going to be warm. Sun was coming through the windows of the visitors' center, and I was glad for my sundress and sandals. Still, I took the cup and thanked her. I wasn't sure why I saw her as the enemy.

......................

* You gotta love an old-fashioned word like "quarrelsome." Today she'd just be a bitch.

"Did you lock the lighthouse?"

"Yes," I said.

"Clara." She leaned one hip against the counter. She sipped her tea. Roger lay in a circle of sun, looking sweet and well-behaved with his chin resting on his paws.

I waited. I studied my palms. I looked at the lines there and wondered about them. My life line was a mess. A "gypsy" told me this during a carnival my school put on, and even though the gypsy was my algebra teacher, Mrs. Yacovich, this still bothered me.

"I know you are worried about your father," she said finally.

Now *she* waited. The truth is, I let her think I was worried about him. But I wasn't, not really. When it came to Sylvie Genovese, anyway, I think I was worried about me.

"Yes," I said.

"I want to let you know something," she said.

The hard thing was, her voice was so beautiful—that rich, musical Italian that made you think of cellos playing, different from the thick, concerto rhythms of Christian's accent. She rarely used our sloppy conjunctions—"I will" and "you have" were never "I'll" and "you've"—new at the language, she sounded careful with it, the way you are with other new things. And she was gorgeous, too. Those dark, dark eyes. Truth was, they made a beautiful couple.

"Okay," I said.

"I do not just say these things. I do not like for people to think I am weak with soft spots like a bad melon." She laughed, but I just looked at her. That long dark hair. My mother had brown hair. In her pictures it is always pulled back in a ponytail or away from her face in a barrette. Her plain hair would never be able to compete with Sylvie's.

"But he is safe with me, all right? I understand broken hearts. I can look out for the lost because I have been lost."

"Well, maybe you should be careful yourself, then." Dad would have killed me for saying that, but if there was one thing I learned from Christian, it was this. "A person who is drowning can grab on to you for help, and you're the one that ends up going under."

"Yes. But your father is not drowning."

Now I really felt pissed. I was *so* glad she knew more about him than I did, someone who'd spent every day of the last seventeen years with the guy. "That's good news," I said.

"There's a difference between drowning and struggling with the . . ." She moved her free arm over her head in a circle. "The swimming stroke."

"The butterfly."

"Yes, all right," she said as if I had just made up the word and she had decided to agree to it. We sat there with each other in that silent, prickly hum of bad feeling. She sighed. "I am taking the boat out for a while," she said.

She had already given up on me. I was not going to get the ass kissing I thought I deserved right then.

"Have fun," I said.

I hated the way my own voice sounded.

I bought a sandwich after work, wrapped part of the roll in a napkin. I stopped and saw Cleo on my way to *Obsession.*

"I brought your seagull a present," I said.

"Oh, my God, don't encourage him," she said when I showed her the roll. "I went outside last night to get a book out of my car, and who do you think I saw on my frickin' front porch? The front porch! Standing there like it was the goddamn bus stop."

"You're his gull-friend."

"Ha ha. Oh, Jesus, don't even say it. I'm just the food, baby. Just the food." She looked over at him. "You know he's really smart? You wouldn't believe this, but he actually has a favorite brand of chips. Doritos Ranch. He can open the bag. You got some Barbecue Lay's? Forget it. Salt 'N' Vinegar? Nope. He picks the Doritos Cool Ranch. I saw him do it—pick only the old bags of Doritos. So I tried an experiment. Sure enough. He *chooses*."

"Hmm," I said. "Bread with mayonnaise maybe won't even turn his head."

"No, bread's fine. It's not good for him to eat so much junk food," she said. "Hey, Clara?"

"Yeah?"

"You should come over for dinner or something. My mom would love to meet you. She can't understand why Finn has been so happy lately. But it aaaaalll makes sense to *me*," she said.

"Maybe I should wait for Finn to ask," I said.

"He's clueless. Hey, Finn!" she shouted. She actually stepped out from The Cove and yelled and then whistled that great whistle some people can do with their fingers. Finn was bent over the lines on the boat, looked up and waved, then hopped off and came our way.

"That is so cool, that whistle. I always wished I could do that."

But Cleo wasn't listening. "I invited Clara over for dinner, okay?"

"Great," he said. He laced his fingers with mine. "You can be overwhelmed with the entire crazy family now." But he was smiling. He was like one great big Sunday afternoon—the kind where you stay in your p.j.'s and watch movies and eat popcorn. Where life is at its uncomplicated best.

And so I went over to Finn's house that night. He'd pointed it out to me before, the small white clapboard not far from the docks. It was a simple house inside—wood paneling, and the kind of couch with a sag that made you work hard to rise from. A wicker chair, a coffee table filled with books, a basket of shells, a lamp made out of a twisting driftwood log, breezy cream curtains. There was a large canvas on one wall, an abstract painting with the varied blues of the sea. I stood before it. Maybe I was only imagining the curve of Possession Point.

"I like this," I said to Finn. I was taking it all in, this place where he grew up. Cleo, in her wild floral blouse and jeans, was finding some music to put on.

"Yeah?" His hand was resting on the small of my back.

"He painted it," Cleo said, over her shoulder. A moment later, on came a gravelly voiced guy singing a soft, thoughtful song.

"You did?"

He shrugged, shy. "One of those things," he said.

"One of those things," Cleo mimicked. "A new age Picasso. Kid's got talent." Cleo grasped him on the shoulders and shook,

and right then their mom opened the door and came in, a grocery bag on one hip. She had long hair, and wore jeans and a
denim jacket with a tank top underneath, a wide belt. She had
eyes that were definite. Cheekbones, too. She looked like an
older Cleo—someone who knew her mind. I was surprised
then, when she gave me a big smile and with her free hand
pointed at me.

"You. You I am glad to meet," she said.

"Clara, Mom. Mom, Clara," Finn said.

"Ness," she said. "As in Vanessa, not Loch."

"Yeah, but sometimes she's a monster," Cleo said.

Ness snagged a brussels sprout right from the bag and
lobbed it right at her, but it missed and rolled under the
television.

"Take your roughhousing outdoors, children," Finn said as
he leaned down to retrieve it. He held up the brussels sprout.
"Don't you know we hate these things?"

"Cleo loves them," Ness said.

"I do not," Cleo said.

"You've always loved them."

"Never." Cleo followed Ness to the kitchen.

"Why do I buy them, then?" Ness said. "I can't stand them
either."

We were alone for a minute. Finn leaned over and kissed my
cheek. "You're in my house."

"I'm in your house," I said. "I like being in your house.
I feel like I've been here a million times." It was true, too. I
remember the time I first went to Christian's, and even the

time I went over to Harrison Daily's.* You could feel the *other-ness* of a person when you went to their house. It could be a weird and wrong other, where a place smelled like a litter box or Pine-Sol or had some reclining chair that gave you the creeps for some reason. You could tell all at once if it was a Super Athlete family or a Gross From Too Many Pets one, and you knew if you fit or not. You knew if you wanted to sit down and eat there, or if you secretly wished you'd brought your own silverware. It could feel too clean, where you were sure you'd spill the drink you were offered. Shakti's house was very different than ours, with its Indian wall hangings and carved wood furniture, but it matched me anyway. I got right in and wanted to stay. And it was like that there at Finn's. A match, for whatever reason.

Finn's mother had a huge music collection, and Finn showed me different CDs and played me bits of songs, and Ness and Cleo shouted out other suggestions, and then dinner was ready. Ness made Parmesan chicken and a salad, and we all sat at a round table in the kitchen. Cleo brought out two chunky wood candlesticks and lit the candles and turned down the light. Their old dog Shane woke from a long nap to sit under the table. We clinked glasses, and Jack came home to change his clothes, snitching a few dinner rolls on his way back out again.

......................

* Homecoming date, freshman year. We all gathered at Harrison's house to take pictures in front of their fireplace. That living room was one of those suburban shrines, unused and untouched, the perfect family photos on the mantel like religious offerings to the Gods of Material Success. I'm sure no one ever usually went in there, except when Harrison's mother made her weekly pilgrimage with the vacuum.

I got up to use the bathroom, and I don't know why I did it, but I looked in their medicine cabinet. Sometimes you get that urge, the bathroom equivalent of googling someone. Inside, there was the usual assortment of Band-Aids and cold medicine, but a whole row, too, of amber plastic bottles with white caps, prescriptions made out for Thomas Bishop, Finn's dad. He'd been dead for years, and I guess Ness couldn't throw those bottles away.

I felt bad when I shut that door. We'd been having this great warm time together, but this family had seen some things, been through layers of life I knew nothing about. Layers I couldn't understand. A father getting thinner and thinner, his skin yellowing, those hospital rooms with sliding curtains. I'd glimpsed their most private moments, and I was still a stranger to them.

I washed my hands, used one of the blue towels folded in neat rectangles on the counter.

It hit me then.

Hospital.

My father's words. *They said at the hospital that there was nothing more that could have been done.*

I felt the spin of confusion starting. Had he gotten mixed up? Had I? I'd always been told my mother died at home. Did they take a person to a hospital anyway? Was that part of the procedure? In my imagination, I had never seen her in an ambulance, a hospital, people in blue scrubs with their hands on her. I'd only pictured what I remembered of our old house. A horrible imagining of her on the living room floor. Being carried out down the stairs. *Hospital* wasn't a word ever used before about her. Was he lying to me? Because that's what it meant when people changed their stories, didn't it?

*Stay*

I was scared. I felt it right there in the Bishops' bathroom, because it seemed like my father kept getting farther away from me, and I needed every anchor I had left. I needed to understand what was real, what I had to be afraid of and what I didn't.

Finn and I did the dishes since Ness and Cleo had cooked. Cleo went out to meet some friends and Ness went to her room to watch a movie. We washed dishes in that candlelight, Finn's arms plunged into the soapy water and me with the towel.

"You've got a great family," I said.

"We're enmeshed, right? I took psych 101. Cleo will probably never leave the house."

"You go through a lot together . . . That's what happens," I said. I had a Disney Movie moment, the thought that if you put Finn's half of family with my half, we'd have a whole.

"We look out for each other," he said.

"Right. Exactly," I said.

He drained the water from the sink, snatched the towel from me, and dried his hands. He pulled me close. His face was so sweet in that candlelight. His eyes, showing me every bit of himself, even if I was not yet that open. I wanted to stay right there, because it was so safe. I don't know if it's what every girl wants, but it's what I wanted, that feeling, being held firmly, the sense that any storm could come and blow the roof right off but in his arms there'd be shelter.

My phone rang then. I could hear it, thrumming in my purse in the living room, muffled but responsibly doing its job.

"Your phone," Finn said, not taking his eyes from mine.

"Stupid phone. I hate that phone," I said, not taking my eyes from his.

He kissed me, then, and it was slow and delicious and his mouth tasted just like mine. I felt the sweet tingle of desire and he pressed hard against me until we finished that kiss and he drew away.

"Wow," he said.

"Wow," I agreed.

He kissed my forehead. "Do you need to check your phone? In case your father twisted his other ankle or something?"

I laughed. "Probably," I said. I went into the living room, sorry that the moment in the kitchen was over, wishing I could have held onto that and onto that. It's wrong, how shortchanged some moments are. So brief, and yet you can sit in some miserable math class for fifty of the longest minutes of your life. You can sit in the DMV, you can have an argument, you can go to the dentist—hours. And yet a sweet kiss is over so fast.

I fished around in my purse and stupidly couldn't find my phone, given that it was one of the biggest things in there. Finally, yes, there it was.

Finn's fingertips were on my waist. I opened the phone. I was an idiot, because it took me by surprise. Every time it happened, I was shocked.

I snapped the cover shut. "Jesus."

"Clara?"

"Jesus, it's him."

"It's okay, Clara."

"It's him already. He found the number already."

"He doesn't know where you are. You're okay."

The phone trilled then, right there in my hand. He was calling again. I dropped it and it fell on the floor. I felt like my breath had been taken. No more air.

"I'll answer it," Finn said. "Let me take care of that prick."

"No!" I said. "No, you can't do that." I tried to breathe. I swear to God, it was like he was right there watching us when we kissed. Like he *felt* that betrayal, knew of it, miles away.

"This is crazy," Finn said.

How can you ever explain this to someone who hasn't been in it? The way that you can still feel that alarmed responsibility, that guilt? You could be away from it for weeks, be there at the beach where your mind could clear and you could see how Finn was right, it *was* crazy, your own responses most of all. And yet there was that phone number, there was his fingers dialing you right then, and you could snap back to that place of panic like you'd never left. You fell right into that way of being, that craziness, same as hooking back up with an old friend you hadn't seen in a while.

"Don't!" I grabbed Finn's arm as he reached for the phone.

"I'm just going to shut it off, okay?"

"Okay," I said.

And then he did. And after he did, I pulled him down beside me on that saggy couch and I told him everything.

# Chapter 17

I parked Dad's car in Christian's driveway. Your mind can sometimes do this interesting thing (mine can, anyway) where it seems it's the mind of two different people, acting and feeling two different ways, because right then I was still not feeling afraid, and yet I remember that I put my keys in my pocket, not in my purse, in case I needed to get out of there in a hurry. Part of me was in charge of being naive and part of me was handling the street smarts. Even though it seems like self-protection leaves you, I think it is probably always there. You don't listen to it for a thousand complicated reasons—your own fear and denial and stupidity and good-heartedness, but it stays on task, shouting truths at you. You turn your back on it, but self-protection never abandons you. Never.

I kept touching those keys with my fingertips in my jacket pocket. I can feel their cold, jagged metal on my fingertips right now, this minute, as if my fingers have their own memory. It was reassuring to know they were there. I imagine it was the same kind of false reassurance people get from a can of mace on their key ring or a deadbolt or some superstitious behavior like knocking on wood, because, really, those things are no protection against someone's strong will.

I'd asked Christian if his parents were going to be home, and he'd said yes. Only one of their cars was parked on the street, though. The driveway looked empty, just a scattering of leaves scritching and doing leaf somersaults in the wind. The house looked dark. My mind was still performing its dual role—it seemed possible Christian wasn't there at all, that he'd stood me up and I'd have to turn around and go back home, and then I flashed on some stupid eleven o'clock news vision of him lying in there in a pool of blood.

Keys in my pocket. Good. I knocked on the door. There was some new, floral wreath type decoration hanging there—dried flowers, a fading smell of potpourri. My stomach started to feel a little sick. I realized I didn't want to see him again. Not at all. Not for a second. Out here it was me in the cold air, trees whispering the far-off rumor of spring, my hands in my pockets, freedom. In there, the dark weight of emotion. Nothing he would say could change my mind. As I've said, he often seemed to know my thoughts before I did and could sense the secret murmurs I didn't dare speak. But at the same time he refused to know what I told him outright, what I wrote to him over and again, what I was most sure of. To face someone with that much hope felt horrible. I felt so cruel.

He must have been watching me out of the living room window, because the door opened right up. "I thought you'd change your mind," he said.

My throat clinched. All at once I felt like crying. I had been worrying about his emotions, but mine were there too. Big, a storm, they could wash me out to sea, because he was still just himself to me in so many ways. I was still drawn to the good parts. But he also looked strange—his cheeks thinner, his eyes different, like they were too far from me and too close to me at the same time.

"You probably won't even come in," he said.

"I'll come in," I said. My voice was shaky from the desire to cry. It was happening already. I was getting sucked in as if I were reading a script and not saying the things I wanted to say myself.

He shut the door behind me. "Let's go upstairs. My parents might just walk in."

"I thought your parents were going to be home," I said. But I followed him upstairs, anyway. I touched the keys with my fingers. "Where are they?"

"They're moving some stuff up to the cabin." Their second home, the A-frame on a rambunctious river. I remembered one time that Christian and I had driven out there alone. We'd spent a short but fantastic afternoon mostly on that couch in front of the fireplace before driving back. I'd felt so close to him then. I couldn't have imagined anything coming between us.

"It's a good two hours away," I said.

"You act like you're afraid to be alone with me," he said. He shut the bedroom door. I felt the closing of it in a way I had never felt before or since, as if we were sealed in a vault, as if the elevator doors were closed with you and a man and a bad feeling. I was aware of myself in relation to where I was in the room, where the door was. That other part of my brain was taking over. I did not want him between me and that door. I could be backed into some corner. He sat at the edge of the bed and reached his hand out to me. "I missed you so much."

I didn't take his hand. "Christian . . ." I said. I meant, *Let's not do this.* I meant, *Things are different now.*

"You won't even hold my hand?"

I wanted to open that door so badly. "You won't even *touch* me?" I could feel his anxiety rise. It started to slowly seep into the closed room, the way poisoned gas does in some action thriller. I felt like gagging.

"Christian, you said you wanted to see me. You said it would give you closure." I could hear the begging in my voice.

"You think we can have *closure?* You think this is something you get *over?* Come on, you know we belong together. You *know* it." Now *he* was pleading. I felt tricked, but it was stupid. Why, why had I believed he only needed this one, last thing? I'd been as morbidly hopeful as he was being now. His hands sat helplessly in his lap. Something looked funny about his arms. I could see scratches disappearing up his sleeves, like he'd been attacked by some cat.

"I'm so sorry you're hurting," I said. I stood there by the door. It was all starting to feel a little unreal. I was taking it in in pieces. His room, that known place, the bed where we had lain together, the brown plaid flannel sheets. His bookcase, where his CD player and speakers sat, a plaster figure of one of those London phone booths, a mug from the world ice hockey championships that his real father had given him, an ashtray of golf tees from the time his stepfather took him out. A framed picture of me that I had given him last Christmas. I was there, looking out at myself. And under his bed, a rope, looped again and again into a figure eight, fastened with twine. A *rope?*

"Hurting? Hurting? You have no idea. This is killing me. You're killing me. You come into my life, you change it. Change it *forever*. You're everything to me. And then you just leave?" He started to cry. Sob. "You have no idea what you're doing." He rocked back and forth.

"Christian . . ." I said. I meant, *Please don't.* I meant, *Get yourself together.*

"I told you, I can change. Whatever you want. What*ever*." His shoulders were shaking. He was sobbing so hard. Howling. I put my arms around him. I was standing up as he sat. He clung to my arms. I could actually feel the wet of his tears through my shirt.

"It's going to be okay," I said. "You'll be okay."

"I'll be *okay?*" He suddenly shoved me back, away from him. "You're probably okay now, aren't you? You probably have already moved on to the next one. Fucking some other guy already."

All right. That was enough now. I stepped back. This could maybe get out of control. It was getting out of control now. "Of course not," I said.

"Right." His face looked hollow; that's the only way I can think to describe it. His eyes were wild, but there was nothing behind them. Some blazing fire at the entrance to a dark, empty cave. "You said you loved me. I guess that word doesn't mean the same thing to me as it does to you."

"Yes it does," I said. My voice was hoarse.

"What about our house?" We'd picked one out, the one that would be ours someday, right across from Greenlake. "What about coming with me to Copenhagen?"

"Christian," I said.

"It all meant nothing. Because you just want to fuck other guys. That's what you want." His face was turning red.

"No," I said.

He stood up. He paced to the window and turned to look at me. "You want to *fuck other guys.*"

"Christian, stop it," I said.

"Don't you?"

I wanted out of there. *Out!* The voice inside shouted. *Out now!* "I'm just going to—"

"You're going to leave?"

My hand was on the doorknob. "No," I said. "I'm not going to leave. I'm just going to go out for a little bit. I'll go out and come right back." My voice—the kind you'd use with a man holding a gun to a hostage. "We'll just take a little break and I'll come right back."

The sound that came from him, then—the sound of an animal. It unfurled from his throat, a roar. *"Goddamn you!"* He brought his hands to his face. He dug his nails in, scratching long red tracks down his face. Long, red, horrible scratches, the same ones on his arms. His own fingers destroying his own flesh.

"I'm going to . . . I'm just going to . . ." I grabbed the handle of the door and flung it open. I started down the hall, but he was screaming. I ran. Somehow he was down on the floor. I was at the top of the stairs. His hand was around my ankle. He gripped me for a moment, and I struggled for balance. My shoe pulled off. I was going to go down, down, but I broke free or he let go, I don't know.

"Go ahead and leave, you bitch! Go ahead! Just go!"

My legs were shaking, my arms, all of me. I ran down those stairs. I looked up for only a second. He stood above me at the rail, his mouth open, shouting. I can tell you, I didn't hear that beautiful accent then, or see those beautiful eyes. He didn't seem human to me.

Keys. Motion. I looked up again, just long enough to see him try to lift himself over the banister. He was heaving his body up by his palms on the rail.

I flung open the front door and ran down the drive. My hand was shaking so hard I could barely get the key in the ignition. Every part of me was shaking. I was so, so cold and shaking and trying to drive and lock the doors and it was dark out. I locked the doors because I didn't know if he'd gone over that rail or if he was right now picking up his own set of keys, heading to that car on the street.

A car honked at me. I didn't understand, and then I realized my headlights were still off. In my rearview mirror in the dark, all the headlights looked the same. His could be there some-where among them. I was shaking and my heart was pounding and something strange was happening, like I wasn't in my own body anymore, just watching this person who was me and not

*Stay*

me. I was scared, he was behind me in his car. I didn't want to drive home because he would know I had gone there. He would be in my driveway. He would be anywhere I went. I just drove. I took streets I didn't know so I could lose him. I saw the freeway entrance and got on, started driving on I-90 east. I was scared he was behind me all the way, even when I turned off thirty miles later in this town called North Bend. There were a lot of trees there, a huge, looming mountain. I had no idea where I was.

I pulled over the first chance I got. I didn't know what to do. I saw his leg going over that rail. I kept seeing it. Those scratches. Him scratching his face. And then I remembered that rope. He had a rope curled under his bed. It had never been there before. I could imagine him holding it—the *yes*, the *no*. I needed to call someone. His parents. I didn't have his parents' number. If they went to their cabin, they could be gone all weekend, no matter what Christian had said. What *had* he said? I opened my phone. No reception. I had no idea where I was, and it was so dark out there and windy, more windy than it got at home, huge dark trees.

I drove in the direction I thought the town might be. I was safe, wasn't I? I was safe if even *I* didn't know where I was? He couldn't know I was here. I still felt he might be behind me. He would jump out when I didn't expect it. I needed a phone. The part of me that had been looking out for me before now told me what I needed to do. A phone, and fast. Were there even pay phones anymore?

The town was a small, old town. An old logging town. An old theater with a long, lit-up sign. A shoe store, a drugstore, a place that sold ammunition, yeah, I was way out of the city. I'd been driving for a while. All the lights were dimmed. The streets were still. I saw an Arco station at the end of the block. Like a gift from God, a phone booth sat in the very outer corner of the lot. A streetlight lit it up.

I got a handful of change from my purse. Even the handful of change looked unreal. I was in some town holding a handful of change. I was so cold and still shaking and so the change danced in my palm. The coins didn't make sense. I couldn't seem to figure out what quarters meant or what dimes meant.

I was in a phone booth, and the trees were blowing and branches were coming down. One landed on the hood of the car. I only had one shoe. I could feel the bumpy asphalt under my sock as I walked. I'd never even used a pay phone before, and I tried to read the directions, but the words didn't mean anything, and then I realized I probably didn't even need money for the number I was calling. I picked up the handle, which was red and felt greasy. I pressed the square silver buttons, which were cold. I remember that, how those silver buttons felt.

9-1-1. The numbers felt monumental. Like a decision. Something huge I could never go back from and Christian would never recover from because it meant that everyone would know the secret places that were between us. He was always afraid of having people know and see what he had done. And so was I; I was just as ashamed. Now I was opening all doors and all windows and shouting for help and everyone would hear. There is no privacy in a crisis. I was revealing more with those numbers than I would ever likely reveal again, about him, but about myself, too.

I don't remember what I said, or the other voice on the

phone, only the magnitude of what I was doing. He could be fine, right? An ambulance could scream up to his house, and all the neighbors would come outside, and he could be sitting on his living room couch, and he would hate me for what I had told people about him with that call. His behavior was his biggest secret. He would never understand why I pushed those buttons. But, the stairs. The scratches. That rope. The desperation.

I spoke. I guess I did. And then I hung up. I thought I might vomit. The ambulance would come. There would be red lights spinning on his street, in front of his house. People would pound on the door. They would take him against his will to a hospital. He'd be scared and pissed and confused and he would not know what to do. He would be all alone. They would find out if he was crazy. He would ride in some ambulance and sit by himself in some room where there were boxes of rubber gloves and syringes, and they would take his blood pressure and ask him questions and a psychiatrist would talk to him, and this was because he had loved me and I had made him love me like that.

I called my father. I had our car. So he came to get me with our neighbor, Russ Mathews, who was a college professor at the university. His wife was one, too. They had a son somewhere in California. Russ was usually friendly and talkative, but he was quiet that night. He dropped my father off and nodded to me and patted my father twice on the shoulder, and now I knew that Russ Mathews and his wife and maybe even the son in California would know this secret of Christian's and mine and would know what I had done.

My father didn't say anything. He held my hand. We drove

down the street and he said, "Ammunition?" when we passed that store, as if he couldn't believe there were whole stores for stuff like that, as if he couldn't believe we were in some town right then with such stores.

He wrapped me in blankets when I got home and brought warm socks, and then I had to shove the blankets off in a hurry to throw up.

I came back and he wrapped the blankets up tight again. He made tea, of course. I wanted the blankets over my face. I wanted to stay in there and not come out ever.

"What will happen to him?" I was so afraid to know. I was scared they would let Christian go and I was scared they would keep him. I couldn't imagine where he was or what was happening to him. *Him* was also still this guy that I had loved. The guy who had brought me four bottles of ginger ale when I was sick once because he didn't know what else to do. The guy who loved the way the air smelled when it was about to snow.

"I think they'll take him to Harborview," my father said. "I'll call over there and find out what's going on."

He got out the big phone book in the kitchen cupboard. It seemed like it had all the answers and no answers, that thick book with yellow pages. He went into his office and shut the door, and that was fine. I tucked the blankets over my face. The shivering had stopped but I was filled with the nausea of horror. I still didn't feel like me in my own body. I didn't even know where *me* was. Those were my hands on that quilt. I thought of my shoe, a brown ballet flat, sitting on the stairway landing of Christian's house. I wished I could get it. I so much wanted it back with me, where it belonged. I felt bad for it there, anxious for it, as if it had been taken prisoner.

My father reappeared. He looked tired. He ran his hands through his hair and I saw the gray underneath. He held his glasses in one hand.

"Don't tell me," I said. "Tell me."

"Fucking idiots," he said. "They let him go."

I started to cry. "Why? Why did they let him go?"

"They said he wasn't a danger to himself. Someone tries to leap over a goddamn stairwell just wants to get down in a hurry? Scratching himself? A person's got to be holding a gun to their head or someone else's before something can be done? Christ."

My father went into the kitchen. I could hear the water running, a pot being noisily freed from the others out of the cupboard, a spoon against a cup.

He reappeared. "We need more than tea." He handed me a mug, and kept one for himself. Hot water, whiskey, honey. He'd made these for me when I was sick and couldn't sleep.* I could feel the warm liquid relax me.

"If that fucker comes near you, I'm having him arrested," my father said. "Just so you know."

He left the hall light on when we went to bed, like he used to when I was little. I tried to sleep but couldn't. They had let Christian go. I didn't know where he was. I imagined him sitting out by my curb, right outside. I imagined him with that rope around his neck. I imagined him creeping up our stairs. I sat

......................
* PTA mothers would disapprove.

up in bed and held my pillow and watched every set of car lights drive down my street, their shine passing across the blinds on my window.

I heard a voice outside. I shot up out of bed. My heart thudded like crazy. Someone was shouting something. I crept to my window as if Christian could hear my footsteps. I cracked the blinds, peered through. When I looked out, I saw our neighbor, Mr. Willows, out on his lawn in his bathrobe, looking for Misty, his cat. The street, our regular street, where Mrs. Porter delivered our mail, where I swept leaves and learned to drive and walked home from school—it seemed still and dangerous in the night. I tried to breathe. I didn't know where I could go to feel safe.

Even in the day that regular street would not look the same to me, no street would. Everything had changed, and everything would stay changed because that's what happens when the fear gets in.

# Chapter 18

I told the rest to Finn, too. All of it. How my father talked to Christian's mother. How Christian had walked fifteen miles home from the hospital after he'd been released. He was scratching his skin with his nails, Christian's mother said. They found that rope. They worried he was suicidal. His mother watched him all the time. They were trying to get him in to "see someone."*

I heard that he had quit his job with Mr. Hooper. I pictured the old man left with only the tired books from his shelf, nothing wonderful and new from the Seattle Library, just waiting. He would be there in his jogging suit and his scuffers. The thought of that jogging suit made me so, so sad.

...........................

* Funny that the only two times we use the phrase "seeing someone" are when we are referring to being in a relationship or getting psychological help.

I didn't hear from Christian for weeks. My phone was silent; there were no e-mails or texts. Two weeks later the messages started up again. My father called Captain Branson, and we followed his advice. I did not answer, except for one e-mail that told him not to contact me anymore. And then, later, that "someone" they were trying to get Christian to see called me. A Dr. Harrelson. He told me that Christian was suffering from an obsession and I was the object of it and that it was best to stay away. I didn't understand what that call meant or why I was even talking to the old, deep-voiced doctor, until Wayne Branson explained it to my father. A mental health professional has a "duty to warn" if they feel a person is in possible danger from their patient.

For the next few months I dragged myself through classes, my senior year. Everyone was talking about prom and graduation and what schools they'd been accepted to, and I was thinking about that rope. I was wondering when the next e-mail would come, or that call from his parents saying that they had found him hanging from the rafters of their back deck. Señora Kingslet asked me to stay after class, tried to talk to me about what was wrong. My grades in her class were slipping. I was so tired. Acceptance letters were coming in the mail, colleges at home and away, but I missed the deadlines for mailing anything back. The future was impossible to think about while trying, trying to swim in the present and the past.

I graduated with my class. My father was there in the audience with our friends Gigi and Lee, who had known me since I was a baby. We didn't see them often. I sat in the sea of purple gowns and mortarboards and camera flashes, and I could only look out in the crowd and wonder if he was there somewhere, watching me. I kept thinking about those old black-and-white movies of President Kennedy and Jacqueline Kennedy, riding in that car. How they didn't know a sniper would fire from an open window.

And then one day after that Christian appeared on our doorstep when my father was arriving home. He saw Christian there as he pulled up. My father said he was so angry he didn't trust himself. He got out and strode up to Christian and yelled at him to get away and stay away. After Christian drove off, he called Christian's stepfather. No more contact, he said. No more updates on Christian's "mental health." No more anything. Right away, right then, he found us the house on Bishop Rock. He wanted us to get out of there. You see something in a person's eyes, he said. You see the way nothing matters.

"Jesus, Clara," Finn said. He was holding my hands on that soft couch in his house.

It was hard to say this, but I needed to. I got it out, a whisper. "I can understand if you don't want to see me anymore."

"Clara, what do you mean? Why would you say this?" He was looking at me hard. He really didn't seem to know what I was talking about.

"How could you want to, after what I did?" The words were stone and thorns, struggling from my throat. "I know people say it wasn't my fault, but it was. I thought you'd be able to understand this."

"I'm sorry, I just don't. It wasn't your fault."

"It was. I know what people really think. What *I* think. *Why didn't you* this, *Why didn't you* that. Why didn't you *stop* it. "

Finn stood. "Let's go for a walk. The beach? What coat did you bring?"

"No coat."

"No worries. We'll borrow one of Cleo's."

He was busy suddenly, rummaging in the closet, pulling out his own jacket and yanking down a blanket from the top shelf and tossing me this black denim coat of Cleo's with *Manny's Tavern* written on the back. Below the letters, there was a skull and crossbones.

"Cleo loves pirates," he said. "She'd be one, if she had the right bird."

It was great timing, because right then he opened the door and that stupid seagull was standing there on the front lawn. I wouldn't have believed it if I hadn't seen it with my own eyes.

"He could work," I said.

"Any old pirate can have a parrot," Finn said. He took my hand. We walked the few blocks toward the ocean. I was glad for Cleo's jacket. It was cold out by the beach, and the night was quiet except for the slow rhythm of the waves. We stepped our way carefully over the rocks and driftwood. We walked along the hard part of the sand, looked out onto the sea. Only the occasional red bobbing of a boat light interrupted its endless blackness.

"You know," Finn said. "I blamed myself when my dad was sick."

"He had *cancer*. You didn't cause that."

"I know. But I still felt all this guilt. Maybe not for *causing* it, but for all the ways I could have made his life better but didn't. I was an ass to him sometimes, you know? The *impact* you have on someone you care about."

"But I *did* cause it." I knew that. "I could have left him alone. If he'd have stayed with this other girl . . ."

"It might not have been any different."

"*I* caused the want and the need. I *liked* it, okay? *I* made it all that important. That *big*. I was *too much*."

Finn stopped walking. He held my arms. He looked at me. "Clara," he said. "Listen."

You read all kinds of books and see all kinds of movies about the man who is obsessed and devoted, whose focus is a single solid beam, same as the lighthouse and that intense, too. It is Heathcliff with Catherine. It is a vampire with a passionate love stronger than death. We crave that kind of focus from someone else. We'd give anything to be that "loved." But that focus is not some soul-deep pinnacle of perfect devotion— it's only darkness and the tormented ghosts of darkness. It's strange, isn't it, to see a person's gaping emotional wounds, their gnawing needs, as our romance? We long for it, I don't know why, but when we have it, it is a knife at our throat on the banks of Greenlake. It is an unwanted power you'd do anything to be rid of. A power that becomes the ultimate powerlessness. Right then, on the beach with Finn Bishop, I learned that the most true-love words are not ones that grasp and hold and bind you, twisting you both up together in some black dance. No, they are ones that leave you free to stand alone on your own solid ground, leave him to do the same, a tender space between you.

"Listen," Finn said. "You're going to believe what you're going to believe. But I could want you and need you and it wouldn't look like that. It could *never* look like that, no matter what you did. What you're saying? It's about his emptiness, not your fullness. You see?"

He wrapped me in his arms. My nose was pressed against his chest, the nylon of his jacket. I breathed in his smell.

"It's not dangerous to be fully yourself," Finn said. "Not with me."

Sylvie's Jeep was parked at our house when I got back. The lights were low. My father had lit candles, and they were sitting on the couch together in flickering yellow light. He seemed fine right then, that was for sure. They both just looked up as if I came home every day while they were on that couch sitting close enough for secrets. Two wineglasses were on the table with only tiny red pools left in the bottoms.

"Clara. You're back."

"I was at Finn's." I tossed my keys on the table. I didn't mean to do it so hard—they slid across the hard surface and dropped off the other side.

"You remember Sylvie." It was a stupid thing to say and he realized it. "That was idiotic," he said.

"Hello, Clara," Sylvie said.

"Roger's home alone?" I said. It came out like an accusation. I'm sure Roger didn't need a babysitter.

"I always thought they should do a remake of that movie with dogs," my father said. "*Home Alone?* The dogs getting the better of the bad guys? Slipping on kibble sprinkled out on the floor? Wearing the dog bowls on both feet? It'd make more money than all my books combined."

"And, of course, that hilarious scene where the robbers both step in—" I added.

"*Fall* in it," my father interrupted.

"Better," I said.

Sylvie smiled down at her hands. I felt sort of triumphant, displaying our usual banter. Still, there was something phony about it. Showing off. Especially since we hadn't exactly been close over the last while, his mood always among us, some big fat unspoken thing, some big fat guest sitting between us in his shorts and undershirt, ugly and distracting.

"I'm going to bed," I said.

I brushed my teeth and got into the cool sheets. I was so tired. My confession had exhausted me the way the longest swim does, but now I couldn't swim anymore. I was too tired to think about my father, my mother in a hospital or not in a hospital, or even about Dad and Sylvie sitting out on that couch right then doing who knew what. I was being pulled into the watery depths of sleep.

I was drifting, and so it could have been one of those half-dream moments where you are part here in this world and part in the unconscious one, but I don't think so. I swear to God, I heard that song. *That* song. Our song. "The Way She Moves" by Slow Change. *Your eyes are on her, on her, on her . . .*

I got out of bed. Was I losing my mind? He'd found my new number so fast . . . Where was the sound coming from? I opened my door to listen for the television, the one tucked in an armoire in the living room. It had only rarely been turned on since we arrived. But in the hallway I could only hear the murmur of voices, Dad's and Sylvie's, her soft laughter. I shut the door again.

I could still hear it. I was awake, and I could. I opened my window. I swear that music was coming from the dunes some-where far off, but it drifted and spun with the wind and I couldn't tell what were night sounds and what weren't.

I realized then that I hadn't played Christian's message. I felt the sudden need to. I picked up my purse on the floor and found the phone. The voice of the message lady sounded as awake and efficient as a fluorescent light in that dark room. *You have*, pause, *one message.*

My heart started to thump. I felt a twist of sick fear. There was his voice. That voice, the accent both rich and icy, now. *I can't believe you would think you had to run from me*, he said. *You had to leave town? You know I would never hurt you. You know that's the last thing I would want.*

Christian knew where I was.

I slammed the phone closed. It was stupid, but I put it in the closet, behind the boxes marked *Winter Clothes*. I shoved one of our mystery host's corduroy jackets on top of it and closed the door. I could still feel it there, like it was someone breathing.

I couldn't hear the music anymore. It could have been Christian somewhere near, listening to it in his car. The song would bring us back together in his mind, our eyes locked, his skin against my skin. He was probably parked on that beach road, the windows rolled down. But I would never know for sure.

# Chapter 19

"I'm sorry I startled you," Sylvie said.

"*I'm* sorry," I said. Sylvie had called my name and I had jumped, sending two pens rolling down the counter. I was on edge. I felt Christian nearby, like people say they feel the souls of their loved ones hovering just after they've died.

"You are tired," she said.

"I didn't sleep much last night." Neither did she, but I didn't mention that little fact. "I have a lot on my mind."

That morning I had tried to call Shakti. No answer and no answer again. It wasn't possible, was it, that she told Christian where I was? I was sure she wouldn't. *Sure.* But she was the only one who knew where I was, right? Captain Branson wasn't exactly going to slip this fact to Christian. But maybe, too, I was making myself crazy. He could know I left town but not know which town. Someone else could have been playing that song. My own head could have been.

I didn't know what was real or not, what happened or hadn't, what might still happen or never happen.

I once went with my father to a reading Stephen King was giving. Afterward there was a small, private party. He was probably the most famous writer I'd ever met with my dad. A few people were standing with him. A woman holding a drink asked, *What do you think would be the scariest thing?* He'd probably been asked it a million times. Someone else in the group answered: *Your child being murdered.* But he shook his head.

*No. Going into your child's room to find him gone.*

Sylvie walked to the windows, folded her arms, and looked out. She reminded me of my father. He stood like that, too. I could see why they liked each other, actually. They were both a deep tumble of thoughts and feelings. *Passionate*, though I cringed at the word. "I know you do not like me all that much," she said.

I looked down. Her words shocked me. Too often we play these little hidden games, motivations not quite buried under our tones and gestures, the truth spoken only behind someone's back. But there Sylvie was, holding the truth right out before me.

"Maybe it's all just a little much right now. It feels sudden, you and him."

"It is sudden only for you," she said. She turned to look at me again. Her words weren't angry, only the flat statement of fact. "He has been grieving for a long time. I have been grieving. We are both perhaps ready to stop."

"Did you lose someone too?" I asked. I thought of the man in the picture. The basket of lemons and the orange house.

"A baby," she said.

Her words startled me. So much so that Sylvie looked like a different person to me all at once. "I'm sorry, Sylvie," I said.

"I was with a man, and I was going to have his child, and he did not want that. I don't tell people this story. I don't tell the whole of it. I went away. To have the child myself. I wanted to save it, and so I ran very far, to a small, small town, San Gemini. He would not find me. I would save it from him, from his not wanting, you see? I would do it on my own. But I was too far away. The baby started to come, too early. A neighbor came. There was no hospital near. I never could see it in my mind, you understand? I could not see things going wrong like that."

"I'm so sorry," I said again.

"We try to hold a storm in our own fist but we are not that strong."

I nodded. I knew about that.

"I am beginning to think there are two kinds of people," she said.

I waited.

"Those who forgive themselves too easily but will not forgive others."

"And?" I asked.

"Those that forgive others too easily but will not forgive themselves."

\* \* \*

We had a lot of visitors that day. An entire bus of senior citizens. I toured them around the grounds and afterward got my picture taken out front with all of them. Then a Winnebago arrived, a big old leaning camper with a license plate that read CAPTAIN ED. A bearded man got out, a camera around his neck, and he toured the museum just as a family with two small children arrived. The kids chased each other on the front lawn and yelled and touched things in the gift shop as Roger ran upstairs to get away. The mother kept shouting, *Inside voices! Inside voices!* as I pictured Roger hiding under the bed with his paws over his ears.

It was finally time to leave, and I wanted to say good-bye to Sylvie. She had reached out to me and I would have reached back, but I couldn't find her. She had taken the boat out, I realized, though I could not see her anywhere on the water. I thought about leaving a note, but all options seemed stupid. *Thanks for telling me about your dead baby* . . . I locked up, headed out.

I called Shakti again from the car. No answer. Why wasn't she answering? There could have been a million reasons that had nothing to do with Christian and me. You can have a crisis in your life, something huge on your mind, and you can forget it's not the first thing on everyone else's. People are out shopping. They are buying shoes and getting manicures and going to Taco Time while your life is falling apart.

I drove down to the docks and parked. I knew Finn would still be out on the afternoon sail that day, so I decided to grab a sandwich at the Portside Café. I was almost to the restaurant when I noticed my father's bike chained up to the lamppost just outside. I was surprised to see it there—he didn't usually go anywhere during writing hours. Still, it was a good surprise. He'd be glad to see me, I thought. I'd go in and he'd be sitting at a table, reading, maybe. He'd give me half of his French dip, or we'd order another one. I needed to tell him about Christian. We could talk about what Sylvie had told me, too. Or maybe we could finally talk about what had come between us over the last weeks.

I pushed open the door. Past the newspaper racks and potted plants I saw the open floor of the café, which was a sensory jumble of tables and booths, loud talking, and the clanking of silverware against plates, the smell of beef and frying onions. I looked around. I saw Jack's girlfriend sitting at a table with two other girls, laughing, and a guy I recognized who kept his boat at the dock—Jim, John, something. And, then, yes, there he was, my father. Annabelle Aurora sat across from him. A stack of books were on the table, as if he'd just been to the library.

I started toward them and then stopped. It looked like they were arguing. Annabelle was leaning forward, her flat hand on the table as if she were making a point. He was leaning back in the booth the way he did when he was pissed. Their voices separated out from the crowd. *You don't know . . . his. You can't keep . . . hers.* Someone else laughed loud, and the voices were gone and then back. *It's her story, too, Bobby.* Annabelle's voice was firm. She would have had command of her class when she'd been a professor.

I backed up toward the plants and the newspaper stands. The hostess asked if I needed a table, and all I could do was shake my head and keep moving backward, out of there. Because I could see that my father had stopped looking angry and now looked destroyed. His face fell, and he looked years older, sitting there. All of that ego swagger that was weirdly one of his best qualities seemed drained from him. His face was pale and defeated. It was that word, *story*, I guessed. He seemed done in by it, and Annabelle's hand went up to his cheek kindly, and something in the gesture bothered me enough that I got out of there.*

I felt shaky. I wanted to be far away from them. I had heard Annabelle's words through the clatter of dishes and voices, and I didn't know what they meant. I didn't know what was happening for my father and me. But I wished we could go back three weeks or three months or two years and start again.**

The shift—I could almost feel it like a real thing under my feet. We'd crossed over into some territory where hidden things had grown too large to stay hidden. So, all right, it was true. There was some big thing about my father and about my mother. *It's her story, too*—Annabelle was talking about me. There was something she didn't understand, though. I didn't *want* to know what he had kept from me. See, I wasn't, never have been, still am not, the type of person who'd want to be told they had three months to live. I didn't like the evening news. Those PBS programs about global warming. Stories about a girl getting her throat slit by her boyfriend on the banks of Greenlake.

............................

* I didn't know what their relationship was, or had been, and I'd never know. Some secrets stay secrets.

** Only, I wouldn't have met Finn then, would I? It's the tricky thing about the starting-over fantasy. You'd want to keep some things, but this somehow seems like breaking the rules of that particular little head game.

I crossed the street, away from that restaurant. I called Shakti again. No answer.

I was hungry, and so I ordered a cheeseburger and some fries from Cleo and sat at one of the picnic tables, keeping Gulliver company. That creepy feeling that Christian was nearby—I couldn't shake it. I knew how stupid it was—he could know I left town and not know the thousands, *thousands*, of places I might be. Still, I kept looking behind me. Checking out the periphery of where I was. I'm sure all of the stuff with Dad wasn't helping any, the ghost of my mother floating around nearby, whatever. But I felt uneasy. It was that nervous energy, that awareness that feels like a shiver about to happen. Still, I'd had that sense a hundred times before, and Christian had not been there. I'd be driving and looking in my rearview mirror; I'd be in the hallway at school. But his car was not behind mine after all, and he was not waiting at my locker.

Finn and Jack and all of their passengers finally arrived. A little while later Finn strolled down the dock, his hands shoved down into his cargo shorts, his grin wide, his cap over his crazy hair. Happiness rushed in where the nerves had been. Something good, a good person, love, can be a great big bulldozer to bad things. It can shove aside a bad moment, or bad years.

I liked it so much, the way he always smelled like outside. His hair was warm from sun.

"Mmm," I said. "You."

"You," he said.

"Oh, God, don't kiss me; I just ate a cheeseburger."

"I love cheeseburgers," he said.

He sat down next to me on the bench. I passed him my basket of fries. He looped one into his mouth. Gulliver ignored the food. Actually he was looking off into the distance as if we were boring him.

"I missed you all day," Finn said. "I missed you before I even got out of bed."

"Me too," I said. "It was the longest morning."

"How was the snake today?" He chose another fry, fed it to me.

"Sylvie?" It didn't seem right to talk about our conversation. What Sylvie had told me—it was too private to speak out loud while slurping Diet Coke out of a paper cup. "She was fine. Rotten kids touching everything, though."

"Ah, man. You get those on the boat all the time. Parents drinking their wine on the sunset sail, oblivious to the kid messing around. Sure, I'll steer a seventy-foot boat, watch for tankers, idiot speedboats, work the sails, and babysit your little monster so he doesn't drown. Nooo problem. You hear anymore from psycho boyfriend?"

"Not yet," I said.

"Did you tell your dad?"

"No chance yet."

"I saw him today. He was riding his bike. He waved, I waved. My mom really liked you, by the way."

"I really liked her. Your whole family . . ."

He grabbed my hands. Looked at me seriously. "You ever think about staying on here after the summer? You graduated. You wouldn't have to go back."

"I never really thought about that as an option. School, you know? I've got to sort out the whole college thing."

"*While* you sorted out the whole college thing . . ."

He was rubbing my fingers with his; our hands were clasped. There was this sweet, sweet space between us and in it sat all this hope, and I stepped into that space and kissed him and he kissed back, and it was so great and that's why it was such a shame that I had been wrong about the uneasy feeling being gone. It was like Christian was there, watching me kiss someone else. I remembered a time when it was Christian and I sitting at a waterfront—in Seattle, at a table at Ivar's, eating fish and chips and hot chowder on a cold day, watching the ships and the ferries crossing the sound. You could see your breath. I had my hands in Christian's pockets. Christian had wrapped his scarf around both of us, pulling us together.

I checked across the street. He would be there, his arms folded in fury. Or worse, his face in his hands.

"Look at this stupid bird," Finn said. "All these french fries sitting here, and he's just watching Cleo read her book."

"Maybe he's waiting for an invitation. He's got better manners, maybe, than the rest of them."

"Or else he just doesn't like the crunchy ones on the bottom, either," Finn said. He started lining up the leftover fries, the narrow dry ones we'd rejected. I smiled. Finn was making a heart out of them. He was talking to Gulliver, telling him how lucky he was. Not every seagull had his food formed into art. It was because he was a particularly intelligent and devoted bird. He shouldn't have to lower himself by going through garbage.

The heart was finished. "Back to work," Finn said. "Crazy amount of tourists today."

"I know. Want to do something tonight?"

He put his arms around my waist, pulled me close. "I hate it, but I can't. I got sunsets all week. Some corporate private charter tonight. But you can come on the one tomorrow night. Casual. Stupid Captain Bishop Inn summer tour. They do it once a month."

"Okay," I said.

"Call me later?" he said.

"Yes," I said.

We held hands, and we started toward the end of the dock where *Obsession* was. I looked back over my shoulder. "Check it out," I said. I pointed back toward our table. Gulliver was eating his way around the heart.

"Hey, you're welcome. No problem," Finn shouted at him, and I laughed. If someone was looking at us right then, this is what they would have seen. Our hands locked together, the effort-less way we had with each other. They would have seen my head tipped toward Finn with happiness as I laughed. It would have looked like I had completely moved on.

Dad was still gone when I got back late that afternoon. His laptop was on the kitchen table, open but turned off. I felt the kind of tired old people must feel, and ancient sea turtles, and trees that had been standing for hundreds of years. I got in my crispy white sheets and put the pillow over my head and shut out everything.

When I woke up, the room had gotten dark, and I was confused for a moment about what day it was and what time until that wake-moment came where the pieces fall into place, where there is either relief or some terrible remembering about what is. I could hear the television on. As I said, my father rarely watches television. It sounded like some nature show, that TV rainforest background of twittering birds and crickets chirping.*

Sometimes a nap makes you feel worse. I got out of bed. My head was draggy and fuzzed.

"Morning, Glory," my father said. He wasn't even wearing his glasses, which meant I knew he couldn't even see that lizard walking along that branch. He was wearing pajama pants and his old Al Gore *Prosperity and Progress 2000* T-shirt. I'd seen him without his glasses a million times, but it still made his face look odd, like a room after the furniture has just been moved around.

"What time is it?"

"A little after nine. You were tired. I got us a pizza." He gestured toward the fridge. The lights from the television flickered across his face.

"We conserving energy around here?" The room was dark; outside those windows it was darker still, only the pink line of the horizon breaking up the wall of gray turning rapidly black.

Dad switched on a table lamp beside him. We both blinked in the sudden brightness. "Never mind," I said.

..........................

* You wonder if it's the same sound track that's been used for years, because, I swear, from the time we watched nature films in elementary school to now, they always sound exactly the same. Those birds and those crickets were probably alive when my parents were growing up.

He turned it back off again, and it was a relief. I went to the fridge and took out a floppy slice of pizza from under the cellophane wrap on the plate. "Mm—love cold pizza."

"Your phone's been ringing in your purse," he said. "I keep hoping your wallet will answer."

"Ha," I said. "My wallet's the strong silent type. Hasn't spoken to anyone in years."

I hadn't woken up all the way yet, because I was just eating that pizza standing by the fridge and joking around and not thinking. And then I did wake up, because I realized the importance of that ringing phone. It could be Shakti. It could be Christian himself. It might be Finn, though it was still a little early for him to be finished at the docks.

"I hate phones," I said.

"We were better off when people didn't talk so much," my father said. A disgusting-looking insect was apparently doing it with another disgusting-looking insect on the television. "When every little feeling anyone had wasn't puked out on someone else."

"Thanks for that image," I said. My phone was blinking the red on-off urgency of a message. "Shit."

"What?" he said. He turned on the couch to face me. I held up a hand.

Shakti. I listened. *Clara, it's me. I'm so sorry. Something terrible happened. I'm just sick about it. Christian called here while I was out . . . He talked to my mom. I'd told her, you know, about you being there . . . Not why, nothing about him. He was just being all nice, looking for information . . . I'm so, so sorry.* She started to cry. I could hear her struggling to talk. *Call me back . . .*

"No," I whispered. *No!*

"Clara?"

My father put the remote control down and came over to me. I handed him the phone. He replayed the message. "Clara," he said. "Clara! Why? Why did you tell her?"

"*She* didn't tell him. Her mother . . ." I wanted to cry. Oh, God. God, I had been such an idiot.

"Jesus," my father said. He rubbed his forehead. "He could be here right now!"

"I'm so tired . . ." I said.

"We're hostages. I'm finished being a hostage, all right? *Finished.*"

He slammed the phone down on the table. He opened one of the kitchen cupboards, decided against getting whatever he was about to get, flung the door shut so that it banged. He sat back down on the couch, clicked through the channels until he came back again to the nature show. He sighed. He took my hand. "Ah, shit, honey."

I didn't say anything. Just held his hand.

"We've got to make a plan, Clara. He could come here. He could *be* here. I've got to get in touch with Branson tomorrow."

"I'm sorry," I said.

"You need to stop being sorry and be this angry, too, Clara Pea. Your guilt is bullshit."

It didn't feel like bullshit. My guilt felt so big, it was like a living thing. I could feel its heart beating. I sat beside him on the couch, drew my knees up, wrapped my arms around them. *Night comes under the canopy, and a hidden world reveals itself* . . . We watched frogs and the glowing eyes of monkeys. I looked over at my father, watched his profile, watched his eyes soften again.

"I saw you at the Portside," I said. "With Annabelle. I would have come over, but it looked like you were arguing."

He kept watching that TV. His face flashed with colors from the lights of the television—yellow and then green and white.

"We were," he said.

"I heard her say something. 'It's her story, too.'"

So much sat there between us, suspended. He'd let it all out of his hands, and what was suspended would be dropped, and things would shatter, and I was not ready for it. "I thought maybe you were arguing about your new book or something," I said.

"Right." His face took on that sagging, old look I'd seen in the restaurant. He didn't look like the same person who was slamming things around just a while ago. "Right. My editor. Her story, too. One could argue. Etcetera, etcetera. I'm trying to decide whether I agree or not," he said.

The rainforest show was over. Upcoming—*Deadliest Sharks!* We sat there. We watched huge, prehistoric bodies snaking through deep waters. Fatal encounters between humans and great whites. We saw what happens when two dangerous creatures end up in the same place at one ill-fated moment in time.

Well, I couldn't sleep after that nap, obviously. Dad went to bed, but I stayed up and talked to Finn and then half-watched some stupid movie. It was late when my phone rang. It buzzed and skirted around the hard surface of the table like a little remote control car. Shakti. I didn't feel like answering. Even her name felt loaded, weighted down by the complicated responsibilities of friendship. But Shakti—she had stayed up all night with me once, helping me color this huge trifold map of ancient Greece for a project due the next day. She was so serious about it, trying to do a good job for me. She would offer her favorite jacket, too, if I ever needed it, the new one any other person would be too selfish to share. On Mother's Day, she brought me flowers. Who would think of that? That's the kind of person she was.

"Oh Clara, I am so sorry. I've been gone all day because Grandma Shia had some stroke or something. She's fine, we just got her home, but I couldn't exactly call. I feel so awful about this. My stupid mother. She feels terrible. She just keeps saying, 'He was such a nice boy. I didn't know. I didn't know.' He called all casual, trying to see if you'd been around. I should have told her the truth a long time ago, but you know how she freaks out about everything. And I was careless. I was so happy to hear from you, I'd said to Mom, 'Oh, I heard from Clara, and she's in Bishop Rock!' and my mother said, 'I thought she went to Europe,' and I said, 'No. They've got a house on the beach.'" Shakti started to cry.

"It was an accident," I said.

"I'm so sorry." She was crying hard. I looked out toward that black, black sea out the windows. A layer of fog slunk along the ground.

"You didn't mean any harm."

"Remember when he checked the mileage of your car?"

"I forgot about that."*

"If anything happens to you . . ."

"Nothing's going to happen. Dad's here. I'll be careful." Shakti stopped crying. I heard her sigh. She sounded exhausted. She'd had her own bad day. "Let's just get some sleep."

"My stupid mother."

"It's okay," I said.

"I didn't tell her in the first place because she couldn't have handled it. So much for protecting anyone."

The conversation with Shakti unsettled me. That dark house did. But I knew if I turned on the lights, it would be worse. Someone could see in when I wouldn't be able to see out. I realized that fear and guilt were both cheap and easy emotions, ready and always available, the salt and pepper to the more exotic herbs that took more effort to gather, like courage or determination or regret.

I was listening too hard, and when you listen too hard you're bound to hear something. An airplane flew overhead; the floor creaked. Silence, and then the distant but insistent hum of a car motor. In the movies, some stupid person always walks outside when they hear a noise and are afraid, but I opened the front door and went outside because I did not want to be afraid any longer. Going outside was an act of confrontation, the anger my father said I needed. I walked down the path through the thick

.........................

* You can forget that other people carry pieces of your own story around in their heads. I've always thought—put together all those random pieces from everyone who's ever known you, from your parents to the guy who once sat next to you on a bus, and you'd probably see a fuller version of your life than you even did while living it.

swath of fog. I could hear the low moan of the foghorn at Pigeon Head Point, could see the slow arc of the lighthouse beam, there and then not there.

Yes, a motor. And now the swing of headlights. Shit, it was too foggy to see the car.

"Are you out here?" I said. *"Are you watching me right now?"* My own voice sliced into that wideness of night. It came to me: I was standing outside in my T-shirt and shorts, in a town far from home, the dewy beach grass wetting my ankles. My father was sleeping inside in our mystery host's bed.

Fury seemed to roll out from the very center of my chest. I hated Christian then. *Hated* him. For what he had done to my father and me, for what he had done, even, to us. I had loved him and worried about him, and he had mattered so much to me, but now he would not go and the hatred filled me.

"I wish I'd never met you."

No one stepped from the haze to answer.

"You," I hissed. *"You* were the one that betrayed *me."*

# Chapter 20

"I told you, Clara. When you take people into the lighthouse, you must lock the door behind you. You were the last one, you and that couple."

"I'm sorry, Sylvie." Roger lay there with his chin on his paws while I stood there and got reprimanded. I guess I wouldn't be told her personal secrets today. I guess I wouldn't be given cups of tea.

"This is my *responsibility*. I am not sure you understand." Her dark eyes bore into mine.

"Sylvie." She'd been going on for five minutes. I'd left the door unlocked, okay. I'd made a mistake.

"It is not safe. People could get hurt."

"I *understand*." An edge crept into my voice. It was wrong, but that edge was there anyway.

"You do not understand. Someone was there this morning. Maybe he was sleeping inside. I saw him coming out, retreating down the rocks. Roger started to bark . . ."

Something slammed in my chest.

"Clara? Are you all right? You need to be able to accept a reprimand when one is due. Clara?"

"Yes. Who was he?"

"A boy, Clara. One of those high school boys who drink at the beach. That is what I am trying to tell you. They have parties on the beach, they drink, they mess around up here. What would happen if he had gone up to the top of the lighthouse? If he went outside, on the upper deck, drunk? There have been beer bottles on the grounds. A condom! Idiots."

"Did you see him?"

"It doesn't matter. He is gone. The police cannot catch someone who is not here. Like smoke, he is gone. We were lucky, do you see? It was a near miss."

"Kids hang out there all the time," Finn said. "It could have been anyone, Clara."

"You're right," I said.

"Maybe it's enough for him to know where you are. It doesn't mean he's here."

I didn't believe it, though. I knew what I knew. I can only explain it as, *I felt him.* The way you feel someone staring at you. The way you know when a person you love is about to drive up, or that it's them on the other end of the ringing phone. Close family, someone you love, *loved*—you operate on another plane besides this one. It is the plane that animals understand, the dogs who smell cancer, the cats who flee before a storm, the coyotes, made crazy by a full moon. Maybe it's the plane where spirits exist, too. Where sand dollars cover the beach and where you hear the bang of shutters even though there is no wind.

I didn't* have actual words for it. I can only say that there was no way I was going to go home that day after work. I called my father, who said he was still waiting to hear back from Captain Branson. I told him I would be back after the sunset cruise with Finn that night. I stayed in the library. I ate my lunch there, same as that bad year in the seventh grade when the girls all turned on each other**, when I always felt alone and the library was the safest place. I sat in the back corner of the Bishop Rock Library, hiding in the protection of the shelves of biographies, stories of people who had gone through much more than I ever would, people who got through. I could see the door from where I sat. This is what those guys in the Mafia did, I remembered. It was in some movie. They would sit where they could see what was coming.

The afternoon turned to dusk. I took my sweater from the arm of the library chair and put it around me. I left the library and went to the marina.

"Are you going to be warm enough?" Finn said when I arrived. "I've still got Cleo's coat."

..........................

* Still don't.

** Seventh grade is *always* the year girls turn on each other.

"Great," I said.

"This is going to be stupid," he said. "Just so you know. It's a tour that the Captain Bishop Inn does every month. But you can hang out with Jack and me."

I took a seat on the small bench behind the wheel. Jack tossed me a blanket from below. "Before the wackos use them all," he said. He had extra energy in his step that night, and I noticed again how alike but not alike he and Finn were. Jack's rumpled white T-shirt half tucked into his dark jeans, his unruly hair, his unshaven face—it all made you think of tangled sheets and sloppy kisses and a grip that was firm but slightly careless. Finn's clothes were not all that different—a wrinkled denim shirt with cowboy snaps and jeans and a leather belt; unshaven and tousled, too, but eyes that were slightly sleepy, a mouth for only thoughtful, careful words.

I could see the van from the inn arrive out by the dock lot. The passengers ducked their heads and came out down the van steps, huddling like children on a field trip. The driver parked the van, stayed there to have a cigarette; I could see his elbow resting out the window, the exhale of smoke that looked like some visible form of relief. He was glad to have that over.

The woman leading the group had that red-purple hair, the misguided magenta that's not seen in nature.* It was cut bluntly, framing her round, energetic face. She was gesturing and talking and walking, shouldering a huge, overloaded purse that meant she liked to be prepared. Behind her was a group of about

..........................

* Okay, beets maybe.

fifteen people, a grab bag of various types, mostly middle-aged. A woman with gray curls in a violet velour jumpsuit, holding the hand of a chunky man with a large, proud belt buckle. Another woman with long straight, gray-black hair to her waist, the kind of hair that looks heavy and burdensome, dead cells from the 1970s, walking next to her friend in an *I only eat organic* tan skirt and *hippies never had shoes this expensive* sandals. A tall, thin man with a pensive, chunky sweater carried a notebook. Two girls about my age in *Bellevue High School Track* sweatshirts clung together, giggling.

"Here they come," I said to Jack. Finn was already at the ramp, getting ready to assist them on board. "What exactly is this again?"

"Jesus," Jack shook his head, smiling that smile that was always more of a grin. "Captain Bishop Inn. First they walk the people around the parts of the hotel that are supposed to be haunted. Some specific bedroom, the old servants' quarters of the kitchen. Then they head down to the William Harvard house. You know it?"

"No," I said.

"He was one of the first people to live here full-time, way the hell back years ago. It's more like a cabin, up near that bank of trees near the north part of the island? Just off Deception Pass? Anyway, he was slaughtered by some Indians. People see him hovering or whatever ghosts do. Moving shit around." Jack laughed. "After that, they bring everyone here, and we go up and down the coast, trying to scare the shit out of the folks."

"You guys sure like your ghosts around here," I said.

"Like? Business . . ." He made that gesture with his thumb rubbing his fingers, indicating money. "Ever since it was on *Evening Seattle* . . . "

"None of it's true?"

"Oh, the things that happened, very true. And people see this shit, so who knows? I don't care, is all I'm saying. Believe what you want. Beliefs don't hurt anyone. Wait, that was brain-dead. Beliefs hurt people all the time. Uh, come on, *religion?*"

"Racism? All the isms?"

"Yeah. But, go ahead and believe in ghosts, right? You got your harmless beliefs, you got your not so harmless. These people never bombed no clinic." We watched them come up the dock, and the idea of those people as dangerous made you laugh. One guy was trying to put film in his camera as he walked.

"You've never seen any ghosts before?" I tried to make my voice sound joking, but I really wanted to know. "On the water? The lighthouse? Your *own* house?"

"We find our washing machine in the middle of the floor sometimes, but that's usually after the spin cycle."

I grinned.

"I laugh my ass off whenever I see that. It reminds me of some kid who partied too hard and wakes up wondering, how'd I get *here?*" The group approached. The woman in velour pulled her jacket closer to her body. "They're going to freeze their butts off," Jack said. "Okay, time to play captain."

Everyone came aboard and found seats on the padded benches and the bow of the boat. Finn untied the ropes and Jack eased us out of port with the motor on. The sun was setting, and the sky turned shades of sherbet. Finn gave his safety talk, and then, as the land fell away from us, he lifted the sails. He grabbed the rope in his two hands and pulled down hard until he was on his knees. The tip of the white sheet touched the sky, you'd swear, rising with clangs and clatters of metal rings against the mast. Jack was right—the summer day fell away sure as that land, and the air was all at once cold.

The magenta-haired guide, Beth Louise, waited until we were underway before she began to speak. She stood near the wheel, off to the side so Jack could safely scan the waters and steer. Jack and Finn had their own shorthand communication, a nonverbal language of nods and gestures and decisions that sent them moving in tandem.

"First of all, you must know that in sailing legend it is bad luck to have a woman aboard ship. . . ." Beth Louise said. Everyone twittered.

"Bad luck's been good to me," Jack sang, and the passengers laughed.

"And a sailor's death at sea will always be avenged, even if this is from the other side."

One of the Bellevue High girls giggled. I wanted to as well. Finn was back again and he must have seen my mouth turn up. He kicked my shoe softly with the toe of his own, made his eyes spooky big. The sun dipped on cue. An older couple wearing matching jackets scooted closer together, and he took her hand.

"You wonder, do you, why seashore towns and lighthouses always have ghosts? Because this is where the violent seas meet turbulent shore, where ships of men leave loved ones behind,

Stay

witnesses to storms and loss and the drowning and crashing of that loss. There are hundreds of dead sailors right here, right below us in these waters. This was a major shipping channel back in the time of the tall ships, and the high winds here made passage deadly. Many ships went missing. The SS *Highport*, the *Williamson*, the *Queen Victoria*, to name just a few. Is it any wonder that the paranormal activity here is so great? Tragic loss and great fear means unsettled spirits."

Beth Louise stopped. You couldn't help yourself. You looked out onto those waters. You imagined.

"The sailing vessels, well, let's come back to those, because right now we are over the spot of a tragic shipwreck that took place on April 1, 1921, the wreck of the SS *Governor*, where the lives lost were not seamen, but a family. The Washbourne family, Harry and Lucy asleep on one side of the cabin and their two young daughters on the other. Imagine the dark night, the deep waters, cold, cold. The family was sound asleep the moment that the captain of the SS *Governor* confused the running lights of the *West Hartland* for the inland light of port and proceeded forward, until the bow of the *West Hartland* slashed through the ship and divided the Washbourne family cabin right in half."

"Oh, God," the woman with the long hair said. Her friend had her hand to her mouth. I didn't feel like joking anymore. Beth Louise's voice was calm and undramatic. None of this seemed silly. This was a real and tragic event, and her voice reflected that. Even Beth Louise herself was not as silly as she first seemed.

"The crew came quickly to their aid, but the young girls were trapped, unable to be freed. Water was coming in. Water everywhere. Harry was brought up top, and, against her will, so was the now hysterical mother, Lucy. The crew worked to move the rest of the stranded passengers of the now sinking ship quickly as possible to the *West Hartland*. But while they were distracted, Lucy broke free of her rescuers and ran to be with her children. She was never seen again. The ship sank within twenty minutes."

Beth Louise looked grim. Now the Bellevue High girls were holding hands. The sky was dark. A half circle moon hung high. Those black waves—they did look so, so cold.

"Lucy is said to haunt the area," Beth Louise said. "She has been seen numerous times, by sailors and fishermen and locals. The Pigeon Head Point Lighthouse keeper at the time, James Shaw, witnessed the accident. Today, members of the U.S. Coast Guard have made reports about seeing the woman in her white nightgown hovering here and at the lighthouse itself, going inside, disappearing. Searching."

*Obsession* sliced through the waters, and then Jack called "Come about!" to Finn, and there was the clatter of boom and sails as the boat turned to parallel the shore. We could see the lighthouse up ahead, and then nearer and nearer it came, looking eerie against the backdrop of that story. Its tall white column held another story now, Lucy Washbourne's, and another, James Shaw's. It was stupid, but I shivered. The whole thing was stupid, but she was a real mother and they were real children. As the boat slowed in front of the lighthouse, I thought of Sylvie in there. I wondered what she and Roger were doing at that very moment. The house looked dark. I thought of Sylvie's own loss, and about loss itself. What loss can do to us. What even the threat of loss can do.

"And now we move to what is perhaps Bishop Rock's most famous spirit, Eliza Bishop. Her husband, Captain Bishop, was one of the town's early leaders. His ship, *Glory,* was hit by a sudden storm right here in front of the land named for his father. It was a terrible wind. The rain slammed hard, waves overtook the boat; the boat, heavy with water, tilted toward the sea. Desperate men were running and clinging and sliding down the slanting floorboards, screaming. Many of the townspeople watched the terrible wreck from the windows of the old meeting hall, which no longer stands. Eliza herself ran through the storm to the hall. She saw that ship sinking, and it was obvious no man would have made it from that wreck alive. She could see the men, her husband somewhere among them, flailing but unable to be rescued in the terrible waters just out of reach. She ran to the lighthouse. The keeper tried to stop her racing up those stairs, to the upper level, but she stepped outside onto that deck and leaped to her death on the rocks below."

"Jesus," the man with the big belt buckle said.

"She has been seen for years at the lighthouse, and the ghost ship *Glory* has been witnessed often, sailing these waters with no crew aboard."

Jack and Finn came about again, the whip and rattle of the sails causing the woman in the expensive hippie sandals to jump and then laugh at herself. Beth Louise was silent. No one else spoke, either. It seemed the respectful thing to do. Eliza and Captain Bishop—they were once living people who felt and loved and who had slept together in their safe bed. The waves looked tipped in silver as the moon glowed on and on and on.

Jack glided the boat back into port. The jovial mood that everyone came with seemed to return once we were off those waters, back in the safety of harbor. People were joking. Someone asked the Bishop brothers whether they had ever spotted any spirits out there, and Jack joked that, no, he hadn't, but he'd once seen the Virgin Mary in an abalone shell.

I tried to shift gears, to pick up the new mood, but I felt weighted down. The deep feelings of other people's grief and passion and tragedy—we drew those things to us; we made them romantic and dreamlike and luridly fascinating. We made them into stories. You could forget, then, that a girl, a real girl, could stand at the banks of Greenlake with her heart beating in her throat, her shoes sinking into the mud. You could forget that Mrs. Bishop felt her life was over. You could come to think that real fear, real danger, was a far-away thing. Romantic and dreamlike and luridly fascinating, but not real, even as you felt it, the phone vibrating in your pocket right then.

Three calls from Christian and one from my father.

Finn jumped from the boat. Took my face in his hands. "I didn't hear a word of any of that, because all I could think was how beautiful you looked in that moonlight," he said.

I smiled. "Kiss me, because I'd better get home," I said.

He did. His face was cold against my cold face.

"Thanks for putting up with that just to see me," he said.

I pretended I thought it was stupid, too. I didn't want to confess that it disturbed me. "So, Mr. Finn. What do you think about all of that? If there are ghosts, *why* are there ghosts?"

*Stay*

He kissed the tip of my nose. "People who can't let go?"

"We feel sorry for them, though. They're 'tormented' . . ."

"Yeah" he said. "But they scare the shit out of people because they can't move on. Selfish."

"Metaphor," I said.

But Finn didn't care about metaphors. He kissed me again. "Do you want me to walk you to your car?"

I did want him to, but I shook my head. I wouldn't let him see how much the dark was scaring me, the sound of the water against the pilings of the dock, the old wood groaning and creaking as it shifted. "See you tomorrow?"

"Great," he said.

I walked away, turned to wave. I wished I could run to my car, but he was watching and it would have been embarrassing. I wanted to, though. Everything inside was *urging*. I unlocked my door in a hurry. I got in and locked all of the doors around me. The street was empty and quiet except for the noise that spilled from Butch's Harbor Bar when a couple opened the door to go in. The steering wheel was cold, the seat, too. I turned on the engine and blasted the heater and drove home too fast, my phone right by my hip in the pocket of Cleo's jacket, those messages from Christian too close to my body.

I drove through town, down the winding beach road that hugged the coast. I watched my rearview mirror for lights, but it was just all darkness stretched out behind me. I saw the house, our house, sitting at the tip of Possession Point, a yellowish glow coming from the windows. As I approached, a Jeep passed me. Sylvie Genovese going home.

I pulled into the driveway. Smoke was coming from our chimney. My father had lit a fire. Intimate ambience, which could have been irritating, only it wasn't. The thought of warmth and home sounded like a great relief, a place to reach that I hadn't yet reached. The distance between the car and the inside seemed so far still, with all that dark space out there, with that endless beach grass high enough to hide in, the black banks of rock, the piles of driftwood right outside my window.

I turned off the engine and looked around before I stepped out, and I almost ran to that front door. I flung it open and shut it hard behind me, safe. I was out of breath. At least, I felt the heaviness in my chest that meant I was trying to get air. Drowning must feel like that.

"Jesus," I said. I put my hand to my heart, like I'd been chased and now I had made it. I looked around. The fire was still popping and snapping, but sleepily, in that winding down way that meant they'd had a long evening together. There were candles in candlesticks on the table. The wax dripped down; the candles were burned to only a few inches high.

My father was in the bathroom. I heard him. And then he came out and stared at me, and his face looked strange. His eyes looked puffy, small slits. I was glad to see him, though. I needed to tell him.

"He called me again. I know he's here."

"We're going on Monday, Clara. There's a courthouse in Anacortes. We're going to get that restraining order as soon as the doors open. But there's something we need to talk about now."

I didn't say anything. My back was still to the front door. I understood something. "Whatever your big secret is, you told Sylvie, didn't you?"

"Come and sit down."

It seemed like a terrible disloyalty, him telling her first. Whatever it was, he was my father and this was my business. It didn't feel safe inside there anymore. Inside, outside—nowhere felt safe. "I don't want to know your big secret."

"Clara Pea."

"Don't call me that."

"I should have told you a long time ago, but I couldn't."

We stayed there, standing. In the movies, you always see people sitting down for Big News. People always say that, too, they urge you to sit before it comes. But sitting is one step further from the chance to flee. Standing is closer to *away*.

"Your mother . . ."

"I don't want this."

"I've lied to you. I've got a hundred good reasons why, but it doesn't change the fact that I never told you the truth."

"I don't need the truth."

"Clara, please." I didn't want to be told, but he needed to tell. You could see it. The words had been pressing at him from the inside for so long and long and long like words do, like secret shame does. Words must finally be said; they press their way out. Words came from his fingertips every day, onto pages that were read by thousands of people, but these private words, they stayed inside where they didn't belong, building strength and weight, shoving harder until they were bigger than he was.

"It's your problem," I said. My back was still to the door.

"She didn't die of an aneurysm," he said.

"No," I said. I shook my head. I felt sick. I kept shaking my head. I didn't want the words to get in. I didn't want to know this.

"We were away for the weekend. A beach house. Near here, but not here."

"You went to a beach house after she died to recover from grief."

He started to pace. He ran his hand through his hair. "We'd been having trouble. I'd had . . . I'd been involved with . . . a woman. Women. Rachel—" A sob escaped his throat. He swallowed. He was fighting back tears. I could feel a grief of my own growing, growing, threatening to spill. "Found out. She found out. It was wrong, I know how wrong. I thought I was hot shit, you know? My book . . . First book. Mr. Everything." He put his palms to his eyes, breathed out, shook his head. "She'd always, she had problems. Depressed. Fragile. It had gotten too much. I felt dragged down . . . She knew. Had known, and we were fighting all the time . . . It was supposed to be some *Let's get this on track* . . . Some weekend where . . . But we were sitting, having a drink. I was. All at once, I wanted out. I said I wanted out."

"No," I said. "Don't say it." The grief rose and spilled. I started to cry. I looked at the floor, the way the slats of wood fit into the other slats of wood. My chest felt like it was sinking into itself. "Please," I said.

He was struggling. "She stood in the doorway. She just stood, and then she ran. I thought she was just leaving, you know, to get away for a while. But she got in this boat. I saw from the window.

The boat—it was right there, in front of the house, on the beach. A rowboat. She dragged it out . . ."

I put my hands over my ears. I was crying. I was crying and shaking my head and my hands were over my ears, but at the same time I was hearing this as if it were a memory, a known thing already, like it was something I had known a long, long time ago and was hearing again. It was searing me, slicing through, a new truth, yet it felt like something I recognized, too. A horrible fact, an ugly deformity that was rising slowly and showing itself again, years later, from behind a mask.

"She got in that boat." He let out a small cry. An *ahh* of pain. "Jesus." His voice was hoarse. "I ran to her. She started it up, and I heard the motor. The boat was going out . . . I went after her. In the water. My clothes on. I ran and the waves were splashing over my head and my clothes were so heavy under the water, and I was yelling and yelling to her and that boat kept going out, and it was so far away but I could see it. I would bob up and see it and scream her name, and I was swallowing water, and then I saw her stand up and go over the side."

He began to sob. His face was in his hands. "Rachel, Jesus."

"No." I saw the boat in my mind, the choppy black waters. The woman who was my mother, throwing it all away. I saw myself in bed at home with some babysitter in another room watching TV. She got in that boat knowing that and not caring.

My father wiped his eyes with his fingertips. He inhaled, exhaled. "I was wrong. What I did was wrong. Clara, I know that. I am so sorry."

I was crying hard and I felt outside my body and my life and

I didn't know what was real and wasn't, because I didn't know who she was anymore or who he was or what our life had been and so I wasn't even sure who I was or what had happened to me. I felt my insides spinning, and he came and put his arms around me and I didn't want them there, but I did want them, too, because we were all each other had, really. He was my family and I was his, and my mother had belonged to us both. He was breathing hard; I could feel his arms gripping me, and what had happened with Christian seemed far away, but also closer than ever, because even through my wracking sobs I understood now why my father had insisted we run. My fear may not have been real, but his was, as real as that water soaking my father's clothes and his screams and that boat too far for him to catch. Fear was the biggest bullshitter, he'd said. But sometimes, too, fear told the truth.

His voice was small. It came from somewhere far away. "I owed her honesty," he said. "But did I owe her everything? Should I have had to hold her life in my hands?"

We clung to each other, and he rocked me, and the house was quiet except for a ticking clock. *What did I owe her?* he wanted to know, and I had no answer for him. None. We cried and held each other because we were two sailors alone in this one boat, out at sea. We exhausted ourselves. We had come away from the door. We were inside that house, which was still better than being outside that house.

"But why did we come here?" I asked. "Why did we come by the sea?"

He held my arms and looked at me. "I don't know." The

words were hushed. I looked back in his eyes, and I realized I was seeing him. All of him, not the joking smart-ass, not the author, not the father, but the man. He looked a lot like me. "Maybe for this," he said. "Maybe for this right here."

Of course I did not sleep. I am guessing I was in that strange place that is not awake but is not entirely dreams, either. I felt sick with grief. Sick with what he had tried to hide from me and what she was guilty of. I spent the night with images flashing— limbs tangled in water, torment tangled with selfishness. The obligations we should feel toward others tangled with the obligations we should never, ever feel.

# Chapter 21

*Lots of kids*, Christian had said.

*Oh really? Are you going to have some of them?*

*They'll look like you.*

*Terrific. They'll get my nose.*

He'd spun my hair around one finger. We were lying on a blanket again near old Denny Hall on the University of Washington campus. It was summer. His skin was warm on mine where our legs touched and his breath smelled like the juice we were sharing. His lips were sticky when he kissed me. We kissed again because it was kind of funny, that stickiness. You could turn to liquid in eyes like that, eyes that looked at you with such love. Mine gave it back to him. That kind of love could feel like a promise. And then I made a real one.

*Promise me you'll stay right here*, he said.

*Stay*

*Right here? You would have to bring me food. People would have to come and visit me.*

*Here.* He lifted his chin, meaning there, in his eyes, with him, where we were. *Promise you'll stay.*

*That is so easy,* I said. *I promise. Of course I promise.*

*Always. Stay always.*

*Always.*

We see a promise as a personal law, and we see the people who break them as private-life criminals. We think it automatically, one of those truths that just *is* to us: breaking a promise is a bad, bad thing. A promise can be buoyant as whispered words or solemn as a marriage vow, but we view it as something pure and untouchable when it should never be either of those things. If a promise is a personal law, a contract, then it ought to be layered with fine print, rules and conditions, promises within those promises, and whether we like it or not, it ought to be something we can snatch back, that we *should* snatch back, if those rules are violated. And if a promise should be offered carefully, it should be accepted with even greater care and with the inherent agreement that it is conditional. Because we offer that promise in good faith—under a tree in the summer or in a church or in the dark holding hands. And then it's fall and winter and there is black jealousy or endless depression or a million other poison arrows, and you are held hostage by that promise. The promises within the promises have also been broken, but that's too complicated for some raging heart to take in. Betrayal—it goes both ways.

When I got out of bed that next morning at the beach, my father was sitting on the back deck holding a coffee cup and watching the ocean. Oh, God, he looked tired. We supposedly age incrementally as we go through life, but looking at him then, I was sure that life sometimes instantly and insistently ages us. I saw it all there, the small and the large—he had searched for nine hundred and twenty-five parking spaces and had forty-two colds; he'd burned one hundred and twenty dinners and fallen over seven or eight tree roots and had three hundred and sixty sleepless nights. He'd lost touch with twelve friends and hung up on fifty-six telemarketers and was late and stuck in traffic four hundred times. And he'd had disappointments too many to count and gotten his heart broken, lost one father, suffered endlessly one tragedy, and it all now caught up with him as he sat in that chair holding that cup.

I shouted out a good-bye. The house still smelled like smoke from the fire in the fireplace the night before. I didn't want to talk anymore or be in that house—I needed to be out, even if *out* meant where Christian was. What was on my mind was my mother and the story that had been my story nearly my whole life long but that was now only truly mine for the last few hours. I didn't know what to do with it.

I parked in the lighthouse parking lot. I felt the kind of boldness that comes before falling apart. The *What does it matter* kind of false courage. If Christian was watching me, if he appeared right then, I'd rip him to shreds with my words. Go ahead and try to hurt me, because I was beyond feeling anything, that's what I told myself. Your hand could be in snow and at first you'd feel the brilliant sharpness of cold and the stinging pain but then only heat and then nothing at all.

# Stay

I'd be lying if I said I didn't look over my shoulder, though, as I made my way down that path and picked my way over the rocks to the beach and Annabelle Aurora's house. I heard that phone vibrate on the nightstand during those hours of tossing and turning, and it rang again in my purse on the drive. I didn't know if it was Christian or Shakti or even Finn, but I didn't look.

It would not be a day where the clouds would eventually burn off and we'd have the blue of summer sky, you could tell. The clouds looked like they planned to stay; they'd settled in. It was cold down there by the water. The gray sky made everything look gray; the water was gray, and even the beach and the houses looked dim. We were used to this in the Northwest—the way the gray would slink in and change how things looked. Our weather was moody. We lived with it for the reasons anyone lives with someone moody—when it was good, it was really good.

But right then, gray. Cold. The water didn't look inviting and wise, but morose and irritable. The wind even picked up a little, slanting the waves and bending the sea grass. I walked faster and pulled my sweatshirt around me.

Annabelle Aurora. I rapped on her door, and she came to it, dressed in some silky kimono, no makeup on, her uncombed, silvery hair looking restless and unsettled. She put her hand to it when she saw me, and you could tell she was probably vain long ago (or still), a person who cared about her attractiveness.

"Clara," she said. "I wasn't expecting company . . ."

"Can I come in?"

"Of course." She stepped aside. "Let me change . . ."

"I don't care," I said.

"All right. I'll make some tea."*

I sat down on her couch, watched her move around in the kitchen, watched the wind ripple the water outside. She came back with two mismatched cups, sat beside me, and folded her kimono around to hide her knees.

"You knew them both. You knew my mother," I said.

"The two of you talked," she said. Her eyes were blue like robins' eggs.

"Why did *you* know what happened? Did everyone know but me?"

"We were close friends then," she said. "And years before, too. He needed to tell someone. I think he told her family. Your grandmother, your uncle. They barely spoke."

"You were close friends," I said.

"Yes."

I wondered again how close. All those years ago—she wouldn't have been this old. It wouldn't have been unheard of. "You knew my mother."

"I did. Not well. I saw her when I'd come to town. I met her briefly before they got married. I was at the wedding."

"She was some depressed person?" My voice sounded small. It started to waver. I felt small.

"Sometimes. You felt how delicate she was. These tiny wrists . . ." She made a circle with her thumb and forefinger.

..........................
\* Everyone in this story, in my *life*, makes tea.

"He liked that, I think. It made him feel . . . *large*. Not just his physical size, yes? But his *being*. "

Maybe I knew how that felt. I had once felt large and powerful with Christian. "What happened, then? If he liked it so much?"

She thought. She spoke gently. "Maybe he stopped feeling large. Maybe he just felt, I don't know. Perhaps burdened."

"I never saw her that way in my mind." I saw her the way she was in photographs—that black-and-white one of her and my father standing on a bridge somewhere. It is raining and her eyes are closed, but her chin is lifted up to him as if she is feeling the rain and feeling his presence at the same time. It looked like joy.

"And she wasn't always that way. A person is never always one way. She laughed—a beautiful laugh. She looked deeply. She had an eye for photography."

"I knew that."

"An excellent cook. One time I visited she made a cheese soufflé, though, and it failed miserably and it looked like she was about to cry. The table was set with these colorful mats and homemade breads . . . She was so mad at herself, and he pulled down cereal boxes and set them on the table. Instant oatmeal, too. Bowls, a carton of milk. He wanted her to laugh. He told her only the company mattered. He seemed to really love her, Clara. You ought to know that."

"What he did was wrong."

"Yes."

"What she did was wrong."

"Very."

"Why did she do it, Annabelle?"

"There are just no answers for some things," Annabelle said.

Grief rose from somewhere deep down, filled my throat, my eyes, rose like some old, old wave that had been waiting until now to break. It hurt so much.

"Oh, Clara," Annabelle Aurora said. She put her arms around me. I cried into her shoulder because it was the shoulder of a woman, a mother's shoulder. I sobbed there. "Clara," she said.

"Didn't she love . . ." I couldn't say it. I needed to know. "Me? Didn't she love me?"

"Honey."

I couldn't get my breath. The grief came and came. "It wasn't enough?" I didn't say the word. *I*.

"Nothing can be enough sometimes, for some people. Nothing." She held my arms and looked me straight in the eye. "You know this. You've seen it."

She held my hands. Old Annabelle Aurora, with her odd and unknown relationship to me, my father, my family. Still, I strangely felt her presence there for me. Her solidity. Her love, even. Maybe this is what she gave my father.

"Why didn't he tell me?" I needed to know this. She would know why.

"Maybe he didn't think he could stand to see what I'm seeing right now," she said.

"Finn's been trying to call you," Cleo said. She chewed on the end of a straw that was stuck in a paper Coke cup. "He was worried when you didn't come by this afternoon. They're not going out tonight. Too windy. He went over to the pizza place to get some dinner. Then he was going to head home. Shit, man, you look awful, no offense."

"One of those . . ." I didn't know what to say. "Days. Maybe I'll try to catch him."

"Good idea," she said. "Vince's? Pizza place around the corner?"

I felt frozen, though. I stood there and looked at Gulliver, who stared off into the distance as if pondering the meaning of his life.

"My stalker," Cleo said. Then, "Oh, shit, I'm such a fucking idiot. I'm sorry."

"You heard, I guess," I said. I didn't know how I felt about this. I felt a flash of something. Anger, maybe. It was my private life. My business.

"Sweetie, I think he's told everyone on this street to make sure they keep an eye out for this asshole. Finn looks out for the people he loves."

The anger left as quick as it came. You could care enough to keep a secret, but you could care enough to tell one, too.

"I've got to go," I said.

I wanted to see Finn so badly right then. The dock was a clanging racket of noise—metal sail rings banging against masts, the sloshing of boat bumpers against dock, a high whistle of wind. I wanted to hurry, too. The wind made me want to hurry. There were only a handful of people out, and no one was in Vince's except the people who worked there and Finn, who sat in a booth. This is what you did in a storm, I guess. You stayed home. The waitress at Vince's sat at a counter stool, watching the television above the bar. Some news story about the weather. A reporter stood behind a microphone, her hair blowing. Finn held his phone, tapped a message. I surprised him—he looked up at me and smiled big.

"I was just sending you a text."

"I'm so glad," I said.

"Clara? Are you okay?"

"Too much is happening."

"Okay. Wait." He slid out of the booth, walked up to the waitress, and spoke to her. She got up, went in back. Finn returned. "We'll get it to go, all right?"

"All right." He put his arms around me. We stood there in Vince's with its red plastic tablecloths. I set my head on his chest.

We stayed there awhile, until Finn said, "Ready." I followed him to the counter where he paid and was handed the box. We walked out together, my arm linked in his. The wind picked up. My hair blew in my mouth.

"Too cold out here," Finn said. "Want to go to my house?"

I wanted to be alone with him. I didn't feel like being polite to mothers or brothers or neighbors we might meet. "My car?" I said.

"Alone," Finn said. He got this.

I nodded. I led us to where I had parked. I unlocked the doors, and after we got in, I locked them again.

"Did I tell you this was my favorite restaurant?" Finn said. We put our seats back. He balanced the box between us. "You want some dinner?"

"You go ahead."

He put a slice on a napkin. I remembered Christian then, in front of the fireplace at my house. *Let's try to think of every time we ever ate pizza.*

*Every time?*

*Every.*

Christian had been smiling. And then, *Pagliacchi Pizza. In the car, with . . . Wait. It's not my turn.*

I remembered the way his face had changed. The way it went from beautiful to something I wanted to run from. *I just can't stand the thought of your mouth on someone else's. Let alone anything* else.

"Not hungry?" Finn said.

"Tired," I said. "Too much."

He folded the rest of his slice into his mouth, put the box into the backseat. He pulled me close. "I think I'll keep it for later. Come here."

I maneuvered. "It's tricky."

"Ow—you okay? Look, we fit."

He set his hand against my face, pulled me softly to his chest so that I could rest there. He rubbed my head, the way you might to get a baby to sleep. I didn't want to talk to him and tell him what I had learned about my mother. I didn't want to talk at all. I thought my father was right, then, that sometimes there were too many words and too many feelings spilled. I just wanted to be there with Finn. His Finn-ness was better than a mountain of spoken feelings.

I watched the trees shaking off the wind. A few fat splatters of rain dropped on the windshield and the hood of the car.

I thought of another car, another night.

*I don't want to lose you.*

*Why would you lose me?*

"Clara?" Finn whispered. "I know we're just getting to know each other, and you're not supposed to say big things, and there are all these rules around that, the no-freaking-someone-out rules, you-can't-love-someone-so-soon rules . . . I'm not making any sense probably."

I didn't say anything. I just kept my head still, felt his chest moving up and down. "But you know what? Shit happens, too, and I keep walking around lately knowing how fragile everything is since my dad died, how fast it goes, how quickly things can change, and so I'm not into bullshit games and rules anymore, okay? I want to let you know that whatever the word is that's more appropriate than love right now . . . I whatever-that-word-is you."

I smiled into his chest. "I whatever-that-word-is you, too," I said.

He kissed me then, and I kissed back, and it was some strange mix of heartbreak and joy and past and present and life rushing in without words to explain it. Just, big. We shifted and I faced him and he held me and we just kissed for a long time, and he pushed the collar of my shirt down so that one shoulder was bare and he kissed it too, like it was a precious thing. I unbuttoned his shirt and put my face against his chest, and that's all that we did. If anyone was watching right then, they would have seen my bare shoulder, his mouth against my skin, but there was nothing else. It could have looked like there was, but there wasn't.

After a while, we separated. It seemed better to keep wanting more than to have too much.

"Can I come over later tonight?" Finn asked. "Maybe after you guys eat?"

"That would be great," I said. It would. I couldn't stand the thought of Dad and I alone together all night with our history between us.

"You should stay tucked in. It's supposed to be really bad tonight."

"Maybe you should stay tucked in."

"Sailors are used to weather," he said.

"Look how dark it's getting," I said.

We untangled. I drove Finn home. When we left, the marina parking lot was empty. I didn't see any other car there. I thought it had been empty all along. But love can wrap you up tight inside love. It can be hard, then, to see a long distance off.

# Chapter 22

As soon as Finn closed the car door, I felt it—the worming finger of unease. I looked all around, but there was only Finn's regular street, a row of mailboxes standing like dutiful soldiers, his neighbor's wisteria snowing white flower petals in a sudden gust of wind. A flash of something? No, just a dog running home as the rain started to fall and splat hard on the car roof and the asphalt and the lids of garbage cans.

The sky had gotten so dark with thick clouds that Dad's automatic headlights came on. The drops of rain were the fat, insistent kind. Then, a deluge, and I had to drive slowly out of town and back to our house. The pummeling rain stopped, and for a moment the clouds cleared and you could see a crack of sunlight and then it was gone again. The black clouds kept rolling in; you could see the next ones approaching, filling the sky once more, an endless stampede, like a pounding, resolute cloud-migration over flat land.

I was driving through the dunes now. Cloud shadows skimmed over the grass. Something heavy sat inside me, something next to the boulder of sorrow. Dread, and maybe knowing. You don't usually feel fate until you see evidence of it afterward, but then I felt fate moving and it moved like those clouds did, definite as they were. It was full like those clouds, too. Full of something needing release. I wondered—did Jennifer Riley feel this, too, when she stood on the muddy banks of Greenlake? Did my father, the night he and my mother were at that beach house? Did he feel it as he sat there holding his drink; did he see fate there in the way she stood, in her eyes, the way her hip leaned against the doorframe? Or did he only recognize it afterward?

I saw our house sitting at the edge of Possession Point, all the lights off. I parked in the gravel driveway, turned the engine off. The house looked still, empty. I walked quickly to the door and found it locked. My hand shook with the key in it, and once inside I shut the door and bolted it again behind me. I felt stupid, because my heart was pounding. I wondered, too, if my mother did not see fate but felt it moving inside of her, held in her grasp, ready to do her bidding. If she felt it rising up within her like some welcome rage, a release of jealousy and too much pain as he sat there with his scotch. The thought of it, even the thought of the smell of that scotch made my stomach swim with nausea.

I called out, but my father wasn't home. I looked out the window, to the side of the house near the back deck where my father

kept his bike, and I was right, he was gone.* The wind was whistling. Everything was sudden angles in that wind—the grass bent
wildly and the waves slanted and the rain, too, fell at a diagonal as
the wind pressed against it. I shut the blinds. It was crazy, but I
went around shutting everything I could shut. Windows and curtains and closet doors. A bathroom drawer that held my father's
shaving kit. The wardrobe that held the television.

I found my phone in my purse and then zipped my purse
up tight, too. I was going to call my father. Wherever he was, I
needed him back. I didn't want to be in that house all alone with
the slanting wind outside. I had never been a baby about being
alone, never. But there was this thrum of inevitability inside me,
and his presence could stop that, I thought. Something needed to
stop it. A person, a conversation, regular keys being dropped on a
regular table, some regular words, dinner being made.

I called him but the phone only rang and there was his voice
leaving his message in that smart-ass voice that was only one side
of him. I hung up. I tried to tell myself I was being stupid when
I knew I was not being stupid, and that's when the phone started
to ring right in my hand and it was him. It was Christian.

I shoved the phone down deep into the couch, under the
cushions. I felt a grip of panic. I opened my purse again and took
out my car keys and put them in my pocket, same as I did that
other day, the last time I had seen him. I could hear the thrum of
ringing under those pillows, and then it stopped. I didn't know
what to do. I needed to do something only I had no idea what.

........................

* An idiot, to ride when a storm was coming.

*Stay*

I went to my father's room. I looked under his bed and took out the paperweight he kept there. It was heavy for its size, shaped like a typewriter, jagged and intricate, with frozen, silent keys. I brought it out to the living room. I set it down on the coffee table in front of me.

I was getting myself worked up over nothing. You could do that. You could make something big in your mind that didn't exist—Christian himself had done that, and what he'd created was as real to him as real actually was. You could see ghosts. How could you tell the difference? How could you tell the fear inside from the danger outside? How could you hear what was real when the wind was battering and the rain coming down and those ghosts were restless and rising from the seas?

# Chapter 23

I sat there on the couch and circled my knees with my arms and watched the sky turn briefly pink and orange in the skylight before it went dark. The phone rang under the cushions again. I knew it might be Finn, but it might not be, too. I couldn't stop to find out, because I needed to listen. The phone stopped. I sat very still and listened hard to the night—the ocean, the wind, the rain, the creak of the joints of the house, so I would hear if he was coming.

And so I did hear it coming from a long way off, that car. The car was one I knew well—the sound of the engine was. A car engine can sound like no other car engine, same as the sound of a particular car door slamming shut, same as particular footsteps, which I did not wait for. I looked out the window when I heard the engine. I saw the headlights and the outline of the driver, and I knew those headlights and that outline.

"Oh, Jesus," I said out loud. My voice was both so big and so small in that room. "Jesus," I whispered.

He had closed that door in his room, and I had been trapped in that corner, I remembered that. I would not be trapped again.

I had the keys in my pocket, but the keys would do no good. The paperweight sat on the table, and it would do no good, either. They were small, silly weapons, pointless objects offering no protection. I saw the headlights swing into the driveway, and they swooped across the living room, same as the lighthouse beam making its slow arc. I went to the sliding door that led to the back deck and opened it, and the blind clattered as I shoved it aside and stepped outside and then remembered that he could hear my shoes on the wooden planks of the deck. I heard him knocking. I heard him calling my name in that voice, and I ran then. I bolted down the dunes toward the beach and I started running and I could still hear him calling out for me.

The rain soaked my blouse in an instant. It clung to my skin, and my hair was wet and rain dripped down my forehead and I stumbled across bits of driftwood and rock to the place on the shore where the sand was hard and I ran and ran until I realized he might see me easily there. He would walk around the house after he had knocked. He would see the open door. Maybe he would walk around inside the place where my father and I had lived, invading our private space, forcing himself where he wasn't wanted. He would get in his car again and drive on the road just above me where he would see my white shirt in the darkness.

I ran back up to the shore again, to a covey of rocks, and I lay down against a huge stone, hidden from the road, feeling the hard slate against my wet clothes, the cold of the rock against my cheek, gritty with sand. My heart was pounding. My phone—it was still under that couch cushion. I felt crazy. I was out of my own body. It was like that other night, when I was driving and there was the ammunition store and the phone booth, and I was in a town where other people lived, not me. I gripped that rock, and the rain soaked my jeans now, and I waited, I don't know for what, just for the right amount of time, the signal inside that it was the right amount of time, and then I climbed up toward the road and crossed it so that I would be farther from where he might look.

I ran. My chest was burning with fire from running. I breathed hard. I prayed I might see my father biking up the road, but then I realized how silly that was. Him on a wobbly bike to save me felt as feeble as those policemen on bikes or horses, the ones you were sure wouldn't be good for much other than stopping some jaywalking citizen. Even my father, though, would not take his bike out now, in this pounding rain and wind. He would stay smartly where he was until he could get a ride back, maybe from Sylvie Genovese's, if that's where he was.

That's where he was, I was sure of it.

It suddenly appeared like the right answer, even though I had been moving that direction all along. The lighthouse. The safest place now, I knew, the safest place in any storm, that column of stone, and inside the keeper's house, Sylvie and my father and Roger, Sylvie's warm rugs and cups of tea and my father, who would not let anything bad happen.

Only, he had let something bad happen. He had let it happen and didn't, couldn't, stop it.

The road was empty—there was no car in sight, not Sylvie's, not Christian's driving slowly past in that rain. It was just me walking now, walking because I couldn't run anymore, and the lights of houses coming on in the dark and the wind whistling and the sound of the waves crashing hard into rock and something banging far off in the wind, some door loose on its hinges.

I could not see the lighthouse in the distance and then I could because the sensors must have gone off, and the beam lit up and it began to swivel in the sky, and I went toward it. It was a long way away when not in the car or on a bike, and I was soaked and started to shiver. A car approached, and I hunched down, and it sped past, a car I did not know. A cat cried out, one of those horrible cat cries, a howl. I felt that howl inside me, curling up from somewhere deep, my own cry. I stood and kept walking, and then I started to run again because I couldn't bear the rain anymore, that night, that road, and the sound of my own steps on pavement.

I ran up the curved drive to the lighthouse. The visitors' center parking lot was empty, but, yes, there was Sylvie's Jeep and my father's bike resting against the gate, and yellow lights blazed upstairs, and in the backdrop was that huge and slowly swiveling beam.

I caught my breath, thankful that I had made it. My father would be shocked to see me there, standing on the porch, soaked and scared. I bent over, rested my hands on my thighs as I let the fire in my chest subside. It seemed crazy and unreal—the headlights, running out that back door, Christian's car. It had been *real*, right? It had been. It was windier up there on the bluff than it had been on the road. The wind had turned from a whistle to a loud, spinning howl, and my teeth were chattering, and I felt so far outside myself that I had a hard time making myself move to that front door, and I just stood there breathing so hard, my hands on my knees.

But I was there, and so I rested a moment. And in the small space of that moment he was in front of me. He was there with the lighthouse behind him.

"Clara!" Christian called, and his voice caught in the wind and carried upward, disappearing.

"No," I said. "No."

He was soaked, too. A striped cotton shirt, his jeans, his hair plastered to his head. His face was much thinner than I remembered. His voice, familiar. He was familiar, too. He was still wearing that leather wristband I had given him that one Christmas. That was the weird thing. I still knew him.

"Stop. Just stop for a minute!"

"Get away from me, Christian."

"You have nothing to be afraid of, Clara! I need you to know that. I would never hurt you."

The rain poured down. I started to cry. "Please, why can't you leave me alone?"

"You need to know I would never hurt you!"

"You came to tell me that? You followed me here for that?"

"I can't believe you would think you needed to run away! You needed to hide from me? From *me*? Do you think I'm a monster?"

He stepped toward me.

"No!" I cried. "Dad!" I yelled. My father would hear me. I was in no danger, with my father just steps away in that house, upstairs where the yellow light was. The door would fling open, the police would come. "Dad!"

My voice lifted up in that wind, too. It lifted and drifted and blew away from that cliff and out to sea.

"You have nothing to be afraid of. It's me! It's only me!"

"Why did you follow me?" I was sobbing. My face was wet with tears and rain, and my nose was running.

"To *talk* to you, Clara. To talk. You won't talk to me! I need you to know I would never hurt you. I just want to explain!"

"I don't want your explanations, don't you see? I don't want them. You may need to give them, but *I don't want them*."

He wouldn't listen, even then. His need was greater than my will always, always: even as we stood on that bluff, he pressed his need over mine, like a hand over my mouth.

I should bolt, I thought. My father couldn't hear me as that rain pummeled down, but he was right there, if I could reach that door. But Christian stood before me, and I knew him, he was familiar in spite of everything, and his arms were out and his palms up as if in pleading, and I could see there was no shiny knife there.

He saw me soften for that second. He saw it. "Clara," he pleaded. He stepped closer to me. "I love you. I would never hurt you. That's all I want you to know. That's all."

"Okay. I know it. Now go."

"I loved you. I will always love you. Christ, Clara. We had so much. Why did you throw it away without giving me a chance?"

This was what happened with him, wasn't it? If you took one of his words, he gave you a thousand more? If you gave him one of your own, he would beg for a million? It was a never-ending need, a pit too deep to see to the bottom of. It was why Captain Branson said no contact, wasn't it? Because a single word was just kindling on a fire, and contact like this was gasoline.

"Please stop."

"I want you to know I've changed. I'm not the person I was. I've learned. A person can learn from their mistakes! I was wrong. How I treated you was wrong." He stepped even closer. He reached his arms out, pleading. He could touch me if he wanted to. I could barely breathe.

"I need to go."

"Clara. I've changed, okay? Just so you know."

Rain rolled down his face. The way he stood was familiar. The rhythm of his words. He was near enough, now, for me to feel his breath. His breath was familiar.

"If you've changed, then you'll understand why you need to leave."

"Stop crying, Jesus, listen to me."

What was happening—it was all feeling further and further away, not closer. "I don't want to ever see you again."

There was a pause, and the lighthouse beam swiveled around, and he held his arm up to his eyes and so did I. I felt some stupid possibility, the ever-hope that he would hear me as he needed to, that this craziness would stop and he would get in his car and drive away. That's how crazy I was too, crazy with naïveté and crazy with hope for the normal and crazy in my desire for other people's reasonableness. *I still believed in reason.* He was proving me wrong by his presence there, but I didn't see that. I still hoped he would turn away; I still believed in that outcome.

And then, like a key turning, a small click, he was in a different place. I saw it in his face. It takes some people a million times to see, but finally it is that millionth time. I saw him clearly, and me clearly. I saw my own stupid hope, and the patterns that made him who he was, patterns that would never change, never. But I could. I could change. I could *see.*

"Because of the sailor? Mr. Pizza? Mr. Fuck *Me* in the Car, too?"

I bolted, and he grabbed my arm, and I knew I didn't have a chance to make it to that door and pound hard enough to be heard upstairs. I ran to the only other route to safety I knew—that path to the beach, that steep slope down the cliff where my father had twisted his ankle. I stumbled and skittered and slid on my ass, and I can say I was finally fully afraid and fully aware in a way I had not yet been. Fully afraid, dear God—a fear that stood up and raged with ugliness and power because I saw, *saw,* that he did not have a knife but he had his own hands. I scraped my way down, ripping the skin from my palms and knees and I could see him above, the light going around again and blinding him.

I reached the ground and ran. I heard him calling me, saying he was sorry, the word *sorry* carrying on the wind and carrying again and again.

He was coming, as I knew he would. I heard his footsteps, heard him running or, at least, I thought I did. I heard hard steps on wood, which I could only connect to Christian,

Christian's nearness, Christian overtaking me. I did not connect them to what they were—the concerned steps of retired Colonel Gerard Yancy in his striped pajamas and slippers on the deck of his beach house, where the wind had carried our voices and finally dropped them. I thought that Christian had overtaken me, and I could no longer see with the rain in my face and my wet hair in my eyes and other visions rolling in like the storm.

I could not make it to Annabelle's shack; I could not even make it to the door of the next house, I was sure. Christian's own voice tumbled to me, calling to me with the clarity brought by the speed and direction of wind, and I did what I had to do. I would go where he could not reach me. I grabbed that rowboat and those two oars stuck upright in the sand, the ones that belonged to retired Colonel Gerard Yancy, only I did not know they belonged to retired Colonel Gerard Yancy. Some strength rose up in me like those pictures you see in old children's books of sea monsters, rearing their heads from the waters. I grabbed the wood bow of that boat, felt its faded green paint flake off in my hand, tossed the oars in. I pulled it across that sand, to the edge of the water.

I pushed the boat far enough out for it to catch the waves, and then I waded in with my shoes still on. I was moving in panic. There was another voice rising now, Colonel Gerard Yancy's, although I couldn't hear it with the wind pounding in my ears. I had to get away, that's all I knew, and there was no other away but this one.

I struggled to get the oars in their oar locks, but my hands were shaking too much, and I gave up and set the oars in the water and began pulling hard. I pulled with such force and panic that I could feel the muscles in my shoulders sear. A thought flashed: I was saving my life as my mother had destroyed hers.

The waves were sloshing hard, slapping the boat, spilling inside. The sea was pulling me farther and farther out, and even through the slatting rain I could see the shore getting smaller. My breath was coming so hard that I had to stop, to try to breathe, to wipe the water from my face, and when I did, I saw the figure on the shore, retired Colonel Gerard Yancy in his pajamas, and I saw the other figure, Christian, who had not come to follow me at all, but who still stood at the top of those cliffs, at the edge near the lighthouse.

Something shifted in me then—the knowing, the under-standing of what was really meant to happen next. I knew what Christian would do, and the sea kept carrying my boat out, and the waves lapped in, and I felt a despair, a confusion in that storm, of who I was—my father or my mother. I stopped rowing. I realized that my fear brought me here, the storm of another's emotions. Christian and I had also been in our own boat together, in a sea of his feelings, and I had stepped in, and I had willingly given myself up to the waves that carried me out. I had let him take me up and keep me in the ways he had wanted, and my father, too, had been taken up, then and for years afterward.

We had let this happen.

The boat bobbed and sloshed, and one of the oars then slipped into the water, and I tried to reach it, but I couldn't. I started to cry as I saw it taken away. I sobbed in despair, and

then I howled, like that cat, like both the mother and her children on the doomed *West Hartland*, their grief, my mother's
grief, my father's, my own. Water was coming in the boat in
great waves, sloshing over the side, and I cried and tried to carry
it out in my cupped hands, but it was too much for me.

Through the rain I could see Gerard Yancy begin to run, and
then I couldn't see him anymore. He was too small. The wind
whistled, and the boat carried on those choppy waves and took
more water in, and I thought of my mother lifting herself, her
leg going over the boat; I thought of Christian lifting himself
over that stair rail and of Eliza Bishop climbing those lighthouse
stairs. I was on my knees, bailing and bailing with my hands,
crying, trying to reach the other side of the boat, trying to save
myself, until I leaned too far and the boat caught, and then it went
over, and I was under and my clothes filled with water, heavy,
heavy weights. My head was underwater, and I couldn't hear anything but bubbles and watery depth, and my nose burned with
the suddenness and cold.

I thrashed and felt the boat near my fingers; I pulled myself
up to breathe but got a mouthful of water. I pulled again; I was
not thinking; my body was only doing what it had to. I fought
the weight of my clothes and the waves splashing against my
face, and then I saw the orange of a life jacket floating nearby.
Those old, summer-camp-type orange life jackets made of
foam, a black strap that went around the waist. I grabbed it and
held and it wasn't enough to lift me above the waves but was
enough to keep me from going under.

I kicked and fought and held to that stupid piece of foam and tried not to think about my mother underwater, how she did not thrash and fight and find what she needed to hold on to. And then, after only a moment, there was the rumble of something, gone as water sloshed into my ears, and then back again. A choke and rumble, and it was getting louder.

I knew that the man on the beach had started to run, but there was much I didn't know. I didn't know what happened to Christian. I didn't know that Finn had called and called my phone and had come to our house and seen the open door. He had gone to the lighthouse and found Gerard Yancy pounding and yelling on the door. *A girl, a boat.* He did not wait for my father and Sylvie to appear—he had instead put the accelerator down and sped furiously back to *Obsession*, where he realized Jack had the fucking key on that string around his neck.

It was right, though, that Jack and Finn had finally only unmoored the boat and were still motoring too far off to save me. And right, too, that the Coast Guard had been called only after Gerard Yancy had arrived at the lighthouse. Because it meant that what I heard, that rumble, was Sylvie and my father racing out to me in Sylvie's bold little boat, and it meant that it was Sylvie who cut the motor where I was clutching that life vest, Sylvie and my father—who was in that feared boat, out in that feared sea—who pulled me in. It was right, because Sylvie needed another chance to save a child, and my father needed another chance to save the one he loved.

He was sobbing into my wet body, and Sylvie was throwing a blanket on me, and I was shaking and clutching them. I was holding on to the ones who cared enough to go out to sea to bring me back, and they were holding on to the one who wanted nothing more than that.

Sylvie took my face in one hand. "I suppose now you will be wanting tomorrow off," she said coolly. And then she kissed my forehead with great tenderness, just before she started that motor again and brought us home.

# Chapter 24

If my life were a movie, this is what would have happened: Christian would have climbed the lighthouse steps and flung himself over the railing, same as Eliza Bishop. Or he would have pitched himself over the rocks of that cliff, landing dead and battered at the bottom. But that's not what happened. He did not kill me, and he did not kill himself. Still, that night in the boat I was sure he had; I was as sure he would kill himself as I'd been previously sure he would never harm me. But I could never really know either of those things, could I? Even though it makes us feel better to think so, we can't predict another person's actions, not really. Another person is, at the heart of it, unknowable. And if you cannot know a person enough to always guess what they're capable of, you certainly cannot know them enough to hold them in your hands, to control their behavior, to fight, manipulate, cajole or nurse or soothe them into doing what they should or shouldn't.

People will do what they will do. The trick is admitting your own helplessness about that little fact.

Christian fled the moment Dad came running from the house. He escaped to his car, crying. My father called the police in a fury. An officer would make a visit to warn him to stay away. Even my father was sure we would never hear from him again after that. But two days later, Christian sent a message asking me if I was all right. As if a text was somehow a smaller and less offensive way to approach me. As if I might not notice it as much, or protest this diminished form of outreach.

We went into the city the next day and got a restraining order.*

...........................

* That, you would like to think, was the end of that. A restraining order, you hope, would give me some sense of peace and safety. Finally, someone is *doing* something, here, right? But Captain Branson knew what he was talking about all along. A bundle of paper is no defense against someone's will. Protection orders are rational documents served to irrational people, a sometimes dangerous solution to a problem there is yet no answer for. I continued to feel uneasy, although I heard nothing from Christian during that time.

As I said before, life is not a movie with expected outcomes and tidy endings. Not my life, anyway. Two months after the restraining order ended, I got a birthday card from Christian. And I do every year. It's unsatisfying to you, isn't it? The lack of a finish? But these kinds of situations are not often satisfying. The truth is, they can go on and on. A card, that's all, nothing threatening. Still—always—a ghost-not-ghost who haunts my mailbox and my memories, both the good ones and the bad.

# Chapter 25

"Clara Pea, you're going to be so pissed," my father said.

His glasses were at the end of his nose. His laptop was open in front of him on the table of the beach house. Outside, the day spread out blue and wide and hopeful.

"What?" I said.

"I know what our mystery host does."

"You cheated! You looked him up!"

"I'm sorry." He didn't look sorry in the least. He looked pleased. He set his coffee cup down hard. "You're not gonna believe it." He started to chuckle. "You're not going to believe what he does."

"Okay, what?"

"Guess."

Oh, God. This could take a while. He loved games like this. "Movie producer."

"Nope."

"Come on, Dad. There are a million professions. A million." He waited.

Shit.

Fine. Whatever. "Actor." Still, that grin. "*Famous* actor."

He laughed a great big *ha!* and slammed his palm on the table.

"This is just getting unfair now, because you're having all the fun at my expense."

"Clara Pea, you are whining."

He was right. Still, I folded my arms.

"Oh, all right," he said. He stood, pushed his chair back. Went to the kitchen, opened the drawer. He held up a knife. One of our mystery host's really nice ones. Black handle, sharp blade. Cut through apples like they were butter.

"A knife." Great. Now we were going to play charades.

He held up another knife. "Another knife," I said. He held up yet another one. He was just chuckling like mad now, and I put my hands on my hips. "Okay! A knife thrower." Silence. "Circus performer."

"Mr. Sharpie," he said. He clapped his hands together happily. The words meant nothing to me.

"No idea," I said.

"Mr. Sharpie?" He looked incredulous that I didn't know what he was talking about.

I shook my head. "Obviously an old people thing."

"Door-to-door knife sales. Scissors, too. My parents got a set as a wedding gift, and it lasted their whole damn life long. Their whole damn life."

"Our mystery host sells knives door-to-door?"

"General manager now. Worked his way up. The whole West Coast is his territory. California, right? Obviously sold a fuckload of knives, my friend. A fuckload of knives."

"You're kidding," I said. I felt disappointed. All of the special things in the house didn't feel so special anymore. Not like back when they were a film producer's things.

"Clara Bean Oates, what? You're disappointed." He set the knives down.

'Well, *yeah*."

"No!"

"No?"

"It would have been too obvious, Bean Sprout. Too expected. Film producer." He waved his hand as if to whoosh the distasteful idea away. "*Knife salesman.*" He nodded at the rightness. "Worked his way up from humble beginnings? Dashed hopes of a career in film? Bought himself a place like this on the tip of this incredible peninsula? It's the real thing, Pea. Honorable. A true accomplishment. Not some stupid fantasy. What *is*."

"Uh-huh."

"Pea." He sighed as if I were hopeless. He stared me down, hard. "We can't get so wrapped up in our own misconceptions that we miss the simple beauty of the truth."

\* \* \*

"I'm worried about something," Finn said.

We sat at that table, our table, outside The Cove, at the end of the dock closest to land.*

"What's that?"

We held hands. He rubbed the top of mine with his thumb. "That after what happened, you'll be afraid of the water."

It was true—at the thought of *water* I remembered suddenly the weight of my clothes, swallowing those waves splashing in my face. How cold, cold, cold I was lying in Sylvie's boat. The shaking. I would close my eyes and see that oar floating away.

"Our bodies are ninety-eight percent water," I said.

"Still." Finn's eyes looked troubled. "My life is ninety-eight percent water."

I looked out at that ocean, waves in, waves out, the ocean being an ocean, same as it had for a billion years. There were ghosts there, surely, but too, there were ghosts at that cabin just outside of town, the William Harvard House, and ghosts, too, at the Captain Bishop Inn, and ghosts on the banks of Greenlake, and in our old house, even. Ghosts, too, in that telephone booth where I called to have Christian taken away, and ghosts in the gym where we met. I thought of skittering down that cliff path, my name carried down by the wind. "I guess I would have to be afraid of land, too."

Finn thought about this. "You'd have to be afraid of your car."

He was right. "The lighthouse," I said.

..........................

* And, yes, thank God, there were french fries again. A reason for living, right there, Mother, dear.

"Even right here. This table."

He was right about that too. We had been watched there. It would be hard to find a place without memories hovering around it. We would have to move to a foreign country. I thought of Sylvie. It didn't seem like even that had helped very much.

"But I love this table," I said.

"I love this table, too," he said.

"So how do you make it all fit together? How do you take it all in? The good memories and the bad and all the in-between ones? The past and the now and the ghosts and the living?" I looked at Finn. I really needed an answer about this.

"You're asking the wrong person," he said.

Still, as I sat there, right then I was full with Finn's sweet company and the sun on my back and Gulliver standing by in his bored but steady way. The water twinkled thoughtfully, a million tiny diamonds on the pinpoints of waves, and that smell, that fantastic smell of the sea—when I breathed it in, it just lifted me right up. "I'm going to keep on loving the water," I said.

"I'm glad," he said. "Because a while back I bet you a trip to the San Juan Islands if you stayed employed by Sylvie Genovese. And, well, Clara Oates, it looks like you're going to make it."

I went to see Annabelle Aurora. I walked down that path which was just a path now, in the daylight. I also walked past the house of retired Colonel Gerard Yancy and saw the boat upturned near his back deck, one oar stuck up in the sand. I made my way to Annabelle's shack. I didn't know why she had taken this place in my life, a woman who knew things, a woman who both stood by you but also who stepped aside, but she had. We were connected, is all. She was the closest thing to family that my father had, and so she was mine, too.

A caftan—that's what she wore that time, the bright orange of a mango, and a long yellow scarf with tasseled ends, her gray hair curved at her chin. She took my hands.

"You came to the end of the earth, too, for your own reasons. I am so thankful we didn't lose you," she said.

"Annabelle—when I first met Christian, I *knew*. I felt this important thing happening. Something that was *supposed* to happen. Love. I went to it. No, worse. I brought *it* to *me*. I'd never been so sure."

"Love or need? Love or desire? Love or ghosts, visiting there in the present? I told you, love isn't often a pure thing."

"But I was so *wrong*."

"Maybe it *was* supposed to happen."

"But look how it turned out!"

"Just because it turned out bad, doesn't mean it wasn't meant."

"Dad's right, then. Fate has a fucking cruel sense of humor."

"Fate." She shrugged. She could give or take it, the shrug said. "We do this, don't we? Put the things in our path to figure out how to finally leave them behind? That is often mistaken for love. But maybe *meant*, yes? Look what you know now."

"You said this thing about instinct. About going away so that you could find it," I said. "About learning to hear and see."

She nodded.

"That night, on the cliff. I did see. I saw it all so clearly. And then I didn't. I mean, I saw what we did, what happened between us, what *always* happened between us, but then I got it wrong. I knew it was in him to kill me or drop himself down those cliffs, too. No matter what he said, I felt the realness of that. But he didn't. He didn't do either of those things."

She took my hand, and we walked outside to the small table on the deck. We sat. Seagulls screeched in the sky, and the long, low horn of a ship passing blew somewhere in the distance. "Oh, this is not about *that boy*," she said. "Listening and seeing—it's not about guessing what someone else might *do*. Ah, if we could do that, this life would be a great deal easier, wouldn't it?"

I nodded. "It would."

"The instinct, the seeing and hearing—it's not about him! It's not about fate! It's not about mysterious forces! It's about *you*, Clara. It's about *you* trusting what *you* feel, hearing the warnings *you* hear. Understanding *your* ghosts. It's about not telling yourself anymore that you don't know what you do know."

"All right," I said. "I see." I think I did see.

"But, dear God, don't listen to me. I'm an old lady in the middle of nowhere without a real toilet."

And then that was that on the subject of Christian Nilsson. Annabelle made a ginger drink for us. We sipped it as she told me which plants were edible on this beach. The sea lettuce and the sea asparagus. The ribbon seaweed. *You could feed yourself,* she said, *with all that you have right here.*

The last days of summer flew too fast out of our hands, the way time does when you most want to savor it. I spent the rest of the month working and going to the library and being with Finn. Shakti and her sister drove up and spent a weekend with us, and my father typed madly and read fat books and brought Sylvie Genovese thoroughly into both of our lives. I could see their chemistry, some odd mix of boiling energy and natural connection that made it work. She had come over one night to cook us dinner,* great steaming plates of pasta with a red pepper sauce, and had left to go home to Roger when my father stopped me before I headed off to bed.

"The summer is ending, Pea," he said.

"I know it," I said. I felt endings everywhere I turned. In the lighthouse gift shop, in the white room of my bedroom at the beach house, in the *tip tip tip* sound of my father's fingers on the keys of his laptop.

"We need to talk," he said.

We did. I had decided some things that I needed to tell him.

I sat by him on the couch. "I've decided some things," he said.

I laughed. "I . . ."

"What?"

"I was just going to say the same thing."

"You were?" He looked nervous.

"I've been scared to tell you," I said.

"Clara, I don't want to go back," he blurted. "I know our life is there, our house, your friends . . . We can keep the house, if that's what you need. We can do that. You're an adult now . . . You could live there on your own. But I want to stay here."

........................

* Dad is a great cook, but Sylvie's meals make his slink off in shame.

"Oh, God, Dad. I don't want to go back either. I didn't know how to tell you. You keep talking about getting back home—"

"Because I thought you missed it. I know you've got Finn and everything, but you've got a whole life there—"

"I applied for a job at the library. You know how I used to love working at the bookstore. Until I get the whole college thing sorted out. And there's this place?"

"Place?" He stopped.

"A room. Don't laugh. Above the taffy shop." I waited. This was the part I was afraid to tell him. "I could afford it."

His eyes suddenly brimmed with tears. Mine, too. Then they spilled over. They rolled down my cheeks. "Pea." He looked surprised, but that kind of surprise that you knew was coming all along. His voice warbled. "You're leaving the nest."

"The new place smells like melting butter." He laughed, we both did, but tears were rolling down his own cheeks now. "I'm gonna be so sick of that smell. I'll need to visit you all the time," I said.

"Pea, I'm so fucking proud of you."

"You are?"

He shook his head with disbelief. "We're *here.*"

"We *are* here."

He just looked at me, and we were a couple of crying idiots. He wiped his eyes with the back of his hand. He sniffed. "Jesus," he said. We kept looking at each other. All we'd been through together was with us right there. "Pea." He squeezed my hand so hard. "There's something . . ." The words were small and ragged, a whisper. "Are you ever going to be able to forgive me?"

"Are you ever going to be able to forgive yourself?" I whispered back.

"Let's both work on that," he said.

"Only a few more trips back and forth over Deception Pass," I said.

*Obsession* was too big to handle on our own all the way out to the San Juan Islands, and so Finn and I took out another of the Bishop family boats, the *Freebird*.* God, the day was grand, the sky so large, and that's the way my heart felt, too, as Finn shouted directions to me and I released the rope that let the sail swoop upward, filling with wind. I had always dreamed of a true and right place, and that's what I felt then as I looked out at the sea and the sky. The rightness stretched farther than I could even see.

"It's all ours," Finn called. He flung both arms out wide.

"We are so lucky," I shouted back.

Our memories and the events of our lives are untidy things. We wish that we could file them away and shut the door, or we wish the opposite—that they would stay with us forever. You want to banish that remembrance of a tight hold on your ankle, a rope under a bed, the amber-colored medicine bottles of your father's, the door your mother slams after a night of too much wine and jealousy. You want to keep close to you always that first sweet kiss, a maple leaf, that growing sense of yourself; you want to hold the sight of your dying father on that last boat trip, the calm you remember as your mother held you. Her voice.

........................

* Finn's father, Thomas Bishop, was a Lynyrd Skynyrd fan.

*Stay*

But the images are all wild things that will do what they wish. They haunt like ghosts; they mingle, like guests at a party, with guilt and hope and revision; they pack up and leave altogether. They spin and collide, even as you anchor the rope and the sail billows on a beautiful September day. Even as he shifts the boat ever so slightly so that the sail is as full as it can be.

When that happens, though, you realize that all of it is there with you still. All of it. You remember. The remembering, and that wind, is what pushes you forward.